PENGUIN BOOKS

THE VIRGIN BLUE

Tracy Chevalier was born in 1962 and grew up in Washington, D C. She moved to London in 1984, where she worked for several years as a reference book editor, publishing encyclopedias on writers and literature. In 1994 she graduated from the M A course in creative writing at the University of East Anglia. She has family in the United States, France and Switzerland.

The Virgin Blue

Tracy Chevalier

PENGUIN BOOKS

PENGUIN BOOKS

Published by the Penguin Group
Penguin Books Ltd, 27 Wrights Lane, London w8 5TZ, England
Penguin Books USA Inc., 375 Hudson Street, New York, New York 10014, USA
Penguin Books Australia Ltd, Ringwood, Victoria, Australia
Penguin Books Canada Ltd, 10 Alcorn Avenue, Toronto, Ontario, Canada M4V 3B2
Penguin Books (NZ) Ltd, 182–190 Wairau Road, Auckland 10, New Zealand

Penguin Books Ltd, Registered Offices: Harmondsworth, Middlesex, England

First published 1997
1 3 5 7 9 10 8 6 4 2

Set in 10.75/13pt Monotype Van Dijck
Typeset by Rowland Phototypesetting Ltd,
Bury St Edmunds, Suffolk
Printed in England by Clays Ltd, St Ives plc

For Jonathan

As yellow is always accompanied with light, so it may be said that blue still brings a principle of darkness with it. This color has a peculiar and almost indescribable effect on the eye. As a hue it is powerful, but it is on the negative side, and in its highest purity is, as it were, a stimulating negation. Its appearance, then, is a kind of contradiction between excitement and repose.

Goethe, *Theory of Colors*,
translated by Charles Lock Eastlake

Contents

Prologue   1

1. The Virgin   3

2. The Dream   22

3. The Flight   56

4. The Search   78

5. The Secrets   110

6. The Bible   126

7. The Dress   157

8. The Farm   175

9. The Chimney   206

10. The Return   225

Epilogue   255

Acknowledgments   257

Prologue

It began with flickering, a movement between dark and light. It wasn't black, it wasn't white; it was blue. I was dreaming in blue.

It moved like it was being buffeted by the wind, undulating toward me and away. It began to press into me, the pressure of water rather than stone. I could hear a voice chanting. Then I was reciting too, the words pouring from me. The other voice began to cry; then I was sobbing. I cried until I couldn't breathe. The pressure of the blue closed in around me. There was a great boom, like the sound of a heavy door falling into place, and the blue was replaced by a black so complete it had never known light. I stared hard into the void; when I couldn't bear it anymore, I closed my eyes.

I woke flat on my back, my hands clutching my neck, my elbows pressed into my breasts. Every part of me was rigid and my heart was racing. I stared up at the ceiling. Over the darkness stretched remnants of blue, fading, vanishing, winking back into sight for a moment. A voice echoed in my mind and I could still feel the tickle of my throat vibrating and the tail-end of a phrase in the air.

Slowly I began to feel the mattress pushing against my back, my thighs, my heels and head, and sensed Rick asleep beside me. I didn't fall back to sleep, but lay looking up at the dark, trying to make sense of the scrambled fragments left behind. They lingered for a few minutes and then disappeared, leaving only the memory of blue. It wasn't a common blue, navy or sky or royal; in the morning I looked at every blue in the house and couldn't find the ink or thread or paint to match it. I could picture the color, but it was the conflicting feelings it generated that I remembered better: a sudden joy and a wrenching sadness.

That was the beginning.

1. The Virgin

She was called Isabelle, and when she was a small girl her hair changed color in the time it takes a bird to call to its mate.

That summer the Duc de l'Aigle brought a statue of the Virgin and Child and a pot of paint back from Paris for the niche over the church door. A feast was held in the village the day the statue was installed. Isabelle sat at the bottom of a ladder watching Jean Tournier paint the niche a deep blue the color of the clear evening sky. As he finished, the sun appeared from behind a wall of clouds and lit up the blue so brightly that Isabelle clasped her hands behind her neck and squeezed her elbows against her chest. When its rays reached her, they touched her hair with a halo of copper that remained even when the sun had gone. From that day she was called La Rousse.

The nickname lost its affection when Monsieur Marcel arrived in the village a few years later, hands stained with tannin and words borrowed from Calvin. In his first sermon, in woods out of sight of the village priest, he told them that the Virgin was barring their way to the Truth.

– La Rousse has been defiled by the statues, the candles, the trinkets. She is contaminated! he proclaimed. She stands between you and God!

The villagers turned to stare at Isabelle. She clutched her mother's arm.

How can he know? she thought. Only Maman knows.

She would not have told him that Isabelle had begun to bleed that day and now had a rough cloth tied between her legs and a pillow of pain in her stomach. *Les fleurs*, her mother had called it, special flowers from God, a gift she was to keep quiet about because it set her apart. She looked up at her mother, who was frowning at Monsieur Marcel and had opened her mouth as if to speak.

Isabelle squeezed her arm and Maman shut her mouth into a tight line.

Afterwards she walked back between her mother and Marie, their twin brothers following more slowly. The other village children lagged behind them at first, whispering. Eventually, bold with curiosity, a boy ran up and grabbed a handful of Isabelle's hair.

— Did you hear him, La Rousse? You're dirty! he shouted.

Isabelle shrieked. Petit Henri and Gérard jumped to defend her, pleased to be useful at last.

The next day Isabelle began wearing a headcloth, every chestnut strand wound out of sight, long before other girls her age.

By the time Isabelle was fourteen two cypress trees were growing in a sunny patch near the house. Each time Petit Henri and Gérard made the trip all the way to Barre-les-Cévennes, a two-day walk, to find one.

The first tree was Marie's. She grew so big all the village women said she must be carrying twins; but Maman's probing fingers felt only one head, though a large one. Maman worried about the size of the head.

— Would that it *were* twins, she muttered to Isabelle. Then it would be easier.

When the time came Maman sent all the men away: husband, father, brothers. It was a bitterly cold night, a strong wind blowing snow into drifts against the house, the stone walls, the clumps of dead rye. The men were slow to leave the fire until they heard Marie's first scream: strong men, accustomed to the sounds of slaughtered pigs, the human tone drove them away quickly.

Isabelle had helped her mother at birthings before, but always in the presence of other women visiting to sing and tell stories. Now the cold kept them away and she and Maman were alone. She stared at her sister, immobile beneath a huge belly, covered with blankets, shivering and sweating and screaming. Her mother's face was tight and anxious; she said little.

Throughout the night Isabelle held Marie's hand, squeezed it during contractions, and wiped her forehead with a damp cloth. She prayed for her, silently appealing to the Virgin and to Saint Margaret to protect her sister, all the while feeling guilty: Monsieur Marcel had told them the Virgin and all the saints were powerless and should not be called upon. None of his words comforted her now. Only the old prayers made sense.

— The head is too big, Maman pronounced finally. We have to cut.

— *Non, Maman*, Marie and Isabelle whispered in unison. Marie's eyes were wild and dilated. In desperation she began to push again, weeping and gasping. Isabelle heard the sound of flesh tearing; Marie shrieked before going limp and grey. The head appeared in a river of blood, black and misshapen, and when Maman pulled the baby out it was already dead, the cord tight around its neck. It was a girl.

The men returned when they saw the fire, smoke from the bloody straw billowing high into the morning air.

They buried mother and child in a sunny spot where Marie had liked to sit when it was warm. The cypress tree was planted over her heart.

The blood left a faint trace on the floor that no amount of sweeping or scrubbing could erase.

The second tree was planted the following summer.

It was twilight, the hour of wolves, not the time for women to be walking on their own. Maman and Isabelle had been at a birthing at Felgérolles. Mother and baby had both lived, breaking a long string of deaths that had begun with Marie and her baby. This evening they had lingered, making the mother and child comfortable, listening to the other women singing and chatting, so that the sun had sunk behind Mont Lozère by the time Maman waved away cautions and invitations to stay the night and they started home.

The wolf lay across the path as if waiting for them. They stopped, set down their sacks, crossed themselves. The wolf did not move. They watched it for a moment, then Maman picked up her sack and took a step toward it. The wolf stood and Isabelle could see even in the dark that it was thin, its grey pelt mangy. Its eyes glowed yellow as if a candle were lit behind them, and it moved in an awkward, off-balance lope. Only when it was so close that Maman could almost reach out and touch the greasy fur did Isabelle see the foam around its mouth and understand. Everyone had seen animals struck with the madness: dogs running aimlessly, foam flecking their mouths, a new meanness in their eyes, their barks muffled. They avoided water; the surest protection from them, besides an axe, was a brimming bucket. Maman and Isabelle had nothing with them but herbs, linen and a knife.

As it leapt Maman raised her arm instinctively, saving twenty days of her life but wishing afterwards that she had let it rip out her throat quickly and mercifully. When it fell back, when the blood was streaking down Maman's arm, the wolf looked at Isabelle briefly and disappeared into the dark without a sound.

While Maman told her husband and sons about the wolf with candles in its eyes, Isabelle cleaned the bite with water boiled with shepherd's purse and laid cobwebs over it before binding the arm with soft wool. Maman refused to sit still, insisted on picking her plums, working in the kitchen garden, continuing as if she had not seen the truth shining in the wolf's eyes. After a day her forearm had swelled to the same size as her upper arm, and the area around the wound went black. Isabelle made an omelet, added rosemary and sage, and mouthed a silent prayer over it. When she brought it to her mother she began to cry. Maman took the bowl from her and ate steadily, her eyes on Isabelle, tasting death in the sage, until the omelet was gone.

Fifteen days later she was drinking water when her throat began to contract in spasms, pumping water down the front of her dress. She looked at the black patch spreading on her chest, then sat in the late summer sun on the bench next to the door.

Fever came fast, and so furious that Isabelle prayed death would come as swiftly to relieve her. But Maman fought, sweating and shouting in her delirium, for four days. On the last day, when the priest from Le Pont de Montvert arrived to perform the last rites,

Isabelle held a broom across the doorway and spat at him until he left. Only when Monsieur Marcel arrived did she drop the broom and stand by to let him pass.

Four days later the twins returned with the second cypress tree.

The crowd gathered in front of the church was not used to victory, nor familiar with the conduct of celebration. The priest had finally slipped away three days before. They were sure now that he was gone – the woodcutter Pierre La Forêt had seen him miles away, all the possessions he could carry piled on his back.

The early winter snow covered the smooth parts of the ground with a thin gauze, wrecked in places by leaves and rocks. There was more to come, with the sky the color of pewter to the north, up beyond the summit of Mont Lozère. A layer of white lay on the thick granite tiles of the church roof. The building was empty. No mass had been said there since the harvest: attendance had dropped as Monsieur Marcel and his followers grew more confident.

Isabelle stood among her neighbors listening to Monsieur Marcel, who paced in front of the door, severe in his black clothes and silver hair. Only his red-stained hands undermined his commanding presence, a reminder to them that he was after all simply a cobbler.

When he spoke he focussed on a point over the crowd's head.

– This place of worship has been the scene of corruption. It is in safe hands now. It is in *your* hands. He gestured before him as if he were sowing seed. A hum rose from the crowd.

– It must be cleansed, he continued. Cleansed of its sin, of these idols. He waved a hand at the building behind him. Isabelle stared up at the Virgin, the blue behind the statue faded but with a power still to move her. She had already touched her forehead and her belly before she realized what she was doing and managed to stop without completing the cross. She glanced around to see if the gesture had been noticed. But her neighbors were looking at Monsieur Marcel, calling to him as he strode through them and continued up the hill toward the bank of dark cloud, tawny hands tucked behind him. He did not look back.

When he was gone the crowd grew louder, more agitated.

Someone shouted: — The window! The cry was taken up. Above the door, a small circular window held the only piece of glass they had ever seen. The Duc de l'Aigle had installed it beneath the niche three summers ago, just before he was touched with the Truth by Calvin. From the outside the window was a dull brown, but from the inside it was green and yellow and blue, with a tiny dot of red in Eve's hand. The Sin. Isabelle had not been inside the church for a long time, but she remembered the scene well, Eve's look of desire, the serpent's smile, Adam's shame.

If they could have seen it once more, the sun lighting up the colors like a field dense with summer flowers, its beauty might have saved it. But there was no sun, and no entering the church: the priest had slipped a large padlock through the bolt across the door. They had not seen one before; several men had examined it, pulled at it, uncertain of its mechanism. An axe would have to be taken to it, carefully, to keep it intact.

Only the knowledge of the window's value held them back. It belonged to the Duc, to whom they owed a quarter of their crops, in turn receiving protection, the assurance of a whisper in the ear of the King. The window and the statue were gifts from him. He might still value them.

No one knew for certain who threw the stone, though afterwards several people claimed they had. It struck the center of the window and shattered it immediately. It was a sound so strange that the crowd hushed. They had not heard glass break before.

In the lull a boy ran over and picked up a shard of glass, then howled and threw it down.

— It bit me! he cried, holding up a bloody finger.

The shouting began again. The boy's mother snatched him and pressed him to her.

— The devil! she screamed. It was the devil!

Etienne Tournier, hair like burnt hay, stepped forward with a long rake. He glanced back at his older brother, Jacques, who nodded. Etienne looked up at the statue and called loudly: — La Rousse!

The crowd shifted, steps sideways that left Isabelle standing alone. Etienne turned around with a smirk on his face, pale blue eyes resting on her like hands pressing into her.

He slid his hand down the handle and hoisted the rake up, letting the metal teeth descend toward her and hover in front of her. They stared at each other. The crowd had gone quiet. Finally Isabelle grabbed the teeth; as she and Etienne held each end of the rake she felt a fire ignite below her stomach.

He smiled and let go, his end tapping the ground. Isabelle grasped the pole and began walking her hands down it, lifting the teeth end of the rake into the air, until she reached him. As she looked up at the Virgin, Etienne took a step back and disappeared from her side. She could feel the press of the crowd, bunched together again, restless, murmuring.

— Do it, La Rousse! someone shouted. Do it!

In the crowd Isabelle's brothers stood staring at the ground. She could not see her father, but if he was there as well he could not help her.

She took a deep breath and raised the rake. A shout rose with it, making her arm shake. She let the rake teeth rest to the left of the niche and looked around at the mass of bright red faces, unfamiliar now, hard and cold. She raised the rake, propped it against the base of the statue and pushed. It did not move.

The shouting became harsher as she began to push harder, tears pricking her eyes. The Child was staring into the distant sky, but Isabelle could feel the Virgin's gaze on her.

— Forgive me, she whispered. Then she pulled the rake back and swung it as hard as she could at the statue. Metal hit stone with a dull clang and the face of the Virgin was sliced off, showering Isabelle and making the crowd shriek with laughter. Desperately she swung the rake again. The mortar loosened with the blow and the statue rocked a little.

— Again, La Rousse! a woman shouted.

I can't do it again, Isabelle thought, but the sight of the red faces made her swing once more. The statue began to rock, the faceless woman rocking the child in her arms. Then it pitched forward and fell, the Virgin's head hitting the ground first and shattering, the body thumping after. In the impact of the fall the child was split from his mother and lay on the ground gazing upward. Isabelle dropped the rake and covered her face with her hands. There were loud cheers and whistles and the crowd surged forward to surround the broken statue.

When Isabelle took her hands from her face Etienne was standing in front of her. He smiled triumphantly, reached over and squeezed her breasts. Then he joined the crowd and began throwing dung at the blue niche.

I will never see such a color again, she thought.

Petit Henri and Gérard needed little convincing. Though Isabelle blamed Monsieur Marcel's persuasiveness, secretly she knew they would have gone anyway, even without his honeyed words.

— God will smile upon you, he had said solemnly. He has chosen you for this war. Fighting for your God, your religion, your freedom. You will return men of courage and strength.

— If you return at all, Henri du Moulin muttered angrily, words only Isabelle heard. He leased two fields of rye and two of potatoes, as well as a fine chestnut grove. He kept pigs and a herd of goats. He needed his sons; he couldn't farm the land with only his daughter left to help him.

— I will plant fewer fields, he told Isabelle. Only one of rye, and I'll give up some of the herd and a few pigs. Then I'll only need one field of potatoes to feed them. I can get more animals again when the twins return.

They won't come back, she thought. She had seen the light in their eyes as they left with other boys from Mont Lozère. They will go to Toulouse, to Paris, to Geneva to see Calvin. They will go to Spain, where men's skin is black, or to the ocean on the edge of the world. But here, no, they will not come back here.

She gathered her courage one evening as her father sat sharpening a plow blade by the fire.

— Papa, she ventured. I could marry and we could live here and work with you.

With one word he stopped her.

– Who? he asked, whetting stone paused over the blade. The room was quiet without the rhythmic sound of metal against stone.

She turned her face away.

– We are alone, you and I, *ma petite*. His tone was gentle. But God is kinder than you think.

Isabelle clasped her neck nervously, still carrying the taste of communion in her mouth – rough, dry bread that remained in the back of her throat long after she had swallowed. Etienne reached up and pulled at her headcloth. He found the end, wound it around his hand and gave a sharp tug. She began to spin, turning and turning out of the cloth, her hair unfurling, seeing flashes of Etienne with a grim smile on his face, then her father's chestnut trees, the fruit small and green and far out of reach.

When she was free of the cloth she stumbled, regained her balance, hesitated. She faced him but stepped backwards. He reached her in two strides, tripped her and tumbled on top of her. With one hand he pulled up her dress while the other buried itself in her hair, fingers splayed, pulling through like a comb to the ends, wrapping the hair around it as it had wound the cloth a moment earlier, until his fist was resting at the nape of her neck.

– La Rousse, he murmured. You've avoided me for a long time. Are you ready?

Isabelle hesitated, then nodded. Etienne pulled her head back by her hair to lift her chin up and bring her mouth to his.

– But the communion of the Pentecost is still in my mouth, she thought, and this is the Sin.

The Tourniers were the only family between Mont Lozère and Florac to own a Bible. Isabelle had seen it at services, when Jean Tournier carried it wrapped in linen and handed it ostentatiously to Monsieur Marcel. He watched it, fretful, throughout the service. It had cost him.

Monsieur Marcel laced his fingers together and held the book in the cradle of his arms, propped against the curve of his paunch. As he read he swayed from side to side as if he were drunk, though

Isabelle knew he could not be, since he had forbidden wine. His eyes moved back and forth, and words appeared in his mouth, but it was not clear to her how they got there.

Once the Truth was established inside the old church, Monsieur Marcel had a Bible brought from Lyons, and Isabelle's father built a wooden stand to hold it. Then the Tourniers' Bible was no longer seen, though Etienne still bragged about it.

— Where do words come from? Isabelle asked him one day after service, ignoring the eyes on them, the glare from Etienne's mother, Hannah. How does Monsieur Marcel get them from the Bible?

Etienne was tossing a stone from hand to hand. He flicked it away; it rustled to a stop in the leaves.

— They fly, he replied firmly. He opens his mouth and the black marks from the page fly to his mouth so quickly you can't see them. Then he spits them out.

— Can you read?

— No, but I can write.

— What do you write?

— I write my name. And I can write your name, he added confidently.

— Show me. Teach me.

Etienne smiled, teeth half-showing. He took a fistful of her skirt and pulled.

— I will teach you, but you must pay, he said softly, his eyes narrowed till the blue barely showed.

It was the Sin again: chestnut leaves crackling in her ears, fear and pain, but also the fierce excitement of feeling the ground under her, the weight of his body on her.

— Yes, she said finally, looking away. But show me first.

He had to gather the materials secretly: the feather from a kestrel, its point cut and sharpened; the fragment of parchment stolen from a corner of one of the pages of the Bible; a dried mushroom that dissolved into black when mixed with water on a piece of slate. Then he led her up the mountain, away from their farms, to a granite boulder with a flat surface that reached her waist. They leaned against it.

Miraculously, he drew six marks to form ET.

Isabelle stared at it.

— I want to write my name, she said. Etienne handed her the feather and stood behind her, his body pressed against the length of her back. She could feel the hard growth at the base of his stomach and a flicker of fearful desire raced through her. He placed his hand over hers and guided it first to the ink, then to the parchment, pushing it to form the six marks. ET, she wrote. She compared the two.

— But they are the same, she said, puzzled. How can that be your name and my name both?

— You wrote it, so it is your name. You don't know that? Whoever writes it, it is theirs.

— But — She stopped, and kept her mouth open, waiting for the marks to fly to her mouth. But when she spoke, it was his name that came out, not hers.

— Now you must pay, Etienne said, smiling. He pushed her over the boulder, stood behind her, and pulled her skirt up and his breeches down. He parted her legs with his knees and with his hand held her apart so that he could enter suddenly, with a quick thrust. Isabelle clung to the boulder as Etienne moved against her. Then with a shout he pushed her shoulders away, bending her forward so that her face and chest pressed hard against the rock.

After he withdrew she stood up shakily. The parchment had been pressed into her cheek and fluttered to the ground. Etienne looked at her face and grinned.

— You've written your name on your face, he said.

She had never been inside the Tourniers' farm, though it was not far from her father's, down along the river. It was the largest farm in the area apart from that of the Duc, who lived further down the valley, half a day's walk toward Florac. It was said to have been built 100 years before, with additions over time: a pigsty, a threshing floor, a tiled roof to replace the thatch. Jean and his cousin Hannah had married late, had only three children, were careful, powerful, remote. Evening visits to their hearth were rare.

Despite their influence, Isabelle's father had never been quiet about his scorn.

— They marry their cousins, Henri du Moulin scoffed. They give money to the church but they wouldn't give a moldy chestnut to a beggar. And they kiss three times, as if two were not enough.

The farm was spread along a slope in an L shape, the entrance in the crux, facing south. Etienne led her inside. His parents and two hired workers were planting in the fields; his sister, Susanne, was working at the bottom of the kitchen garden.

Inside it was quiet and still. All Isabelle could hear were the muted grunts of pigs. She admired the sty, the barn twice the size of her father's. She stood in the common room, touching the long wooden table lightly with her fingertips as if to steady herself. The room was tidy, newly swept, pots hung at even intervals from hooks on the walls. The hearth took up a whole end of the room, so big all of her family and the Tourniers could stand in it together — all of her family before she began to lose them. Her sister, dead. Her mother, dead. Her brothers, soldiers. Just she and her father now.

— La Rousse.

She turned around, saw Etienne's eyes, the swagger in his stride, and backed up until granite touched her back. He matched her step and put his hands on her hips.

— Not here, she said. Not in your parents' house, on the hearth. If your mother —

Etienne dropped his hands. The mention of his mother was enough to tame him.

— Have you asked them?

He was silent. His broad shoulders sagged and he stared off into a corner.

— You have not asked them.

— I'll be twenty-five soon and I can do what I want then. I won't need their permission then.

Of course they don't want us to marry, Isabelle thought. My family is poor, we have nothing, but they are rich, they have a Bible, a horse, they can write. They marry their cousins, they are friends with Monsieur Marcel. Jean Tournier is the Duc de l'Aigle's *syndic*, collecting tax from us. They would never accept as their daughter a girl they call La Rousse.

— We could live with my father, she suggested. It has been hard for him without my brothers. He needs —

— Never.

— So we must live here.

— Yes.

— Without their consent.

Etienne shifted his weight from one leg to the other, leaned against the edge of the table, crossed his arms. He looked at her directly.

— If they don't like you, he said softly, it's your own fault, La Rousse.

Isabelle's arms stiffened, her hands curled into fists.

— I have done nothing wrong! she cried. I believe in the Truth.

He smiled.

— But you love the Virgin, yes?

She bowed her head, fists still clenched.

— And your mother was a witch.

— What did you say? she whispered.

— That wolf that bit your mother, he was sent by the devil to bring her to him. And all those babies dying.

She glared at him.

— You think my mother made her own daughter die? Her own granddaughter die?

— When you are my wife, he said, you will not be a midwife. He took her hand and pulled her toward the barn, away from his parents' hearth.

— Why do you want me? she asked in a low voice he could not hear. She answered herself: Because I am the one his mother hates most.

The kestrel hovered directly overhead, fluttering against the wind. Grey: male. Isabelle narrowed her eyes. No. Reddish-brown, the color of her hair: female.

Alone she had learned to remain on the surface of the water, lying on her back, arms stroking out from her sides, breasts flattened, hair floating in the river like leaves around her face. She looked up again. The kestrel was diving to her right. The brief moment of impact was hidden by a clump of broom. When the bird reappeared it was carrying a tiny creature, a mouse or a sparrow. It flew up fast then and out of sight.

She sat up abruptly, crouching on the long smooth rock of the river bed, her breasts regaining their roundness. The sounds arose out of nothing, a tinkle here and there, then suddenly joined together into a chorus of hundreds of bells. The *estiver* – Isabelle's father had predicted they would arrive in two days' time. Their dogs must be good this summer. If she didn't hurry she would be surrounded by hundreds of sheep. She stood up quickly and picked her way to the bank, where she brushed the water from her skin with the flat of her hand and wrung the river from her hair. Her shameful hair. She pulled on her dress and smock and wound her hair out of sight in a long piece of white linen.

She was tucking in the end of the linen when she froze, feeling eyes on her. She searched as much of the surrounding land as she could without moving her head but could see nothing. The bells were still far away. With her fingers she felt for loose strands of hair and pushed them under the cloth, then dropped her arms, pulled her dress up away from her feet, and began to run down the path next to the river. Soon she turned off it and crossed a field of scrubby broom and heather.

She reached the crest of a hill and looked down. Far below a field rippled with sheep making their way up the mountain. Two men, one in front, one in back, and a dog on each side were keeping the flock together. Occasionally a few strays darted to one side, to be herded quickly back into the fold. They would have been walking for five days now, all the way from Alès, but at this final summit they showed no signs of flagging. They would have the whole summer to recover.

Over the bells she could hear the whistles and shouts of the men, the sharp barks of the dogs. The man in front looked up, straight at her it seemed, and whistled shrilly. Immediately a young man appeared from behind a boulder a stone's throw to her right. Isabelle clutched her neck. He was small and wiry, sweaty and very dark from the sun. He carried a walking stick and the leather sack of a shepherd and wore a close-fitting round cap, black curls framing the brim. When she felt his dark eyes on her she knew he had seen her in the river. He smiled at her, friendly, knowing, and for a moment Isabelle felt the touch of the river on her body. She looked down, pressed her elbows to her breasts, could not smile back.

With a leap the man started down the hill. Isabelle watched his progress until he reached the flock. Then she fled.

— There is a child here. Isabelle placed a hand on her belly and stared defiantly at Etienne.

In an instant his pale eyes darkened like the shadow of a cloud crossing a field. He looked at her hand, calculating.

— I will tell my father, then we must tell your parents. She swallowed. What will they say?

— They'll let us marry now. It would look worse if they said no when there is a child.

— They'll think I did it deliberately.

— Did you? His eyes met hers. They were cold now.

— It was you who wanted the Sin, Etienne.

— Ah, but you wanted it too, La Rousse.

— I wish Maman were here, she said softly. I wish Marie were here.

Her father acted as if he had not heard her. He sat on the bench by the door and scraped at a branch with his knife; he was making a new pole for the hoe he had broken earlier that day. Isabelle stood motionless in front of him. She had said it so quietly that she began to think she would have to repeat herself. She opened her mouth to speak when he said: — You will all have left me, then.

— I'm sorry, Papa. He says he won't live here.

– I wouldn't have a Tournier in my house. This farm won't go to you when I die. You'll get your dowry, but I will leave the farm to my nephews over at l'Hôpital. A Tournier will never get my land.

– The twins will return from the wars, she suggested, fighting tears.

– No. They will die. They're not soldiers, but farmers. You know that. Two years and no word from them. Plenty have passed through from the north and no news.

Isabelle left her father sitting on the bench and walked across their fields, along the river, down to the Tournier farm. It was late, more dark than light, long shadows cast along the hills and the terraced fields full of half-grown rye. A flock of starlings sang in the trees. The route between the two farms seemed long now, at the end of it Etienne's mother. Isabelle began walking more slowly.

She had reached the Tourniers' empty *cleda*, the season's chestnuts long since dried, when she saw the grey shadow emerge skittishly from the trees to stand in the path.

– *Sainte Vierge, aide-moi*, she prayed automatically. She watched the wolf watching her, its yellow eyes bright despite the gloom. When it began to move toward her, Isabelle heard a voice in her head: – Don't let this happen to you too.

She crouched and picked up a large branch. The wolf stopped. She stood up and advanced, waving the stick and shouting. The wolf began to move backwards, and when Isabelle pretended to throw the branch, it turned and skittered sideways, disappearing into the trees.

Isabelle ran from the woods and across a field, rye cutting into her calves. She reached the rock shaped like a mushroom that marked the bottom of the Tourniers' kitchen garden and stopped to catch her breath. Her fear of Etienne's mother was gone.

– Thank you, Maman, she said softly. I won't forget.

Jean, Hannah and Etienne were sitting by the fire while Susanne cleared the last of their *bajanas*, the same chestnut soup Isabelle had served her father earlier, and dark, sweet-smelling bread. All four froze when Isabelle entered.

— What is it, La Rousse? Jean Tournier asked as she stood in the middle of the room, her hand once more resting on the table as if to secure her a place among them.

Isabelle said nothing but looked steadily at Etienne. At last he stood up and moved to her side. She nodded and he turned to face his parents.

The room was silent. Hannah's face looked like granite.

— Isabelle is going to have a child, Etienne said in a low voice. With your permission we would like to marry.

It was the first time he had ever used Isabelle's name.

Hannah's voice pierced.

— You carry whose child, La Rousse? Not Etienne's.

— It is Etienne's child.

— No!

Jean Tournier put his hands on the table and stood up. His silver hair was smooth like a cap against his skull, his face gaunt. He said nothing, but his wife stopped speaking and sat back. He looked at Etienne. There was a long pause before Etienne spoke.

— It is my child. We will marry anyway when I am twenty-five. Soon.

Jean and Hannah exchanged glances.

— What does your father say? Jean asked Isabelle.

— He has given his permission and will provide the dowry. She said nothing about his hatred.

— Go and wait outside, La Rousse, Jean said quietly. You go with her, Susanne.

The girls sat side by side on the door bench. They had seen little of each other since they were children. Many years ago, even before Isabelle's hair turned red, Susanne had played with Marie, helping with the haying, the goats, splashing in the river.

For a while they sat, looking out over the valley.

— I saw a wolf out by the *cleda*, Isabelle said suddenly.

Susanne stared, brown eyes wide. She had the thin face and pointed chin of her father.

— What did you do?

— Chased it with a stick. She smiled, pleased with herself.

— Isabelle —

— What is it?

— I know Maman is upset, but I am glad you will live with us. I never believed what they said about you, about your hair and — She stopped. Isabelle did not ask.

— And you will be safe here. This house is safe, protected by —

She stopped again, glanced at the door, bowed her head. Isabelle let her eyes rest on the shadowy humps of the hills in the distance.

It will always be like this, she thought. Silence in this house.

The door opened and Jean and Etienne emerged with a flickering torch and an axe.

— We will take you back, La Rousse, Jean said. I must speak with your father.

He handed a piece of bread to Etienne.

— Take this bread together and give her your hand.

Etienne tore the bread in two and gave the smaller piece to Isabelle. She put it in her mouth and placed her hand in his. His fingers were cold. The bread stuck in the back of her throat like a whisper.

Petit Jean was born in blood and was a fearless child.

Jacob was born blue. He was a quiet child: even when Hannah smacked his back to start his breath he did not scream.

Isabelle lay in the river again, many summers later. There were marks on her body from the two boys, and another child pushing her belly above the water. The baby kicked. She cupped the mound with her hands.

— Please let the Virgin make it a girl, she prayed. And when she is born I will name her after you, after my sister. Marie. I will fight everyone to name her that.

This time there were no warnings at all, no bells, no sense of eyes on her. He was just there, sitting on his heels on the river bank. She sat up and looked at him. She did not cover her breasts.

He looked the same, a little older, with a long scar down the right side of his face, from his cheekbone to his chin, touching the corner of his mouth. This time she would have smiled back at him if he had smiled. He did not smile. He simply nodded at her, cupped his hands, splashed water on his face, then turned and walked in the direction of the river's source.

Marie was born in a flood of clear liquid, her eyes open. She was a hopeful child.

2. The Dream

When Rick and I moved to France, I figured my life would change a little. I just didn't know how.

To begin with, the new country was a banquet where we were ready to try every dish. Our first week there, while Rick was sharpening his pencils at his new office, I knocked the rust from my high-school French and set out to explore the countryside surrounding Toulouse and to find us a place to live. A small town was what we wanted; an interesting town. I sped along little roads in a new grey Renault, driving fast through long lines of sycamores. Occasionally when I wasn't paying attention I thought I was in Ohio or Indiana, but the landscape snapped back into itself the moment I saw a house with a red tile roof, green shutters, window boxes full of geraniums. Everywhere farmers in bright blue work pants stood in fields dusted with pale April green and watched my car pass across their horizon. I smiled and waved; sometimes they waved back, hesitantly. 'Who was *that*?' they were probably asking themselves.

I saw a lot of towns and rejected them all, sometimes for frivolous reasons, but ultimately because I was looking for a place that would sing to me, that would tell me my search was over.

I arrived in Lisle-sur-Tarn by crossing a long narrow bridge over the River Tarn. At the end of it a church and a café marked the town's edge. I parked next to the café and began to walk; by the time I reached the center of town I knew we would live there. It was a *bastide*, a fortified town preserved from the Middle Ages; when there were invasions in medieval times the villagers would gather in the market square and close off its four entrances. I stood in the middle of the square next to a fountain with lavender bushes planted around it and felt contained and content.

The square was surrounded on all four sides by an arched,

covered walkway, with shops on the ground level and shuttered houses above. The arches were built of long narrow bricks; the same bricks made up the top two levels of the houses, laid horizontally or diagonally in decorative patterns between brown timbers, held together with dull pink mortar.

This is what I need, I thought. Seeing this every day will make me happy.

Immediately I began having doubts. It seemed absurd to decide on a town because of one beautiful square. I began to walk again, looking for that deciding factor, the sign that would make me stay or go.

It didn't take long. After exploring the surrounding streets I entered a *boulangerie* on the square. The woman behind the counter was short and wore a navy blue and white housecoat I'd seen for sale at every market I had visited. When she finished with another customer she turned to me, black eyes scrutinizing me from a lined face, hair pulled back in a loose bun.

'*Bonjour, Madame*,' she said in the singsong intonation French women use in shops.

'*Bonjour*,' I replied, glancing at the bread on the shelves behind her and thinking: This will be my *boulangerie* now. But when I looked back at her, expecting a warm welcome, my confidence fell away. She stood solidly behind the counter, her face like armor.

I opened my mouth: nothing came out. I swallowed. She stared at me and said, '*Oui, Madame?*' in exactly the same tone she'd first used, as if the last few awkward seconds hadn't occurred.

I hesitated, then pointed at a baguette. '*Un*,' I managed to say, though it sounded more like a grunt. The woman's face modulated into the stiffness of disapproval. She reached behind her without looking, eyes still fixed on me.

'*Quelque chose d'autre, Madame?*'

For a moment I stepped outside myself and saw myself as she must see me: foreign, transient, thick tongue stumbling over peculiar sounds, dependent on a map to locate me in a strange landscape and a phrasebook and dictionary to communicate. She made me feel lost the very moment I thought I'd found home.

I looked at the display, desperate to show her I wasn't as ridiculous as I seemed. I pointed at some onion quiches and managed to say, '*Et un quiche.*' A split second afterwards I knew I'd used the wrong article – *quiche* was feminine and should be used with *une* – and groaned inwardly.

She put one in a small bag and laid it on the counter next to the baguette. '*Quelque chose d'autre, Madame?*' she repeated.

'*Non.*'

She rang up the purchases on the cash register. Mutely I handed her the money, then realized when she placed my change on a small tray on the counter that I should have put the money there rather than directly into her hand. I frowned. It was a lesson I ought to have learned already.

'*Merci, Madame,*' she intoned with a blank face and flinty eyes.

'*Merci,*' I mumbled.

'*Au revoir, Madame.*'

I turned to go, then stopped, thinking there must be a way to salvage this. I looked at her: she had crossed her arms over her vast bosom.

'*Je – nous – nous habitons près d'ici, là-bas,*' I lied, gesturing wildly behind me, clawing out a territory somewhere in her town.

She nodded once. '*Oui, Madame. Au revoir, Madame.*'

'*Au revoir, Madame,*' I replied, spinning around and out the door.

Oh Ella, I thought as I trudged across the square, what are you doing, lying to save face?

'So don't lie, then. Live here. Confront Madame every day over the croissants,' I muttered in reply. I found myself by the fountain and reached over to a lavender bush, pulled off a few leaves and crushed them between my fingers. The sharp woody scent said: *Reste.*

Rick loved Lisle-sur-Tarn when he saw it, and made me feel better about my choice by kissing me and spinning me around in his arms. 'Hah!' he shouted at the old houses.

'Shh, Rick,' I said. It was market day in the square and I could feel all eyes on us. 'Put me down,' I hissed.

He just smiled and held me more tightly.

'This is my kind of town,' he said. 'Just look at the detail in that brickwork!'

We wandered all over, picking out our favorite houses. Later we stopped at the *boulangerie* for more onion quiches. I turned red the moment Madame looked at me, but she directed most of her remarks at Rick, who found her hilarious and chuckled at her without appearing to offend her in the slightest. I could see she found him handsome: his blond ponytail in this land of short dark hair was a novelty and his Californian tan hadn't faded yet. To me she was polite, but I detected an underlying hostility that made me tense.

'It's a shame those quiches are so good,' I remarked to Rick out on the street. 'Otherwise I'd never go in there again.'

'Oh babe, there you go, taking things to heart. Don't go all east-coast paranoid on me, now.'

'She just makes me feel unwelcome.'

'Bad customer relations. Tut-tut! Better get a personnel consultant in to sort her out.'

I grinned at him. 'Yeah, I'd like to see her file.'

'Positively *riddled* with complaints. She's on her last legs, it's obvious. Have a little pity on the old thing.'

It was tempting to live in one of the old houses in or near the square, but when we found out none were for rent I was secretly relieved: they were serious houses, for established members of town. Instead we found a place a few minutes' walk from the center, still old but without the fancy brickwork, with thick walls and tiled floors and a small back patio sheltered by a vine-covered trellis. There was no front yard: the front door opened directly onto the narrow street. The house was dark inside, though Rick reminded me that it would be cool during the summer. All of the houses we'd seen were like that. I fought against the dimness by keeping the shutters open, and caught my neighbors peeking through the windows several times before they learned not to look.

One day I decided to surprise Rick: when he came home from work that night I'd painted over the dull brown of the shutters with a rich burgundy and hung boxes of geraniums from the windows. He stood in front of the house smiling up at me as I leaned over the window sill, framed in pink and white and red blossoms.

'Welcome to France,' I said. 'Welcome home.'

When my father found out Rick and I were going to live in France he encouraged me to write to a cousin several times removed who lived in Moutier, a small town in northwest Switzerland. Dad had visited Moutier once, long ago. 'You'll love it, I promise,' he kept saying when he called to give me the address.

'Dad, France and Switzerland are two different countries! I probably won't get anywhere near Switzerland.'

'Sure, kid, but it's always good to have family nearby.'

'Nearby? Moutier must be 400, 500 miles from where we'll be.'

'You see? Just a day's drive. And that's a lot closer than I'll be to you.'

'Dad –'

'Just take the address, Ella. Humor me.'

How could I say no? I wrote down the address and laughed. 'This is silly. What do I write to him: "Hello, I'm a distant cousin you've never heard of before and I'm on the continent, so let's meet up"?'

'Why not? Listen, as an opening you could ask him about the family history, where we come from, what our family did. Use some of that time you'll have on your hands.'

Dad was driven by the Protestant work ethic, and the prospect of me not having a job made him nervous. He kept making suggestions about useful things I could do. His anxiety fuelled my own: I wasn't used to having free time – I'd always been busy either training or working long hours. Having time on my hands took some getting used to; I went through a phase of sleeping late and moping around the house before I devised three projects to keep me occupied.

I started by working on my dormant French, taking lessons twice a week in Toulouse with Madame Sentier, an older woman with bright eyes and a narrow face like a bird. She had a beautiful accent, and the first thing she did was to tackle mine. She hated sloppy pronunciation, and yelled at me when I began saying *Oui* in that throwaway manner many French have of barely moving their lips and letting the sound come out like a duck quacking. She made me pronounce it precisely, sounding all three letters, whistling the air through my teeth at the end. She was adamant that how I said things was more important than what I said. I tried to argue against her priorities, but I was no match for her.

'If you do not pronounce the words well, no one will understand what you say,' she declared. 'Moreover, they will know that you are foreign and will not listen to you. The French are like that.'

I refrained from pointing out that she was French too. Anyway I liked her, liked her opinions and her firm hand, so I did her mouth exercises, pulling my lips around like they were made of bubblegum.

She encouraged me to talk as much as possible, wherever I was. 'If you think of something, say it!' she cried. 'No matter what it is, however small, say it. Talk to everyone.' Sometimes she made me talk non-stop for a set period of time, starting with one minute and working up to five minutes. I found it exhausting and impossible.

'You are thinking a thought in English and then translating it word by word into French,' Madame Sentier pointed out. 'Language does not work like that. It has a grand shape. What you must do is to *think* in French. There should be no English in your head. Think as much as you can in French. If you cannot think in paragraphs, think in sentences, at least in words. Build it up into grand thoughts!' She gestured, taking in the whole room and all of human intellect.

She was delighted to find out that I had Swiss relations; it was she who made me sit down and write. 'They may have been from France originally, you know,' she said. 'It would be good for you to find out about your French ancestors. You will feel more connected to this country and its people. Then it will not be so hard to think in French.'

I shrugged inwardly. Genealogy was one of those middle-aged things I lumped together with all-talk radio stations, knitting and staying in on Saturday nights: I knew I would eventually indulge in all of them, but I was in no hurry about it. My ancestors didn't have anything to do with my life right now. But to humor Madame Sentier, as part of my homework I pieced together a few sentences asking my cousin about the history of the family. When she'd checked it for grammar and spelling I sent the letter off to Switzerland.

The French lessons in turn helped me with my second project. 'What a wonderful profession for a woman!' Madame Sentier crowed when she heard I was studying to qualify as a midwife in France. 'What noble work!' I liked her too much to be annoyed by her romantic notions, so I didn't mention the suspicion my colleagues and I were treated with by doctors, hospitals, insurance companies, even pregnant women. Nor did I bring up the sleepless nights, the blood, the trauma when something went wrong. Because it *was* a good job, and I hoped to be able to practice in France once I'd taken the required classes and exams.

The final project had an uncertain future, but it would certainly keep me busy when the time came. No one would have been surprised by it: I was twenty-eight, Rick and I had been married two years, and the pressure from everyone, ourselves included, was beginning to mount.

One night when we had lived in Lisle-sur-Tarn just a few weeks we went out to dinner at the one good restaurant in town. We talked idly – about Rick's work, my day – through the crudités, the pâté, trout from the Tarn and filet mignon. When the waiter brought Rick's *crème brûlée* and my *tarte au citron* I decided this was the moment to speak. I bit into the lemon slice garnish; my mouth puckered.

'Rick,' I began, setting down my fork.

'Great *brûlée*,' he said. 'Especially the *brûléed* part. Here, try some.'

'No thanks. Look, I've been thinking about things.'

'Ah, is this gonna be serious talk?'

At that moment a couple entered the restaurant and were seated at the table next to us. The woman's belly was just visible against her elegant black dress. Five months pregnant, I thought automatically, and carrying it very high.

I lowered my voice. 'You know how every now and then we talk about having kids?'

'You want to have kids now?'

'Well, I was thinking about it.'

'OK.'

'OK what?'

'OK let's do it.'

'Just like that? "Let's do it"?'

'Why not? We know we want them. Why agonize over it?'

I felt let down, though I knew Rick too well to be surprised by his attitude. He always made decisions quickly, even big ones, whereas I wanted the decisions to be more complicated.

'I feel –' I considered how to explain it. 'It's kind of like a parachute jump. Remember when we did that last year? You're up in this tiny plane and you keep thinking, Two minutes till I can't say no anymore, One minute till I can't turn back, then, Here I am balancing by the door, but I can still say no. And then you jump and you can't get back in, no matter how you feel about the experience. That's how I feel now. I'm standing by the open door of the plane.'

'I just remember that fantastic sensation of falling. And the beautiful view floating down. It was so quiet up there.'

I sucked at the inside of my cheek, then took a big bite of tart.

'It's a big decision,' I said with my mouth full.

'A big decision made.' Rick leaned over and kissed me. 'Mmm, nice lemon.'

Later that night I slipped out of the house and went to the bridge. I could hear the river far below but it was too dark to see the water. I looked around; with no one in sight I pulled out a pack of contraceptive pills and began to push the tablets one by one out of their metal foil. They disappeared toward the water, tiny white flashes pinpointed in the dark for a second. After they were gone I leaned against the railing for a long time, willing myself to feel different.

Something did change that night. That night I had the dream for the first time: the fog, the voices, the boom, the blue.

Friends had told me that when you try to conceive, you have either lots more sex or lots less. You can go at it all the time, the way a shotgun sprays its pellets everywhere in the hope of hitting something. Or you can strike strategically, saving your ammunition for the appropriate moment.

To start with, Rick and I went for the first approach. When he got home from work we made love before dinner. We went to bed early, woke up early to do it, fit it in whenever we could.

Rick loved this abundance, but for me it was different. For one thing, I'd never had sex because I felt I had to — it had always been because I wanted to. Now, though, there was an unspoken mission behind the activity that made it feel deliberate and calculated. I was also ambivalent about not using contraception: all the energy I'd put into prevention over the years, all the lessons and caution drilled into me — were they to be tossed away in a moment? I'd heard that this could be a great turn-on, but I felt fear when I'd expected exhilaration.

Above all, I was exhausted. I was sleeping badly, dragged into a room of blue each night. I didn't say anything to Rick, never woke him or explained the next day why I was so tired. Usually I told him everything; now there was a block in my throat and a lock on my lips.

One night I was lying in bed, staring at the blue dancing above me, when it finally dawned on me: the only two nights I hadn't had the dream in the last ten days were when we hadn't had sex.

Part of me was relieved to make that connection, to be able to explain it: I was anxious about conceiving, and that was bringing on the nightmare. Knowing that made it a little less frightening.

Still, I needed sleep; I had to convince Rick to cut down on sex without explaining why. I couldn't bring myself to tell him I had nightmares after he made love to me.

Instead, when my period came and it was clear we hadn't conceived, I suggested to Rick that we try the strategic approach. I used every textbook argument I knew, threw in some technical words and tried to be cheerful. He was disappointed but gave in gracefully.

'You know more about this than me,' he said. 'I'm just the hired gun. You tell me what to do.'

Unfortunately, though the dream came less frequently, the damage had been done: I found it harder to sleep deeply, and often lay awake in a state of non-specific anxiety, waiting for the blue, thinking that some night it would return anyway, unaccompanied by sex.

One night – a strategic night – Rick was kissing his way from my shoulder down my arm when he paused. I could feel his lips hovering above the crease in my arm. I waited but he didn't continue. 'Um, Ella,' he said at last. I opened my eyes. He was staring at the crease; as my eyes followed his gaze my arm jerked away from him.

'Oh,' I said simply. I studied the circle of red, scaly skin.

'What is it?'

'Psoriasis. I had it once, when I was thirteen. When Mom and Dad divorced.'

Rick looked at it, then leaned over and kissed my eyelids shut.

When I opened my eyes again I just caught a flicker of distaste cross his face before he controlled himself and smiled at me.

Over the next week I watched helplessly as the original patch widened, then jumped to my other arm and both elbows. It would reach my ankles and calves soon.

At Rick's insistence I went to see a doctor. He was young and brusque, lacking the patter American doctors use to soften up their patients. I had to concentrate hard on his rapid French.

'You have had this before?' he asked as he studied my arms.

'Yes, when I was young.'

'But not since?'

'No.'

'How long have you been in France?'

31

'Six weeks.'

'And you will stay?'

'Yes, for a few years. My husband has a job with an architectural firm in Toulouse.'

'You have children?'

'No. Not yet.' I turned red. Pull yourself together, Ella, I thought. You're twenty-eight years old, you don't have to be embarrassed about sex anymore.

'And you work now?'

'No. That is, I did, in the United States. I was a midwife.'

He raised his eyebrows. '*Une sage-femme?* Do you want to practice in France?'

'I would like to work but I haven't been able to get a work permit yet. Also the medical system is different here, so I have to pass an exam before I can practice. So now I study French and this autumn I begin a course for midwives in Toulouse to study for the exam.'

'You look tired.' He changed the subject abruptly, as if to suggest I was wasting his time by talking about my career.

'I've been having nightmares, but –' I stopped. I didn't want to get into this with him.

'You are unhappy, Madame Turner?' he asked more gently.

'No, no, not unhappy,' I replied uncertainly. Sometimes it's hard to tell when I'm so tired, I added to myself.

'You know psoriasis appears sometimes when you do not get enough sleep.'

I nodded. So much for psychological analysis.

The doctor prescribed cortisone cream, suppositories to bring down the swelling and sleeping pills in case the itching kept me awake, then told me to come back in a month. As I was leaving he added, 'And come to see me when you are pregnant. I am also an *obstétricien*.'

I blushed again.

My infatuation with Lisle-sur-Tarn didn't last much longer than my unbroken sleep had.

It was a beautiful, peaceful town, moving at a pace I knew was healthier than what I'd been used to in the States, and the quality of life was undeniably better. The produce at the Saturday market in the square, the meat at the *boucherie*, the bread at the *boulangerie* – all tasted wonderful to someone brought up on bland supermarket products. In Lisle lunch was still the biggest meal of the day, children ran freely with no fear of strangers or cars, and there was time for small talk. People were never in too much of a hurry to stop and chat with everyone.

With everyone but me, that is. As far as I knew, Rick and I were the only foreigners in town. We were treated that way. Conversations stopped when I entered stores, and when resumed I was sure the subject had been changed to something innocuous. People were polite to me, but after several weeks I still felt I hadn't had a real conversation with anyone. I made a point of saying hello to people I recognized, and they said hello back, but no one said hello to me first or stopped to talk to me. I tried to follow Madame Sentier's advice about talking as much as I could, but I was given so little encouragement that my thoughts dried up. Only when a transaction took place, when I was buying things or asking where something was, did the townspeople spare a few words for me.

One morning I was sitting in a café on the square, drinking coffee and reading the paper. Several other people were scattered among the tables. The proprietor passed among us, chatting and joking, handing out candy to the children. I had been there a few times; he and I were on nodding terms now but had not progressed to conversation. Give that about ten years, I thought sourly.

A few tables away, a woman younger than me sat with a five-month-old baby who was lying in a car seat set on a chair, shaking a rattle. The woman wore tight jeans and had an irritating laugh. She soon got up and went inside. The baby didn't seem to notice she'd gone.

I concentrated on *Le Monde*. I was forcing myself to read the entire front page before I was allowed to touch the *International Herald Tribune*. It was like wading through mud: not just because of the language, but also all the names I didn't recognize, the political situations I knew nothing about. Even when I understood a story I wasn't necessarily interested in it.

I was plowing through a piece about an imminent postal strike – a phenomenon I wasn't accustomed to in the States – when I heard a strange noise, or rather, silence. I looked up. The baby had stopped shaking the rattle and let it drop into his lap. His face began to crumple like a napkin being scrunched after a meal. Right, here comes the crying, I thought. I glanced into the café: his mother was leaning against the bar, talking on the phone and playing idly with a coaster.

The baby didn't cry: his face grew redder and redder, as if he were trying to but couldn't. Then he turned purple and blue in quick succession.

I jumped up, my chair falling backwards with a bang. 'He's choking!' I shouted.

I was only ten feet away but by the time I reached him a ring of customers had formed around him. A man was crouched in front of the baby, patting his blue cheeks. I tried to squeeze through but the proprietor, his back to me, kept stepping in front of me.

'Hang on, he's choking!' I cried. I was facing a wall of shoulders. I ran to the other side of the circle. 'I'm a midwife, I can help him!'

The people I was pushing between looked at me, their faces hard and cold.

'You have to pound him on the back, he's not getting any air. Now! He'll get brain damage if you don't do it quickly!'

I stopped. I had been speaking in English.

The mother appeared, melting through the barricade of people. She began frantically hitting the baby's back, too hard, I thought. Everyone stood watching her in an eerie silence. I was wondering how to say 'Heimlich maneuver' in French when the baby suddenly coughed and a red candy lozenge shot out of his mouth. He gasped for air, then began to cry, his face going bright red again.

There was a collective sigh and the ring of people broke up. I caught the proprietor's eye; he looked at me coolly. I opened my mouth to say something, but he turned away, picked up his tray and went inside. I gathered up my newspapers and left without paying.

After that I felt uncomfortable in town. I avoided the café and the woman with her baby. I found it hard to look people in the eye. My French became less confident and my accent deteriorated.

Madame Sentier noticed immediately. 'But what has happened?' she asked. 'You were progressing so well!'

An image of a ring of shoulders came to mind. I said nothing.

One day at the *boulangerie* I heard the woman ahead of me say she was on her way to '*la bibliothèque*', gesturing as if it were just around the corner. Madame handed her a plastic-covered book; it was a cheap romance. I bought my baguettes and quiches in a rush, cutting short my awkward ritual conversation with Madame. I ducked out and trailed the other woman as she made her daily purchases around the square. She stopped to say hello to several people and argued with all the storekeepers while I sat on a bench in the square and kept an eye on her over my newspaper. She made stops on three sides of the square before abruptly entering the town hall on the last side. I folded my paper and raced after her, then found myself having to hover in the lobby examining wedding banns and planning permission notices while she labored up a long flight of stairs. I took the stairs two at a time and slipped through the door after her. Shutting it behind me, I turned to face the first place in town that felt familiar.

The library had exactly that mixture of seediness and comforting quiet that made me love public libraries back home. Though it was small — only two rooms — it had high ceilings and several unshuttered windows, giving it an unusually airy feel for such an old building. Several people looked up from what they were doing to stare at me, but their attention was mercifully short and one by one they went back to reading or talking together in low voices.

I had a look around and then went to the main desk to apply for a library card. A pleasant, middle-aged woman in a smart olive suit told me I would need to bring in something with my French address on it as proof of residence. She also tactfully pointed me in the direction of a multi-volume French–English dictionary and a small English-language section.

The woman wasn't behind the desk the second time I visited the library; in her place a man stood talking on the phone, his sharp brown eyes focussed on a point out in the square, a sardonic smile on his angular face. About my height, he was wearing black trousers and a white shirt without a tie, buttoned at the collar, sleeves rolled up above his elbows. He fell into my lone-wolf category of men. I smiled to myself: one to avoid.

I veered away from him and headed for the English-language section. It looked like some tourists had donated a sackful of vacation reading: it was full of thrillers and sex-and-shopping novels. There was also a good selection of Agatha Christie. I found one I hadn't read, then browsed in the French fiction section. Madame Sentier had recommended Françoise Sagan as a painless way to ease myself into reading in French; I chose *Bonjour Tristesse*. I started toward the front desk, glanced at the wolf behind it, then at my two frivolous books, and stopped. I went back to the English section, dug around and added *Portrait of a Lady* to my pile.

I dawdled for a while, poring over a copy of *Paris-Match*. Finally I carried my books up to the desk. The man behind it looked hard at me, made some mental calculation as he glanced at the books and, with the faintest smirk at the corner of his mouth, said in English, 'Your card?'

Damn you, I thought. I hated that sneering appraisal, the assumption that I couldn't speak French, that I looked so American.

'I would like to apply for a card,' I replied carefully in French, trying to pronounce the words without any trace of an American accent.

He handed me a form. 'Fill out this,' he commanded in English.

I was so annoyed that when I filled in the application I wrote down my last name as Tournier rather than Turner. I pushed the sheet defiantly toward him along with driver's license, credit card and a letter from the bank with our French address on it. He glanced at the pieces of identification, then frowned at the sheet.

'What is this "Tournier"?' he asked, tapping his finger on my name. 'It is Turner, yes? Like Tina Turner?'

I continued to answer in French. 'Yes, but my family name was originally Tournier. They changed it when they moved to the United States. In the nineteenth century. They took out the "o" and the "i" so that the name would be more American.' This was the one bit of family lore I knew and I was proud of it, but it was clear he wasn't impressed. 'Lots of families changed their names when they emigrated –' I trailed off and looked away from his mocking eyes.

'Your name is Turner, so there must be Turner on the card, yes?'

I lapsed into English. 'I – since I'm living here now I thought I'd start using Tournier.'

'But you have no card or letter with Tournier on it, no?'

I shook my head and scowled at the stack of books, elbows clenched to my sides. To my mortification my eyes began to fill with tears. 'Never mind, it's nothing,' I muttered. Careful not to look at him, I scooped up the cards and letter, turned around and pushed my way out.

That night I opened the front door of our house to shoo away two cats fighting in the street and stumbled over the stack of books on the front step. The library card was sitting on top and was made out to Ella Tournier.

I stayed away from the library, stifling my urge to make a special trip to thank the librarian. I hadn't yet learned how to thank French people. When I was buying something they seemed to thank me too many times during the exchange, yet I always doubted their sincerity. It was hard to analyze the tone of their words. But the librarian's sarcasm had been undeniable; I couldn't imagine him accepting thanks with grace.

A few days after the card appeared I was walking along the road by the river and saw him sitting in a patch of sunlight in front of the café by the bridge, where I'd begun going for coffee. He seemed mesmerized by the water far below and I stopped, trying to decide whether or not to say something to him, wondering if I could pass by quietly so he wouldn't notice. He glanced up then and caught me watching him. His expression didn't change; he looked as if his thoughts were far away.

'*Bonjour*,' I said, feeling foolish.

'*Bonjour*.' He shifted slightly in his seat and gestured to the chair next to him. '*Café?*'

I hesitated. '*Oui, s'il vous plaît*,' I said at last. I sat down and he nodded at the waiter. For a moment I felt acutely embarrassed and cast my eyes out over the Tarn so I wouldn't have to look at him. It was a big river, about 100 yards wide, green and placid and seemingly still. But as I watched I noticed there was a slow roll to the water; I kept my eyes on it and saw occasional flashes of a dark, rust-red substance boiling to the surface and then disappearing again. Fascinated, I followed the red patches with my eyes. Each time one disappeared I felt a strange dual sense of relief and disappointment and then a gathering excitement as I waited for the next one to appear. When it did I found myself shivering involuntarily but watching closely until it slipped out of sight.

The waiter arrived with the coffee on a silver tray, blocking my view of the river. I turned to the librarian. 'That red there in the Tarn, what is it?' I asked in French.

He answered in English. 'Clay deposits from the hills. There was a landslide recently that exposed the clay under the soil. It washes down into the river.'

My eyes were drawn back to the water. Still watching the clay I switched to English. 'What's your name?'

'Jean-Paul.'

'Thank you for the library card, Jean-Paul. That was very nice of you.'

He shrugged and I was glad I hadn't made a bigger deal of it.

We sat without speaking for a long time, drinking our coffee and looking at the river. It was warm in the late May sun and I would have taken off my jacket but I didn't want him to see the psoriasis on my arms.

'Why aren't you at the library?' I asked abruptly.

He looked up. 'It's Wednesday. Library's closed.'

'Ah. How long have you worked there?'

'Three years. Before that I was at a library in Nîmes.'

'So that's your career? You're a librarian?'

He gave me a sideways look as he lit a cigarette. 'Yes. Why do you ask?'

'It's just – you don't seem like a librarian.'

'What do I seem like?'

I looked him over. He was wearing black jeans and a soft salmon-colored cotton shirt; a black blazer was draped over the back of his chair. His arms were tanned, the forearms densely covered with black hair.

'A gangster,' I replied. 'Except you need sunglasses.'

Jean-Paul smiled slightly and let smoke trickle from his mouth so that it formed a blue curtain around his face. 'What is it you Americans say? "Don't judge a book by its cover".'

I smiled back. '*Touché.*'

'So why are you here in France, Ella Tournier?'

'My husband is working as an architect in Toulouse.'

'And why are you here?'

'We wanted to try living in a small town rather than in Toulouse. We were in San Francisco before, and I grew up in Boston, so I thought a small town would be an interesting change.'

'I asked why are *you* here?'

'Oh.' I paused. 'Because my husband is here.'

He raised his eyebrows and stubbed out his cigarette.

'I mean, I *wanted* to come. I was glad for the change.'

'You *were* glad or you *are* glad?'

I snorted. 'Your English is very good. Where did you learn it?'

'I lived in New York for two years. I was studying for a library science degree at Columbia University.'

'You lived in New York and then came back *here*?'

'To Nîmes and then here, yes.' He gave me a little smile. 'Why is that so surprising, Ella Tournier? This is my home.'

I wished he would stop using Tournier. He was looking at me

with the smirk I'd first seen on his face at the library, impenetrable and condescending. I would've liked to see his face as he wrote out my library card: had he made that into a superior act as well?

I stood up abruptly and fumbled in my purse for some coins. 'It's been nice talking, but I have to go.' I laid the money on the table. Jean-Paul looked at it and frowned, shaking his head almost imperceptibly. I turned red, scraped the coins up and turned to go.

'*Au revoir, Ella Tournier*. Enjoy the Henry James.'

I spun around. '*Why* do you keep using my last name like that?'

He leaned back, the sun in his eyes so that I couldn't see his expression. 'So you will grow accustomed to it. Then it will become your name.'

Delayed by the postal strike, my cousin's reply arrived on June 1st, about a month after I'd written to him. Jacob Tournier had written two pages of large, almost indecipherable scrawl. I got out my dictionary and began to work through the letter, but it was so hard to read that after looking up several words without success I gave up and decided to use the bigger dictionary at the library.

Jean-Paul was talking to another man at his desk as I walked in. There was no change in his demeanor or expression but I noted with a satisfaction that surprised me that he glanced at me as I passed. I took the dictionary volumes to a desk and sat with my back to him, annoyed with myself for being so aware of him.

The library dictionary was more helpful but there were still words I couldn't find, and more words I simply couldn't read. After spending fifteen minutes on one paragraph, I sat back, dazed and frustrated. It was then that I saw Jean-Paul, leaning against the wall to my left and watching me with an amused expression that made me want to slap him. I jumped up and thrust the letter at him, muttering, 'Here, *you* do it!'

He took the sheets, gave them a cursory glance and nodded. 'Leave it with me,' he said. 'See you Wednesday at the café.'

On Wednesday morning he was sitting at the same table, in the same chair, but it was cloudy this time and there were no bubbling clay deposits in the river. I sat opposite him rather than in the adjacent seat, so that the river was at my back and we had to look at each other. Beyond him I could see into the empty café: the waiter, reading a newspaper, glanced up as I sat down and abandoned his paper when I nodded.

Neither of us said anything while we waited for our coffee. I was too tired to make small talk; it was the strategic time of the month and the dream had woken me three nights running. I hadn't been able to get back to sleep and had lain hour after hour listening to Rick's even breathing. I'd been resorting to cat naps in the afternoons, but they made me feel ill and disoriented. For the first time I'd begun to understand the look I had seen on the faces of new mothers I'd worked with: the bewildered, shattered expression of someone robbed of sleep.

After the coffee came Jean-Paul placed Jacob Tournier's letter on the table. 'There are some Swiss expressions in it,' he said, 'which maybe you would not understand. And the handwriting was difficult, though I have read worse.' He handed me a neatly written page of translation.

My dear cousin,

What a pleasure to receive your letter! I remember well your father from his brief visit to Moutier long ago and am happy to make the acquaintance of his daughter.

I am sorry for the delay in my reply to your questions, but they required that I should look through my grandfather's old notes about the Tourniers. It was he who had a great interest in the family, you see, and he undertook many researches. In fact he made a family tree – it is difficult to read or reproduce it for you in this letter, so you will have to visit us and see it.

Nonetheless I can give you some facts. The first mention of a Tournier in Moutier was of Etienne Tournier, on a military list in 1576. Then there was a baptism registered in 1590 of another Etienne Tournier, the son of Jean Tournier and Marthe Rougemont. There are few records left from that time, but later there are many mentions of Tourniers – the family tree is abundant from the eighteenth century to the present.

The Tourniers have had many occupations: tailor, innkeeper, watchmaker, schoolteacher. A Jean Tournier was even elected mayor in the early nineteenth century.

You ask about French origins. My grandfather sometimes said that the family originally came from the Cévennes. I do not know from where he had this information.

It pleases me that you have interest in the family, and I hope you and your husband will visit us sometime soon. A new member of the Tournier family is always welcome to Moutier.

Yours etc.

Jacob Tournier

I looked up. 'Where's Cévennes?' I asked.

Jean-Paul gestured over my shoulder. 'Northeast of here. It's an area in the mountains north of Montpellier, west of the Rhône. Around the Tarn and to the south.'

I fastened on to the one familiar bit of geography. 'This Tarn?' I pointed with my chin at the river below, hoping he hadn't noticed that I'd thought Cévennes was a town.

'Yes. It's a very different river further east, closer to its source. Much smaller, quicker.'

'And where's the Rhône?'

He flicked me a look, then reached into his jacket pocket for a pen, and quickly sketched the outline of France on a napkin. The shape reminded me of a cow's head: the east and west points the ears, the top point the tuft of hair between the ears, the border with Spain the square muzzle. He drew dots for Paris, Toulouse, Lyons, Marseilles, Montpellier, squiggly vertical and horizontal lines for the Rhône and the Tarn. As an afterthought he added a dot next to the Tarn and to the right of Toulouse to mark Lisle-sur-Tarn. Then he circled part of the cow's left cheek just above the Riviera. 'That's the Cévennes.'

'You mean they were from a place nearby?'

Jean-Paul blew out his lips. 'From here to the Cévennes is at least 200 kilometers. You think that is near?'

'It is to an American,' I replied defensively, well aware that I'd recently chided my father for making the same assumption. 'Some Americans will drive 100 miles to a party. But look, it's an amazing coincidence that in your big country –' I gestured at the cow's head – 'my ancestors came from a place pretty close to where I live now.'

'An amazing coincidence,' Jean-Paul repeated in a way that made me wish I'd left off the adjective.

'Maybe it wouldn't be so hard then to find out more about them, since it's nearby.' I was remembering Madame Sentier saying that to know about my French ancestors would make me feel more at home. 'I could just go there and –' I stopped. What would I do there exactly?

'You know your cousin said it is a family story that they came from there. So it is not certain information. Not concrete.' He sat back, shook a cigarette out of the pack on the table and lit it in one fluid movement. 'Besides, you already know this information about your Swiss ancestors, and there exists a family tree. They have traced the family back to 1576, more information than most people know about their families. That is enough, no?'

'But it would be fun to dig around. Do some research. I could look up records or something.'

He looked amused. 'What kind of records, Ella Tournier?'

'Well, birth records. Death records. Marriages. That kind of thing.'

'And where are you finding these records?'

I flung out my hands. '*I* don't know. That's *your* job. *You're* the librarian!'

'OK.' Appealing to his vocation seemed to settle him; he squared himself in his chair. 'You could start with the archives at Mende, which is the capital of Lozère, one of the *départements* of the Cévennes. But I think you do not understand this word "research" you are so easy to use. There are not so many records from the sixteenth century. They did not keep records then the way the government began to do after the revolution. There were church records, yes, but many were destroyed during the religious wars. And especially the Huguenot records were not kept securely. So it is all very unusual that you find something about the Tourniers if you go to Mende.'

'Wait a minute. How do you know they were, uh, Huguenots?'

'Most of the French who went to Switzerland then were Huguenots looking for a safe place, or who wanted to be close to Calvin at Geneva. There were two main waves of migration, in 1572 and 1685, first after the Massacre of Saint Bartholomew, then with the revocation of the Edict of Nantes. You can read about them at the library. I won't do all your work for you,' he added tauntingly.

I ignored his gibe. I was beginning to like the idea of exploring a part of France where I might have ancestors. 'So you think it's worth me going to the archives at Mende?' I asked, foolishly optimistic.

He blew smoke straight up into the air. 'No.'

My disappointment must have been obvious, for Jean-Paul tapped the table impatiently and remarked, 'Cheer up, Ella Tournier. It is not so easy, finding out about the past. You Americans who come over here looking for your roots think you will find it out all in one day, no? And then you go to the place and take a photograph and you feel good, you feel French for one day, yes? And the next day you go looking for ancestors in other countries. That way you claim the whole world for yourselves.'

I grabbed my bag and stood up. 'You're really enjoying this, aren't you?' I said sharply. 'Thanks for your advice. I've really learned a lot about French optimism.' I deliberately tossed a ten-franc coin on the table; it rolled past Jean-Paul's elbow and fell to the ground, where it bounced on the concrete a few times.

He touched my elbow as I began to walk away. 'Wait, Ella. Don't go. I did not know I was upsetting for you. I try just to be realistic.'

I turned on him. 'Why should I stay? You're arrogant and pessimistic, and you make fun of everything I do. I'm mildly curious about my French ancestors and you act like I'm tattooing the French flag on my butt. It's hard enough living here without you making me feel even more alien.' I turned away once more but to my surprise found I was shaking; I felt so dizzy that I had to grab onto the table.

Jean-Paul jumped up and pulled out a chair for me. As I dropped into it he called inside to the waiter, '*Un verre d'eau, Dominique, vite, s'il te plaît.*'

The water and several deep breaths helped. I fanned my face with my hands; I'd turned red and was sweating. Jean-Paul sat across from me and watched me closely.

'Maybe you take your jacket off,' he suggested quietly; for the first time his voice was gentle.

'I –' But this was not the moment for modesty and I was too tired to argue; my anger at him had faded the moment I sat back down. Reluctantly I shrugged my jacket off. 'I've got psoriasis,' I announced lightly, trying to pre-empt any awkwardness about the state of my arms. 'The doctor says it's from stress and lack of sleep.'

Jean-Paul looked at the patches of scaly skin like they were a curious modern painting.

'You do not sleep?' he asked.

'I've been having nightmares. Well, *a* nightmare.'

'And you tell your husband about it? Your friends?'

'I haven't told anyone.'

'Why you do not talk to your husband?'

'I don't want him to think I'm unhappy here.' I didn't add that Rick might feel threatened by the dream's connection to sex.

'Are you unhappy?'

'Yes,' I said, looking straight at Jean-Paul. It was a relief to say it.

He nodded. 'So what is the nightmare? Describe it to me.'

I looked out over the river. 'I only remember bits of it. There's no real story. There's a voice – no, two voices, one speaking in French, the other crying, really hysterical crying. All of this is in a fog, like the air is very heavy, like water. And there's a thud at the end, like a door being shut. And most of all there's the color blue everywhere. Everywhere. I don't know what it is that scares me so much, but every time I have the dream I want to go home.

It's the atmosphere more than what actually happens that frightens me. And the fact that I keep having it, that it won't go away, like it's with me for life. That's the worst of all.' I stopped. I hadn't realized how much I'd wanted to tell someone about it.

'You want to go back to the States?'

'Sometimes. Then I get mad at myself for being scared off by a dream.'

'What does the blue look like? Like that?' He pointed to a sign advertising ice cream for sale in the café. I shook my head.

'No, that's too bright. I mean, the dream blue *is* bright. Very vivid. But it's bright and yet dark too. I don't know the technical words to describe it. It reflects lots of light. It's beautiful but in the dream it makes me sad. Elated too. It's like there are two sides to the color. Funny that I remember the color. I always thought I dreamed in black and white.'

'And the voices? Who are they?'

'I don't know. Sometimes it's my voice. Sometimes I wake up and I've been saying the words. I can almost hear them, as if the room has just then gone silent.'

'What are the words? What are you saying?'

I thought for a minute, then shook my head. 'I don't remember.'

He fixed his eyes on me. 'Try. Close your eyes.'

I did as he said, sitting still as long as I could, Jean-Paul silent next to me. Just as I was about to give up, a fragment floated into my mind. '*Je suis un pot cassé*,' I said suddenly.

I opened my eyes. 'I am a broken pot? Where did that come from?'

Jean-Paul looked startled.

'Can you remember any more?'

I closed my eyes again. '*Tu es ma tour et forteresse*,' I murmured at last.

I opened my eyes. Jean-Paul's face was screwed up in concentration and he seemed far away. I could see his mind working, travelling over a vast plain of memory, scanning and rejecting, until something clicked and he returned to me. He fixed his eyes on the ice-cream sign and began to recite:

Entre tous ceux-là qui me haient
Mes voisins j'aperçois
Avoir honte de moi:
Il semble que mes amis aient
Horreur de ma rencontre,
Quand dehors je me montre.
Je suis hors de leur souvenance,
Ainsi qu'un trespassé.
Je suis un pot cassé.

As he spoke I felt a pressure in my throat and behind my eyes.
It was grief.

I held tightly to the arms of my chair, pushing my body hard
against its back as if to brace myself. When he finished I swallowed
to ease my throat.

'What is it?' I asked quietly.

'The thirty-first psalm.'

I frowned at him. 'A psalm? From the Bible?'

He smiled tightly. 'Yes.'

'But how could I know it? I don't know any psalms! Hardly
in English, and certainly not in French. But those words are
so familiar. I *must* have heard it somewhere. How do *you* know
it?'

'Church. When I was young we had to memorize many psalms.
But also it was in my studying at one time.'

'You studied psalms for a library science degree?'

'No, no, before that, when I studied history. The history of the
Languedoc. That is what I really do. That is my real love.'

'What's Languedoc?'

'An area all around us. From Toulouse and the Pyrenees all
the way to the Rhône.' He drew another circle on his napkin
map, encompassing the smaller circle of the Cévennes and a lot
of the cow's neck and muzzle. 'It was named for the language once
spoken there. *Oc* was their word for *oui*. *Langue d'oc* – language
of *oc*.'

'What did the psalm have to do with Languedoc?'

He hesitated. 'Well, that's curious. It was a psalm the Huguenots used to recite when bad things happened.'

That night after supper I finally told Rick about the dream, describing the blue, the voices, the atmosphere, as accurately as I could. I left out some things too: I didn't tell him that I'd been over this territory with Jean-Paul, that the words were a psalm, that I only had the dream after sex. Since I had to pick and choose what I told him, the process was more self-conscious and not nearly as therapeutic as it had been with Jean-Paul, when it had come out involuntarily and naturally. Now that I was telling it for Rick's sake rather than my own, I found I had to shape it more into a story, and it began to detach itself from me and take on its own fictional life.

Rick took it that way too. Maybe it was the way I told it, but he listened as if he were half paying attention to something else at the same time, a radio on in the background or a conversation in the street. He didn't ask any questions the way Jean-Paul had.

'Rick, are you listening to me?' I asked finally, reaching over and pulling his ponytail.

'Of course I am. You've been having nightmares. About the color blue.'

'I just wanted you to know. That's why I've been so tired recently.'

'You should wake me up when you have them.'

'I know.' But I knew I wouldn't. In California I would have woken him immediately the first time I had the dream. Something had changed; since Rick seemed to be himself, it must be me.

'How's the studying going?'

I shrugged, irritated that he'd changed the subject. 'OK. No. Terrible. No. I don't know. Sometimes I wonder how I'm ever going to deliver babies in French. I couldn't say the right thing when that baby was choking. If I can't even do that, how can I possibly coach a woman through labor?'

'But you delivered babies from Hispanic women back home and managed.'

'That's different. Maybe they didn't speak English, but they didn't expect me to speak Spanish either. And here all the hospital equipment, all the medicine and the dosages, all that will be in *French*.'

Rick leaned forward, elbows anchored on the table, plate pushed to one side. 'Hey, Ella, what's happened to your optimism? You're not going to start acting French, are you? I get enough of that at work.'

Even knowing I'd just been critical of Jean-Paul's pessimism, I found myself repeating his words. 'I'm just trying to be realistic.'

'Yeah, I've heard that at the office too.'

I opened my mouth for a sharp retort, but stopped myself. It was true that my optimism had diminished in France; maybe I was taking on the cynical nature of the people around me. Rick put a positive spin on everything; it was his positive attitude that had made him successful. That was why the French firm approached him; that was why we were here. I shut my mouth, swallowing my pessimistic words.

That night we made love, Rick carefully avoiding my psoriasis. Afterwards I lay patiently waiting for sleep and the dream. When it came it was less impressionistic, more tangible than ever. The blue hung over me like a bright sheet, billowing in and out, taking on texture and shape. I woke with tears running down my face and my voice in my ears. I lay still.

'A dress,' I whispered. 'It was a dress.'

In the morning I hurried to the library. The woman was at the desk and I had to turn away to hide my disappointment and irritation that Jean-Paul wasn't there. I wandered aimlessly around the two rooms, the librarian's gaze following me. At last I asked her if Jean-Paul would be in any time that day. 'Oh no,' she replied with a small frown. 'He won't be here for a few days. He has gone to Paris.'

'Paris? But why?'

She looked surprised that I should ask. 'Well, his sister is getting married. He will return after the weekend.'

'Oh. *Merci*,' I said and left. It was strange to think of him having a sister, a family. Dammit, I thought, pounding down the stairs and out into the square. Madame from the *boulangerie* was standing next to the fountain talking to the woman who had first led me to the library. Both stopped talking and stared at me for a long moment before turning back to each other. Damn you, I thought. I'd never felt so isolated and conspicuous.

That Sunday we were invited to lunch at the home of one of Rick's colleagues, the first real socializing we'd done since moving to France, not counting the occasional quick drink with people Rick had met through work. I was nervous about going and focussed my worries on what to wear. I had no idea what Sunday lunch meant in French terms, whether it was formal or casual.

'Should I wear a dress?' I kept pestering Rick.

'Wear what you want,' he replied usefully. 'They won't mind.'

But I will, I thought, if I wear the wrong thing.

There was the added problem of my arms – it was a hot day but I couldn't bear the furtive glances at my erupted skin. Finally I chose a stone-colored sleeveless dress that reached my mid-calf and a white linen jacket. I thought I would fit in with more or less any occasion in such an outfit, but when the couple opened the door of their big suburban house and I took in Chantal's jeans and white T-shirt, Olivier's khaki shorts, I felt simultaneously overdressed and frumpy. They smiled politely at me, and smiled again at the flowers and wine we brought, but I noticed that Chantal abandoned the flowers, still wrapped, on a sideboard in the dining room, and our carefully chosen bottle of wine never made an appearance.

They had two children, a girl and a boy, who were so polite and quiet that I never even found out their names. At the end of the meal they stood up and disappeared inside as if summoned by a bell only children could hear. They were probably watching television, and I secretly wished I could join them: I found conversation among us adults tiring and at times demoralizing. Rick and Olivier spent most of the time discussing the firm's business, and spoke in English. Chantal and I chatted awkwardly in a mixture of French and English. I tried to speak only French with her, but she kept switching to English when she felt I wasn't keeping up. It would have been impolite for me to continue in French, so I switched to English until there was a pause; then I'd start another subject in French. It turned into a polite struggle between us; I think she took quiet pleasure in showing off how good her English was compared to my French. And she wasn't one for small talk; within ten minutes she had covered most of the hot spots in the world – Bosnia, Israel, Northern Ireland – and looked scornful when I didn't have a decisive answer to every problem.

Both Olivier and Chantal hung onto every word Rick uttered, even though I made more of an effort than he did to speak to them in their own language. For all my struggle to communicate they barely listened to me. I hated comparing my performance with Rick's: I'd never done such a thing in the States.

We left in the late afternoon, with polite kisses and promises to have them over in Lisle. That'll be a lot of fun, I thought as we drove away. When we were out of sight I pulled off my sweaty jacket. If we had been in the States with friends it wouldn't have mattered what my arms looked like. But then, if we were still in the States I wouldn't have psoriasis.

'Hey, they were nice, weren't they?' Rick started off our ritual debriefing.

'They didn't touch the wine or flowers.'

'Yeah, but with a wine cellar like theirs, no wonder! Great place.'

'I guess I wasn't thinking about their material possessions.'

Rick glanced at me sideways. 'You didn't seem too happy there, babe. What's wrong?'

'I don't know. I just feel – I just feel I don't *fit*, that's all. I can't seem to talk to people here the way I can in the States. Until now the only person I've had any sustained conversation with besides Madame Sentier is Jean-Paul, and even that isn't real conversation. More like a battle, more like –'

'Who's Jean-Paul?'

I tried to sound casual. 'A librarian in Lisle. He's helping me look into my family history. He's away right now,' I added irrelevantly.

'And what have you two found out?'

'Not much. A little from my cousin in Switzerland. You know, I was starting to think that knowing more about my French background would make me feel more comfortable here, but now I think I'm wrong. People still see me as American.'

'You *are* American, Ella.'

'Yeah, I know. But I have to change a little while I'm here.'

'Why?'

'Why? Because – because otherwise I stick out too much. People want me to be what they expect; they want me to be like them. And anyway I can't help but be affected by the landscape around me, the people and the way they think and the language. It's going to make me different, a little different at least.'

Rick looked puzzled. 'But you already *are* yourself,' he said, switching lanes so suddenly that cars behind us honked indignantly. 'You don't need to change for other people.'

'It's not like that. It's more like adapting. It's like – cafés here don't serve decaffeinated coffee, so I'm getting used to having less real coffee or no coffee at all.'

'I get my secretary to make decaf at the office.'

'Rick –' I stopped and counted to ten. He seemed to be willfully misunderstanding my metaphors, putting that positive spin on things.

'I think you'd be a lot happier if you didn't worry so much about fitting in. People will like you the way you are.'

'Maybe.' I stared out the window. Rick had the knack of not trying to fit in but being accepted anyway. It was like his ponytail: he wore it so naturally that no one stared or thought him odd. I, on the other hand, despite my attempts to fit in, stood out like a skyscraper.

Rick had to stop by the office for an hour; I had planned to sit and read or play with one of the computers, but I was in such a bad mood that I went for a walk instead. His office was right in the center of Toulouse, in an area of narrow streets and boutiques now full of Sunday strollers window-shopping. I began to wander, looking in windows at tasteful clothes, gold jewelry, artful lingerie. The cult of French lingerie always surprised me; even small towns like Lisle-sur-Tarn had a store specializing in it. It was hard to imagine wearing the things on display, with their intricate straps and lace and designs that mapped out the body's erogenous zones. There was something un-American about it, this formalized sexiness.

In fact French women in the city were so different from me that I often felt invisible around them, a dishevelled ghost standing aside to let them pass. Women out strolling in Toulouse wore tailored blazers with jeans and understated chunks of gold at their ears and throats. Their shoes always had heels. Their haircuts were neat, expensive, their eyebrows plucked smooth, their skin clear. It was easy to imagine them in complicated bras or camisoles, silk underwear cut high on the thigh, stockings, suspenders. They took the presentation of their images seriously. As I walked around I could feel them glancing at me discreetly, scrutinizing the shoulder-length hair I'd left a little too long in cutting, the absence of make-up, the persistently wrinkled linen, the flat clunky sandals I'd thought so fashionable in San Francisco. I was sure I saw pity flash over their faces.

Do they know I'm American? I thought. Is it that obvious?

It was; I myself could spot the middle-aged American couple ahead of me a mile off just from what they were wearing and the way they stood. They were looking at a display of chocolate and as I passed were discussing whether or not to return the next day and buy some to take home with them.

'Won't it melt in the plane?' the woman asked. She had wide, low-slung hips and wore a loose pastel blouse and pants and running shoes. She stood with her legs wide apart, knees locked.

'Naw, honey, it's *cold* 35,000 feet up. It's not gonna melt, but it might get squished. Maybe there's something else in this town we can take home.' He carried a substantial gut, emphasized by the belt bisecting and hugging it. He wasn't wearing a baseball cap but he might as well have been. Probably left it at the hotel.

They looked up and smiled brightly, a wistful hope shining in their faces. Their openness pained me; I quickly turned down a side street. Behind me I heard the man say, 'Excuse me, miss, *sea-view-play*.' I didn't turn around. I felt like a kid who's embarrassed by her parents in front of her friends.

I came out at the end of the street next to the Musée des Augustins, an old brick complex that held a collection of paintings and sculpture. I glanced around: the couple hadn't followed me. I ducked inside.

After paying I pushed through the door and entered cloisters, a peaceful, sunny spot, the square walkways lined with sculpture, a neatly planted garden of flowers and vegetables and herbs in the center. On one walkway there was a long line of stone dogs, snouts pointed upwards, howling joyously. I walked all the way around the square, then strolled through the garden, admiring the strawberry plants, the lettuces in neat rows, the patches of tarragon and sage and three kinds of mint, the large rosemary bush. I sat for a while, taking off my jacket and letting the psoriasis soak up the sun. I closed my eyes and thought of nothing.

Finally I roused myself and got up to look at the attached church. It was a huge place, as big as a cathedral, but all the chairs and the altar had been removed, and paintings were hung on all the walls. I'd never seen a church blatantly used as a gallery. I stood in the doorway admiring the effect of a large empty space hanging over the paintings, swamping and diminishing them.

A flash in my peripheral vision made me look toward a painting on the opposite wall. A shaft of light had fallen across it and all I could see was a patch of blue. I began to walk toward it, blinking, my stomach tightening.

It was a painting of Christ taken off the cross, lying on a sheet on the ground, his head resting in an old man's lap. He was watched over by a younger man, a young woman in a yellow dress, and in the center the Virgin Mary, wearing a robe the very blue I'd been dreaming of, draped around an astonishing face. The painting itself was static, a meticulously balanced tableau, each person placed carefully, each tilt of the head and gesture of the hands calculated for effect. Only the Virgin's face, dead center in the painting, moved and changed, pain and a strange peace battling in her features as she gazed down at her dead son, framed by a color that reflected her agony.

As I stood in front of it, my right hand jerked up and involuntarily made the sign of the cross. I had never made such a gesture in my life.

I looked at the label to the side of the painting and read the title and the name of the painter. I stood still for a long time, the space of the church suspended around me. Then I crossed myself again, said, 'Holy Mother, help me,' and began to laugh.

I would never have guessed there had been a painter in the family.

3. The Flight

Isabelle sat up straight and glanced across to the children's bed. Jacob was already awake, arms around his legs, chin on his knees. He had the best ears of all of them.

— One horse, he said quietly.

Isabelle nudged Etienne.

— A horse, she whispered.

Her husband jumped up, half-asleep, his hair dark with sweat. Pulling on his breeches, he reached over and shook Bertrand awake. Together they slipped down the ladder as someone began pounding on the door. Isabelle peered over the edge of the loft and watched the men gather, clutching axes and knives. Hannah appeared from the back room with a candle. After whispering through the crack in the door, Jean set down the axe and drew back the bolt.

The Duc de l'Aigle's steward was no stranger. He appeared periodically to confer with Jean Tournier and used the house to collect tithes from the surrounding farms, carefully recording them in a calfskin-bound book. Short, fat, completely bald, he made up for his lack of height with a booming voice that Jean tried in vain now to stifle. There could be no secrets with such a voice.

— The Duc has been murdered in Paris!

Hannah gasped and dropped the candle. Isabelle unthinkingly crossed herself, then clutched her neck and looked around. All four children were now sitting up in a row, Susanne perched next to them on the edge, balancing precariously, her belly huge and distended. She'll be ready soon, Isabelle thought, automatically assessing her. Though never used now, the old knowledge was still with her.

Petit Jean had begun whittling with the knife that he kept with him even in bed. Jacob was silent, eyes large and brown like his

56

mother's. Marie and Deborah leaned against each other, Deborah looking sleepy, Marie's eyes bright.

— Maman, what is murder? she called out in a voice that rang like a copper pan being beaten.

— Hush, Isabelle whispered. She moved to the end of the bed to hear what the steward was saying. Susanne came to sit beside her and the two leaned forward, resting their arms on the railing.

— . . . ten days ago, at the wedding of Henri de Navarre. The gates were locked and thousands of followers of the Truth slaughtered. Coligny as well as our Duc. And it is spreading to the countryside. Everywhere they are killing honest people.

— But we are far from Paris and we are all followers of the Truth here, Jean replied. We are safe from Catholics here.

— They say a garrison is coming from Mende, the steward boomed. To take advantage of the Duc's death. They will come for you, a *syndic* for the Duc. The Duchesse is fleeing to Alès and passes this way in a few hours. You should come with us, to save your family. She is not offering to take others. Just the Tourniers.

— No.

It was Hannah who replied. She had relit the candle and stood solidly in the middle of the room, back slightly humped, silver braid running down her spine.

— We do not need to leave this house, she continued. We are protected here.

— And we have crops to harvest, Jean added.

— May you change your mind. Your family — any of your family — is welcome to join the Duchesse.

Isabelle thought she caught the flash of the steward's eyes directed toward Bertrand. Watching her husband, Susanne shifted uneasily. Isabelle reached for her hand: it was as cold as the river. She glanced at the children. The girls, too young to understand, had fallen back to sleep; Jacob was still sitting with his chin on his knees; Petit Jean had dressed and was leaning against the railing, watching the men.

The steward left to warn other families. Jean bolted the door and set the axe beside it while Etienne and Bertrand disappeared into the barn to secure it from within. Hannah moved to the hearth, set the candle on the mantel and knelt beside the fire, banked for the night under ashes. Isabelle thought at first that she was going to build it up, but the old woman did not touch the fire.

She squeezed Susanne's hand and nodded toward the hearth.

— What is she doing?

Susanne watched her mother, wiping her cheek where a tear had strayed.

— The magic is in the hearth, she whispered finally. The magic that protects this house. Maman is praying to it.

The magic. It had been referred to obliquely over the years, but Etienne and Susanne would never explain, and she had never dared ask Jean or Hannah.

She tried once more.

— But what is it? What is there?

Susanne shook her head.

— I don't know. Anyway, to speak of it is to ruin its power. I have already said too much.

— But why is she praying? Monsieur Marcel says there is no magic in praying.

— This is older than praying, older than Monsieur Marcel and his teachings.

— But not older than God. Not older than — the Virgin, she finished silently.

Susanne had no answer.

— If we go, she said instead, if we go with the Duchesse, we will no longer be protected.

— Protected by the Duchesse's men, by swords, yes, Isabelle responded.

— Will you come?

Isabelle did not answer. What would it take to draw Etienne away? The steward had not looked at him when urging them to go. He knew Etienne would not leave.

Etienne and Bertrand returned from the barn, Etienne joining his parents at the table. Jean glanced up at Isabelle and Susanne.

– Go to sleep, he said. We will keep watch.

But their eyes were on Bertrand, standing uncertainly in the middle of the room. He looked up at Susanne as if searching for a sign. Isabelle leaned toward her.

– God will protect you, she whispered in Susanne's ear. God and the Duchesse's men.

She sat back, caught Hannah's glare, met it. All these years you have taunted me because of my hair, she thought, yet you pray to your own magic. She and Hannah stared at each other. Hannah looked away first.

Isabelle missed Susanne's nod but not its result. Bertrand turned resolutely toward Jean.

– Susanne, Deborah and I, we will go to Alès with the Duchesse de l'Aigle, he stated.

Jean gazed at Bertrand.

– You understand that you will lose everything if you go, he said quietly.

– We will lose everything if we stay. Susanne is near her time, she cannot walk far. She cannot run. There will be no chance for her when the Catholics come.

– You do not believe in this house? Where no babies have died? Where Tourniers have thrived for 100 years?

– I believe in the Truth, he replied. That is what I believe in. With his words he seemed to grow, his defiance giving him height and girth. Isabelle realized for the first time that he was actually taller than his father-in-law.

– With our marriage you gave no dowry because we live here with you. All I ask for now is one horse. That will be dowry enough.

Jean looked incredulous.

– You want me to give you a horse so you can take away my daughter and grandchildren?

– I want to *save* your daughter and grandchildren.

– I am the master of this family, yes?

– God is my master. I must follow the Truth, not this magic you are so convinced by.

Isabelle would never have guessed Bertrand could be so rebellious. After Jean and Hannah chose him for Susanne, he had worked hard and never crossed Jean. He had brought an ease to the house, arm-wrestling with Etienne every day, teaching Petit Jean to whittle, making them laugh by the fire at night with his stories of the wolf and the fox. He treated Susanne with a gentleness that Isabelle envied. Once or twice she had seen him swallow his defiance; it appeared to have grown in his stomach, waiting for a moment such as this.

Then Jean surprised everyone.

— Go, he said gruffly. But take the ass, not the horse. He turned and strode to the barn door, yanked it open and disappeared inside.

Etienne glanced up at Isabelle before looking down at his hands; she was certain then that they would not follow Bertrand. Etienne's marriage to her had been his one act of defiance. He had no will left for another.

Isabelle turned to her sister-in-law.

— When you ride the ass, she whispered, you must ride sideways to support the baby with your legs. That will keep it from coming too soon. Ride sideways, she repeated, for Susanne was staring into space as if in shock. She turned to look at Isabelle.

— You mean like the Virgin riding into Egypt?

— Yes. Yes, just like the Virgin.

They had not mentioned Her for a long time.

Deborah and Marie were sleeping with a sheet twined around them when Susanne and Isabelle went to wake Deborah just before dawn. They tried not to disturb the others but Marie woke up and began to say loudly: — Why is Deborah leaving? Why is she leaving? Jacob opened his eyes, his features pinched. Then Petit Jean, still dressed, sat up.

— Maman, where are they going? he whispered hoarsely. Will they see soldiers? And horses and flags? Will they see Uncle Jacques?

— Uncle Jacques is not a Catholic soldier; he fights with Coligny's army in the north.

— But the steward said Coligny was killed.

– Yes.

– So Uncle Jacques may come back.

Isabelle did not answer. Jacques Tournier had gone to the army ten years before, at the same time as other young men from Mont Lozère. He had returned once, scarred, raucous, full of tales, one of them about Isabelle's brothers, run through with the same pike. – As twins should be, Jacques had added brutally, laughing when Isabelle turned away. Petit Jean worshipped Jacques. Isabelle hated him, whose eyes had followed her everywhere, never resting on her face. He encouraged a hard boisterousness in Etienne that disturbed her. But Jacques had not stayed long: the call of blood and excitement had been too strong, stronger even than the claims of family.

The children followed the women down the ladder and out into the yard, where the men had loaded the ass with a few possessions and food: goat's cheese and hard dark loaves of chestnut bread that Isabelle had quickly made during the few hours before dawn.

– Come, Susanne, Bertrand gestured.

Susanne looked for her mother, but Hannah had not come outside. She turned to Isabelle, kissed her three times and put her arms around her neck.

– Ride sideways, Isabelle whispered in her ear. And make them stop if you begin to have pains. And may the Virgin and Saint Margaret keep you and bring you safe to Alès.

They lifted Susanne onto the ass, where she sat among the packs, legs to one side.

– *Adieu, Papa, petits,* she said, nodding to Jean and the children. Deborah climbed onto Bertrand's back. He gathered the rope attached to the ass's halter, clucked and kicked, and started down the mountain path at a quick pace. Etienne and Petit Jean followed, to accompany them as far as the road to Alès, where they would meet the Duchesse. Susanne looked back at Isabelle, her face small and white, until she was out of sight.

– Grandpapa, why are they leaving? Why is Deborah leaving? Marie asked. Born only a week apart, the cousins had been inseparable until now. Jean turned away. Marie followed Isabelle inside and stood by Hannah, busy at the fire.

– Why, Mémé, why is Deborah leaving? she kept saying until Hannah reached out and slapped her.

Soldiers or not, the crops were waiting. The men went to the fields as usual, but Jean chose a field near the house to scythe, and Isabelle did not follow with the rake as she normally would – she and Marie remained at the house with Hannah and helped with preserving. Petit Jean and Jacob worked behind their father and grandfather, raking the rye into bundles, Jacob barely tall enough to handle the rake.

In the house Isabelle and Hannah said little, the hole left behind by Susanne shutting their mouths. Twice Isabelle stopped stirring, staring into space, and cursed when hot plum spattered her arms. Finally Hannah pushed her away.

– Honey is too precious to be wasted by idle hands, she muttered.

Isabelle, boiling crockery instead, often went to the door in search of a cooling breeze and to listen to the silence of the valley. Once Marie followed and stood next to her in the doorway, her tiny hands stained purple from picking through the plums to find the unripe or rotten.

– Maman, she said quietly, knowing now to keep her voice down. Maman, why did they leave?

– They left because they were afraid, Isabelle replied after a moment, wiping sweat from her temples.

– Afraid of what?

– Of bad men who want to hurt them.

– Bad men are coming here?

Isabelle tucked her hands under her smock so Marie would not see they were shaking.

– No, *chérie*, I think not. But they were worried about Susanne with the baby.

– Will I see Deborah soon?

– Yes.

Marie had her father's pale blue eyes and, to Isabelle's relief, his blond hair as well. If it had been red, Isabelle would have dyed it with the juice of black walnuts. Marie's bright eyes gazed up at her now, perturbed, uncertain. Isabelle had never been able to lie to her.

Pierre La Forêt visited the field at midday just as Isabelle was bringing the men their dinner. He told them who had fled – not so many, only those with wealth to be looted, daughters to be raped, connections with the Duc.

He saved the most surprising news for last.

– Monsieur Marcel has left, he announced with poorly disguised glee. He has gone north, over Mont Lozère.

There was silence. Jean picked up his scythe.

– He will return, he said shortly, turning back to the rye. Pierre La Forêt watched him begin his rhythmic swinging, then glanced fearfully around, as if just remembering that soldiers might descend at any moment. He left quickly, whistling for his dog.

Their progress in the field that morning had been slow. Besides the absence of Bertrand and Susanne, the workers Jean had hired for the harvest never appeared, fearful of the farm's connection with the Duc. The boys had not been able to keep up with the men, so that now and then Jean or Etienne had been forced to drop a scythe and to rake for a time to catch up.

– Let me rake, Isabelle suggested now, eager to escape Hannah and the stifling house. Your mother – Maman can handle the preserves alone. Jacob and Marie will help her. Please. She rarely called Hannah Maman, only when wheedling was necessary.

To her relief the men agreed, sending Jacob back to the house. She and Petit Jean followed in the wake of the scythes, raking as fast as they could, bundling the rye, leaning the bundles upright against one another to dry. They worked quickly, sweat soaking their clothes. Occasionally Isabelle stopped to look around and listen. The sky was yellow with haze, wide and empty. It seemed the world itself had paused and was waiting with her.

It was Jacob who heard them. Late in the afternoon he appeared at the edge of the field, running fast. They all stopped and watched him, Isabelle's heart beginning to race. When he reached them he leaned over, hands on his thighs, gasping for breath.

– *Ecoute, Papa*, was all he said when he could speak, gesturing toward the valley. They listened. At first Isabelle could hear nothing except birds and her own breathing. Then a dull rumble emerged from the countryside.

– Ten. Ten horses, Jacob announced. Isabelle dropped her rake, took Jacob's hand and ran.

Petit Jean was the fastest; only nine, even after a day's work he outran his father easily. He reached the barn and raced to draw the bolts. Etienne and Jean brought water from the nearby stream while Isabelle and Jacob began closing shutters.

Marie stood in the middle of the room, pressing an armful of lavender to her chest. Hannah continued to work at the fire, as if oblivious of the activity around her. Once they had all gathered around the table, the old woman turned and said simply: – We are safe.

They were the last words Isabelle ever heard her speak.

They took their time appearing.

The family sat silently around the table in their usual places but with no meal before them. It was dark inside: the fire was low, no candles had been lit and the only light came through cracks in the shutters. Isabelle perched on a bench, Marie close at her side holding her hand, the lavender in her lap. Jean sat very straight at the head of the table. Etienne was staring down at his clasped hands. His cheek twitched; otherwise he was as impassive as his father. Hannah rubbed her face, pressed the bridge of her nose with thumb and forefinger, eyes closed. Petit Jean had taken out his knife and laid it on the table in front of him. He kept picking it up, flashing it, testing its blade, setting it down again. Jacob, slumped alone on the bench where Susanne, Bertrand and Deborah usually sat, held a round stone in his hand. The rest were in his pocket. He had always loved the brightly colored stones in the Tarn, preferring deep reds and yellows. He kept them even when they dried into dull browns and greys. When he wanted to see their true colors he licked them.

The gaps along the bench seemed to Isabelle to be filled with the ghosts of her family – her mother, her sister, her brothers. She shook her head and closed her eyes, trying to imagine where Susanne was now, safe with the Duchesse. When that failed she thought of the blue of the Virgin, a color she had not seen in years but could picture at this moment as if the walls of the house were painted with it. She took a deep breath and her heartbeat slowed. She opened her eyes. The empty spaces at the table were shimmering with blue light.

When the horses arrived there were shouts and whistles, then a loud banging at the door that made everyone jump.

– Let us sing, Jean said firmly and began in a deep, confident bass: *J'ai mis en toi mon espérance: Garde-moi donc, Seigneur, D'éternel déshonneur: Octroye-moi ma délivrance, Par ta grande bonté haute, Qui jamais ne fit faute.* Everyone joined in but Hannah, who had always said singing was frivolous and preferred to mumble the words under her breath. The children sang in high-pitched voices, Marie hiccuping with fear.

They finished the psalm to the accompaniment of rattling shutters and a rhythmic pounding on the door. They had begun another psalm when the pounding stopped. After a moment they heard a scraping thud against the bottom of the door, then crackling and the smell of smoke. Etienne and Jean stood up and strode to the door. Etienne picked up a bucket of water and nodded. Jean quietly drew the bolt and swung open the door a crack. Etienne dashed the water out just as the door was kicked violently open and a wave of flames leapt inside. Two hands grabbed Jean by his throat and shirt and pulled him violently outside, the door slamming shut after him.

Etienne scrambled for the door, flung it open again and was engulfed in smoke and fire.

– Papa! he shouted and disappeared into the yard.

Inside there was a strange, frozen silence. Then Isabelle stood up calmly, feeling the blue light surround and protect her. She picked up Marie.

– Hold on to me, she whispered, and Marie wound her arms

65

around her mother's neck, her legs around her waist, the lavender crushed between them. Isabelle took Jacob's hand, gesturing to Petit Jean to take his other hand. As if in a dream she led the children across the room, drew back the bolt and entered the barn. They skirted around the horse, now stepping sideways and whinnying at the smell of smoke and the sounds of other horses in the yard. At the far end of the barn, Isabelle unbolted a small door that led into the kitchen garden. Together they picked their way through cabbages and tomatoes, carrots, onions, herbs. Isabelle's skirt brushed against the sage plant, releasing into the air the familiar tangy odor.

They reached the mushroom rock at the bottom of the garden and stopped. Jacob pressed his hands briefly against the stone. Beyond it was a fallow field the goats had cropped short, dry and brown now from a full summer of sun. The four began to run across it, the boys ahead, Isabelle behind with Marie still clinging to her.

Halfway across she realized Hannah had not followed them. She cursed aloud.

They reached the chestnut trees safely. At the *cleda* Isabelle put Marie down and turned to Petit Jean.

— I have to go back, to get Mémé. You are good at hiding. Wait here until I return. But don't hide in the *cleda*; they might set fire to it. And if they come and you have to run, go toward my father's house, through the fields, not on the path. *D'accord?*

Petit Jean nodded and pulled his knife from his pocket, his blue eyes sparkling.

Isabelle turned and looked back. The farm was alight now. The pigs were screaming, the dogs howling, howls taken up by the dogs all around the valley. The village knows what is happening, she thought. Will they come and help? Will they hide? She glanced at the children, Marie and Jacob wide-eyed and still, Petit Jean scanning the woods.

— *Allez*, she said. Without a word Petit Jean led the other two into the undergrowth.

Isabelle left the trees and skirted the edge of the field. In the distance she could see the field they had worked in that day: all the bundles she and Petit Jean and Jacob had raked together were smoking. She heard distant shouts, and laughter, a sound that made the hair on her arms stand on end. As she got closer she smelled burning flesh, a scent both familiar and strange. The pigs, she thought. The pigs and – she realized what the soldiers had done.

– *Sainte Vierge, aide-nous*, she breathed and crossed herself.

So much smoke filled the bottom of the garden that it seemed night had fallen. She crept through the vegetables and halfway up the row found Hannah on her knees, clutching a cabbage to her breast, tears cutting grooves down her blackened face.

– *Viens, Mémé*, Isabelle whispered, putting her arms around Hannah's shoulders and lifting her. *Viens*.

The old woman made no sound as she wept, letting Isabelle lead her back through the garden to the field. Behind them they heard the soldiers galloping into the garden, but the wall of smoke kept the women hidden. They stayed at the edge of the field, following the low granite wall Jean had built many years before. Hannah kept stopping and looking behind her, and Isabelle had to urge her on, putting an arm around her, pulling her forward.

The soldier appeared so suddenly he seemed to have been dropped by God from the sky. They would have expected him behind them; instead he emerged from the very woods they were heading toward. He crossed the field at a full gallop, sword raised and, as Isabelle saw when he got closer, a smile on his face. She moaned and began stumbling backwards, pulling Hannah with her.

When the horseman was so close she could smell his sweat, a grey mass detached itself from the ground and rose, casually shaking a back leg. Immediately the horse reared up, screaming. The soldier lost his seat and fell heavily to the ground. His horse wheeled around and headed wildly back across the field to the chestnut grove.

Hannah looked from the wolf to Isabelle and back to the wolf. It stood watching them calmly, its yellow eyes alert. It did not even glance at the soldier, who lay without moving.

— *Merci*, Isabelle said quietly, nodding at the wolf. *Merci, Maman.*

Hannah's eyes widened.

They waited until the wolf turned and trotted away, leaping over the low wall, disappearing into the next field. Then Hannah moved forward again. Isabelle began to follow, then stopped and looked around, staring at the soldier and shivering. Finally she turned and approached him warily. She barely looked at him; instead she crouched next to his sword and studied it intently. Hannah waited for her, arms crossed, head bowed.

Isabelle rose abruptly.

— No blood, she said.

When they reached the woods Isabelle began calling quietly for the children. In the distance she could hear the riderless horse tearing through the trees. Presumably it reached the edge of the forest, for the sound stopped.

The children did not appear.

— They must have gone ahead, Isabelle murmured. There was no blood on the sword. Please let them have gone ahead. They have gone ahead, she repeated more loudly for Hannah's benefit.

When there was no reply she added: — Eh, Mémé? You think they have gone ahead?

Hannah only shrugged.

They began the trek across the fields to Isabelle's father's farm, listening for the soldiers, the children, the horse, anyone. They met nothing.

It was dark by the time they stumbled into the farmyard. The house was black and bolted shut, but when Isabelle knocked softly on the door and whispered, *Papa, c'est moi*, they were let in. The children were sitting in the dark with their grandfather. Marie jumped up and ran to her mother, pressing her face into Isabelle's side.

Henri du Moulin nodded briefly to Hannah, who looked away. He turned to Isabelle.

— Where are they?

Isabelle shook her head.

– I don't know. I think – She looked at the children and stopped.

– We will wait, her father said grimly.

– Yes.

They waited for hours, the children falling asleep one by one, the adults seated stiffly around the table in the dark. Hannah closed her eyes but sat very straight, hands clasped on the table before her. At every sound she opened her eyes and jerked her head toward the door.

Isabelle and her father were silent. She gazed around her sadly. Even in the dark it was clear the house was falling apart. When Henri du Moulin learned his twin sons were dead, he stopped keeping up the farm: fields lay fallow, roofs leaked, goats wandered away, mice nested in the grain. It was dirty and dank inside, damp even in the heat and dryness of the harvest season.

Isabelle listened to the mice rustling in the dark.

– You need a cat, she whispered.

– I had one, her father replied. It left. Nothing remains here.

Just before dawn they heard a movement in the yard, the muffled sound of a horse. Jacob sat up quickly.

– It's our horse, he said.

At first they didn't recognize Etienne. The figure swaying in the doorway had no hair left except for a few patches of singed black stubble on his scalp. His fair eyebrows and lashes were gone, making his eyes seem to float anchorless in his face. His clothes were burnt and he was dusted all over with soot.

They stood frozen except for Petit Jean, who took the figure's hand with both of his.

– Come, Papa, he said, and led Etienne to a bench at the table.

Etienne gestured behind him.

– The horse, he whispered as he sat. The horse stood patiently in the yard, hooves wrapped in cloth to muffle them. Mane and tail had been burnt off; otherwise it appeared unharmed.

When Etienne's hair grew back, a few months later and many miles away, it was grey. His eyebrows and lashes never reappeared.

★

Etienne and his mother sat at Henri du Moulin's table in a daze, unable to think or act. All day Isabelle and her father tried to talk to them, without success. Hannah would say nothing, and Etienne simply stated, I'm thirsty, or I'm tired, and closed his eyes.

Finally Isabelle roused them by crying in desperation: — We *must* leave here soon. The soldiers will be looking for us still, and eventually someone will tell them to look here.

She knew the villagers: they were loyal. Offered enough, though, or threatened enough, they would give away a secret, even to a Catholic.

— Where do we go? Etienne asked.

— You could hide in the woods until it's safe to return, Henri du Moulin suggested.

— We cannot return there, Isabelle replied. The crops are ruined, the house is gone. Without the Duc we have no protection from the Catholics. They will continue to search for us. And — she hesitated, careful to convince them with their own words — without the house, it is no longer safe.

And I do not want to return to that misery, she added silently.

Etienne and his mother looked at each other.

— We could go to Alès, Isabelle continued. To join Susanne and Bertrand.

— No, Etienne said firmly. They made their choice. They left this family.

— But they — Isabelle stopped, not wanting to ruin with argument what little influence she now had. She had a sudden vision of Susanne's belly sliced open by the soldier in the field and knew they had made the right decision.

— The road to Alès will be dangerous, her father said. It could happen there, what has happened here.

The children had been listening silently. Now Marie spoke.

— Maman, where can we be safe? she demanded. Tell God we want to be safe.

Isabelle nodded.

– Calvin, she announced. We could go to Calvin. To Geneva, where it is safe. Where the Truth is free.

They waited till nightfall, hot and restless. Isabelle had the children clean the house while she baked as much bread as she could in the chimney shelf. She and her sister and mother had used that shelf daily; now she had to brush off mouse droppings and cobwebs. The hearth looked unused and she wondered what her father ate.

Henri du Moulin refused to go with them, though his connection to the Tourniers made him a target.

– This is my farm, he said roughly. No Catholic will drive me from it.

He insisted they take his cart, the only valuable possession he had left besides his plow. He brushed it out, repaired one of the wheels, set the plank in its place across the box to sit on. When darkness came he pulled it into the yard and loaded it with an axe, three blankets, two sacks.

– Chestnuts and potatoes, he explained to Isabelle.

– Potatoes?

– For the horse and for you.

Hannah overheard him and stiffened. Petit Jean, leading the horse from the barn, laughed.

– People don't eat potatoes, Grandpapa! Only poor beggars.

Isabelle's father tightened his hands into fists.

– You will be thankful enough to have them to eat, *mon petit*. All men are poor in the eyes of God.

When they were ready, Isabelle looked at her father closely, trying to take in every part of his face to keep in her mind always.

– Be careful, Papa, she whispered. The soldiers may come.

– I will fight for the Truth, he replied. I am not afraid. He looked at her and with a brief upward flick of his chin added: – *Courage*, Isabelle.

She tightened the corners of her mouth into a smile that kept back the tears, then put her hands on his shoulders and, standing on tiptoe, kissed him three times.

– Bah, you have picked up the Tournier kiss, he muttered.

– Hush, Papa. I am a Tournier now.

– But your name is still du Moulin. Don't forget that.

– No. She paused. Remember me.

Marie, who never cried, cried for an hour after they left him standing in the road.

The horse could not pull all of them. Hannah and Marie sat in the cart while the rest walked behind, with Etienne or Petit Jean leading the horse. Occasionally one of them got in to rest and the horse went on more slowly.

They took the road over Mont Lozère, the moon bright, lighting their way but making them conspicuous. Whenever they heard a strange noise they pulled off the road. They reached the Col de Finiels at the summit and hid the cart while Etienne took the horse and went in search of the shepherds. They would know the route toward Geneva.

Isabelle waited by the cart, the others sleeping. She listened for every sound. Close by she knew the source of the Tarn welled up and began its long descent down the mountain. She would never see the river again, never feel its touch. Silently she began to weep for the first time since the Duc's steward woke them in the night.

Then she felt eyes upon her, but not a stranger's eyes. A familiar feel, the feel of the river on her skin. Glancing around, she saw him leaning against a rock not a stone's throw away. He didn't move when she looked at him.

Isabelle wiped her wet face and walked over to the shepherd. They held each other's eyes. Isabelle reached up and touched the scar on his cheek.

– How did you get this?

– From life.

– What is your name?

– Paul.

– We're leaving. To Switzerland.

He nodded, his dark eyes calming her.

– Remember me.

He nodded again.

– Come, Isabelle, she heard Etienne whisper behind her. What are you doing there?

– Isabelle, Paul repeated softly. He smiled, his teeth bright with moonlight. Then he was gone.

– The house. The barn. Our bed. The big pig and her four babies. The bucket in the well. Mémé's brown shawl. My doll that Bertrand made for me. The Bible.

Marie was listing all the things they had lost. At first Isabelle couldn't hear her over the sound of the wheels. Then she understood.

– Hush! she cried.

Marie stopped. Or at least stopped saying them aloud: Isabelle could see her lips move.

She never referred to Jean.

Isabelle's stomach tightened when she thought of the Bible.

– Could it still be there? she asked Etienne softly. They had reached the River Lot at the bottom of the other side of Mont Lozère; Isabelle was helping Etienne guide the horse through the water.

– Hidden in that niche in the chimney, she added, it might have been protected from the fire. They would never have found it.

He glanced at her wearily.

– We have nothing left and Papa is dead, he replied. The Bible is no help now. It is not worth anything to us now.

But its words are worth everything, she thought. Isn't that why we are leaving, for those very words?

Sometimes when Isabelle rested in the cart, facing backwards out over the land they had covered, she thought she saw her father running along the road after them. She would squeeze her eyes shut for a moment; when she opened them he had disappeared. Occasionally a real person took his place, a woman standing by the road, men scything or raking or digging in the fields, a man riding an ass. All stood still and watched them pass.

Sometimes boys Jacob's age threw stones at them and Etienne had to keep Petit Jean from fighting back. Marie would stand at the very end of the cart, looking back at the strange boys. She was never hit by the rocks. Once Hannah was: it was only when Etienne turned to speak to her long after the boys were gone that he saw blood trickling down the side of her face from the top of her head. She continued to stare straight ahead as Isabelle leaned over to dab gently at the blood with a piece of dampened cloth.

Marie began listing everything she could see.

– There's a barn. And there's a crow. And there's a plow. And there's a dog. And there's a church needle. And there's a pile of hay on fire. And there's a fence. And there's a log. And there's an axe. And there's a tree. And there's a man in the tree.

Isabelle looked up when Marie's litany ceased.

The man had been hanged from the branch of a small olive tree that could barely hold his weight. They stopped and stared at the body, naked but for a black hat rammed over his brow. His penis stood out stiffly like a branch. Then Isabelle saw the red hands, looked more closely at the face and drew in her breath sharply.

– It's Monsieur Marcel! she cried before she could stop herself.

Etienne clucked and began to run, pulling the horse with him, and they quickly left the vision behind, the boys glancing back several times until the body was out of sight.

For a few hours afterwards Marie was silent. When she began to list things once more, she avoided mentioning anything made by men. They reached a village and she simply repeated: – And there's the ground. And there's the ground – over and over until they had passed through.

They had halted at a stream to let the horse drink when an old man appeared on the opposite bank.

– Don't stop here, he said abruptly. Don't stop at all until you reach Vienne. It is very bad here. And don't go near St. Etienne or Lyons. He disappeared into the woods.

They did not stop that night. The horse plodded on exhausted while Hannah and the children slept in the cart and Etienne and Isabelle took turns leading. They hid during the day in a pine forest. When it was dark Etienne hitched up the horse and led it back onto the road. A moment later a group of men emerged from the trees on either side and surrounded them.

Etienne halted the horse. One of the men lit a torch; Isabelle could see the axes and pitchforks among them. Etienne handed the horse's rope to Isabelle, reached into the cart and pulled out the axe. He set the head carefully on the ground and gripped the end of the handle.

Everyone stood motionless. Only Hannah's lips moved in a silent prayer.

The men seemed unsure how to begin. Isabelle stared at the one who held the torch, watching his Adam's apple dart up and down. Then she felt a tickling at her ear: Marie had moved to the side of the cart and was whispering something.

— What is it? Isabelle murmured, still looking at the man and trying not to move her lips.

— That man with the fire. Tell him about God. Tell him what God wants him to do.

— What does God want him to do?

— To be good and not to sin, she replied firmly. And tell him we are not staying here.

Isabelle licked her lips. Her mouth was dry.

— Monsieur, she began, addressing the man with the torch. Etienne and Hannah jerked their heads at the sound of her voice.

— Monsieur, we are on our way to Geneva. We are not stopping here. Please let us pass.

The men stamped their feet. A few chuckled. The man with the torch stopped swallowing.

— Why should we? he demanded.

— Because God does not want you to sin. Because murder is a sin.

She was shaking and could say nothing more. The man with the torch took a step forward and Isabelle saw the long hunting knife in his belt.

Then Marie spoke, the metal in her voice ringing out through the woods.

— *Notre Père qui es aux cieux, ton nom soit sanctifié*, she called out. The man stopped.

— *Ton règne vienne, ta volonté soit faite sur la terre comme au ciel.*

A pause, then two voices continued.

— *Donne-nous aujourd'hui notre pain quotidien.* Jacob's voice rattled like pebbles underfoot. *Pardonne-nous nos péchés, comme aussi nous pardonnons ceux qui nous ont offensés.*

Isabelle, taking a deep breath, added her voice to theirs.

— *Et ne nous induis point dans la tentation, mais délivre-nous du malin; car à toi appartient le règne, la puissance, et la gloire à jamais. Amen.*

The man with the torch stood between them and the group of men. He stared at Marie, the silence stronger than ever.

— If you hurt us, she said, God will hurt you. He will hurt you very very badly.

— And what will he do to us, *ma petite*? the man asked, amused.

— Hush, Marie! Isabelle whispered.

— He will throw you in the fire! And you won't die, not right away. You will lie in it and then your guts will begin to ooze and boil. And your eyes will get bigger and bigger until pop! They explode!

This was no lesson from Monsieur Marcel. Isabelle recognized the details: Petit Jean had thrown a frog into the fire once and the children had gathered around to watch its demise.

The man did something Isabelle never would have expected from such a man in such a place: he laughed.

— You are very brave, *ma pauvre*, he said to Marie, but a little foolish. I would like you to be my daughter.

Isabelle clutched Marie's hand and the man laughed again.

— But why would I want a girl? he chuckled. What use are they?

He jerked his head at the others and extinguished the torch. All of them disappeared into the woods.

They waited for a long time; no one returned. Finally Etienne clicked his tongue and the horse continued, more slowly than before.

In the morning Isabelle found the first strand of red in Marie's hair. She pulled it out and burned it.

4. The Search

I ran back to the office, clutching a postcard of the Tournier painting. Rick was sitting on a high stool at his drawing board, a Tensor lamp picking out his cheekbones and the arrow of his jaw. Though he was staring at the sketch in front of him, his mind had clearly moved beyond the paper. He often sat for hours, visualizing in detail what he had just designed: fixtures, electrical system, plumbing, windows, ventilation. He imagined the whole thing and held it in his head, walking through it, sitting in it, living in it, combing through it for faults.

I watched him, then stuffed the postcard in my bag and sat down, my elation ebbing. Suddenly I didn't want to share my discovery with him.

But I *should* tell him, I argued with myself. I *will* tell him.

Rick looked up from the board and smiled. 'Hey there,' he said.

'Hey yourself. Everything OK? Structure sound?'

'Structure sound so far. And good news.' He waved a fax. 'A German firm wants me to present to them in a week or two. If it comes off we'll get a huge contract. This office will be busy for years.'

'Really? What a star you are!' I smiled and let him talk on about it for a few minutes.

'Listen, Rick,' I began when he had finished, 'I found something at a museum nearby. Look.' I pulled out the card and handed it to him. He held it under the spotlight.

'That's the blue you were telling me about, right?'

'Yes.' I stood behind him and wrapped my arms around his neck. He stiffened momentarily; I checked to make sure none of the psoriasis was touching his skin.

'Guess who it's by?' I rested my chin on his shoulder.

He started to turn the card over but I stopped him. 'Guess.'

Rick chuckled. 'C'mon, babe, you know I don't know anything about painting.' He studied it. 'One of those Italian Renaissance painters, I guess.'

'Nope. He's French.'

'Oh, well, one of your ancestors, then.'

'Rick!' I punched him on the arm. 'You looked!'

'No, I didn't! I was just joking.' He turned the card over. 'This really is one of your relatives?'

'Yeah. Something makes me think so.'

'That's great!'

'It is, isn't it?' I grinned at him. Rick slid an arm around my waist and kissed me while reaching around to unzip my dress. He had peeled it down to my waist before I realized he was serious. 'Hang on a minute,' I gasped. 'Let's wait till we get home!'

He laughed and grabbed a stapler. 'What, you don't like my stapler? How about my straight-edge?' He twisted the Tensor spot so the light bounced off the ceiling. 'My mood lighting doesn't turn you on?'

I kissed him and zipped up my dress. 'It's not that. I just think we should – maybe this isn't a good time to talk about it, but I've been thinking I'm not so sure about the baby thing. Maybe we should wait a little longer before we try.'

He looked surprised. 'But we made a decision.' Rick liked to stick to decisions.

'Yeah, but it's been more traumatic than I'd expected.'

'Traumatic?'

'Maybe that's too strong a word.' Wait a minute, Ella, I thought, it *has* been traumatic. Why are you trying to shelter him from this?

Rick was waiting for me to say something else. When I didn't he sighed. 'OK, Ella, if you feel that way.' He began to gather up his drawing pens. 'I don't want you going through with it unless you're sure.'

We drove home in a funny mood, both of us excited for different reasons, both chastened by my bad timing. We had just passed the square in Lisle when Rick stopped the car. 'Hang on a second,' he said. He jumped out and disappeared around the corner. When he returned a minute later he tossed something into my lap. I began to laugh. 'You didn't,' I said.

'I did.' He smiled mischievously. We'd often joked about the forlorn condom machine on one of the main streets and the kinds of emergency that would make anyone use it.

That night we made love and slept soundly.

The day Jean-Paul returned from Paris I was so distracted at my French lesson that Madame Sentier began to tease me.

'*Vous êtes dans la lune*,' she taught me. In turn I taught her, 'The light's on but nobody's home.' It took some explaining, but once she got it she laughed and went on about my *drôle* American humor.

'I never know what you will say next,' she said. 'But at least your accent is improving.'

Finally she dismissed me, assigning extra homework to make up for the wasted lesson.

I hurried to catch the train back to Lisle. When I got to the square and looked across at the *hôtel de ville*, though, I was suddenly reluctant to see him, like the feeling you get when throwing a party and an hour before the guests arrive you want to back out of it. I made myself walk across the square, enter the building, climb the stairs, open the door.

Several people were waiting for help from the two librarians. They both looked up, and Jean-Paul nodded politely. I sat down at a desk, disconcerted. I hadn't expected to have to wait, to tell him with so many people around. I began working on Madame Sentier's assignment half-heartedly.

After fifteen minutes the library cleared a little and Jean-Paul came over. 'May I help you, Madame?' he asked quietly in English, leaning over, one hand on my desk. I'd never been so close to him and as I looked up, caught the particular smell of him, of sun on skin, and stared at his jaw line peppered with stubble, I thought, Oh no. No, not this. This is not what I came here for. A quivery panic rose in my stomach.

I shook myself and whispered, 'Yes, Jean-Paul, I have –' A slight movement of his head stopped me. 'Yes, Monsieur,' I corrected myself. 'I have something to show you.' I gave him the postcard. He glanced at it, turned it over and nodded. 'Ah, the Musée des Augustins. You saw the Romanesque sculpture, yes?'

'No, no, look at the name! The name of the painter!'

He read aloud in a low voice, 'Nicolas Tournier, 1590 to 1639.' He looked at me and smiled.

'Look at the blue,' I whispered, touching the card. 'It's *that* blue. And you know the dream I told you about? I figured out even before I saw this that I was dreaming of a dress. A blue dress. That blue.'

'Ah, the blue of the Renaissance. You know there is lapis lazuli in this blue. It was so expensive they could only use it for important things like the Virgin's robe.'

Always a lecture ready.

'Don't you see? He's my ancestor!'

Jean-Paul glanced around, shifted on the desk, looked at the card again.

'Why do you think this painter is your ancestor?'

'Because of the name, obviously, and the dates, but mostly because of the blue. It matches perfectly with the dream. Not just the color itself, but the feeling around it. That look on her face.'

'You did not see this painting before you had the dream?'

'No.'

'But your family was in Switzerland by that time. This Tournier is French, yes?'

'Yes, but he was born in Montbéliard. I checked, and guess where that is? Thirty miles from Moutier! Just inside the French border. His parents could easily have moved from Moutier to Montbéliard.'

'There was no information about his family?'

'No, there wasn't much about him at the museum, just that he was born in Montbéliard in 1590, spent some time in Rome, then came to Toulouse and died in 1639. That's all they know.'

Jean-Paul tapped the postcard against his knuckles. 'If they know his birth date they will know his parents' names. Birth and baptism records always list the parents.'

I gripped the table. Rick's response was so different from this, I thought.

'I will look for information about him for you.' He stood up and handed me the postcard.

'No, I don't want you to,' I said loudly. Several people looked up and the other librarian frowned at us.

Jean-Paul raised his eyebrows.

'Monsieur, I will do it. I will find out about him.'

'I see. Very well, Madame.' He bowed slightly and walked away, leaving me feeling shaky and deflated. 'Damn him,' I muttered, staring at the Virgin. 'Damn him!'

Jean-Paul's skepticism affected me more than I wanted to admit. When I discovered the painter it didn't occur to me to find out more about him. I knew who he was; my gut feeling was all the proof I needed. Names and dates and places would make no difference to that certainty. Or so I thought.

But it only takes one comment to cast doubt. For a couple of days I tried to ignore what he had said, but the next time I went into Toulouse I took the postcard with me and after my lesson headed for the university library. I'd been there before to use their medical books but I'd never ventured into the arts section. It was packed with students studying for exams, writing papers, talking in stairwells in excited tones.

It took longer than I'd expected to find out anything about Nicolas Tournier. He was part of a group of painters called the Caravagesques, Frenchmen who studied in Rome in the early seventeenth century, copying Caravaggio's use of strong light and shadow. These painters often didn't sign their works, and there were long-running debates about who had painted what. Tournier was mentioned briefly here and there. He wasn't famous, though two of his paintings were in the Louvre. The little information I found was different from what I'd read at the museum: the earliest source listed him as *Robert* Tournier, born in Toulouse in 1604, died around 1670. I was only sure it was the same painter because I recognized the paintings. Other sources gave different dates again and corrected his name to Nicolas.

Finally I pinpointed three books that were the most up-to-date sources. When I looked for them on the shelves they were all missing. I talked to a hassled student behind the information desk who probably had his own exams to study for; he looked up the books on his computer and confirmed that they'd all been taken out.

'It is very busy now, as you can see,' he said. 'Maybe someone is using them to research a paper.'

'Can you find out who has them?'

He glanced at the screen. 'Another library has requested them.'

'In Lisle-sur-Tarn?'

'Yes.' He looked surprised, even more so when I muttered, 'Bastard! Not you, I mean. Thanks very much.'

I should have known Jean-Paul wouldn't sit on his hands and let me do it myself. He was too intrusive to stay away, too intent on proving his own theories. The question was whether or not I was willing to chase after him to find out more.

In the end I didn't have to decide. Up the street from the Lisle train station I ran into Jean-Paul on his way home from work. He nodded and said '*Bonsoir*,' and before I could think I blurted out, 'You've got the books I've been looking for all afternoon. Why did you do that? I asked you not to look into him for me but you're doing it anyway!'

He looked almost bored. 'Who said I do this research for you, Ella Tournier? I was curious about him, so I look for myself. If you want the books you can see them at the library tomorrow.'

I leaned against a wall and crossed my arms. 'All right, all right. You've won. Just tell me what you found out. Hurry up and get it over with.'

'You are sure you don't want to see the books yourself?'

'Just tell me.'

He lit a cigarette, inhaled and blew out toward his feet. 'OK. Maybe you find out today that there is not so much information on Nicolas Tournier for a long time. But in 1951 was found a record of his baptism, in July 1590 in a Protestant church in Montbéliard. His father was André Tournier, who was a painter from Besançon – that is not so far from Montbéliard. His grandfather was called Claude Tournier. The father, André Tournier, came to Montbéliard in 1572 because of religious troubles – maybe because of the Massacre of Saint Bartholomew. Your painter, Nicolas, was one of several children. There are mentions of him in Rome between 1619 and 1626. Then a mention of him in Carcassonne in 1627, and in Toulouse in 1632. For a long time they thought he died later in the seventeenth century, after 1657. But in 1974 was discovered his will with the date 30 December 1638. He died probably soon after.'

I studied the ground and was quiet for so long that Jean-Paul grew restless and flicked his cigarette into the street.

Finally I spoke. 'Tell me, were baptisms back then performed right after the birth?'

'Usually, yes. Not always.'

'So it could be put off for some reason, right? The date of baptism doesn't necessarily indicate the date of birth. Nicolas Tournier could have been a month or two years or ten years old when he was baptized for all we know. Maybe he was even an adult!'

'That is not likely.'

'No, but it's *possible*. What I'm saying is that the source doesn't tell us exactly. And his will has that date you mentioned, but that doesn't mean we know when he died. We don't know, do we? Maybe he died ten years after making it.'

'Ella, he was ill, he made his will, he died. That is what usually happens.'

'Yes, but we don't know *for sure*. We don't know *exactly* when he was born or when he died. These records don't prove anything. All the basic details about him are still open to question.' I paused to suppress the rising hysteria in my voice.

He leaned against the wall and folded his arms. 'You just don't want to hear that this painter's father was André Tournier and not any of your ancestors. No Etienne or Jean or Jacob. But he was not from the Cévennes or from Moutier. He is not your relative.'

'Look at it this way,' I continued more calmly. 'Until recently — until the 1950s — they didn't know *anything* about him. They got all his vital statistics wrong except for his last name and the city he died in. Everything else was wrong: his first name, his birth and death dates, where he was born, some of his paintings which turned out to be by other painters. And all of this wrong information was *published*; I saw it at the library. If I hadn't found out there were more recent sources I'd have all the wrong information about him. I'd even be calling him by the wrong name! Even now art historians are arguing over which paintings are his. If they can't get that basic information right — if it's all got to be based on speculation, where a baptism equals birth and a will equals death — well, that's just shifting evidence. It's not concrete, so why should I believe it? What *does* seem concrete to me is that his last name is my last name, that he worked only thirty miles from where I live, that he painted the same blue I dream about all the time. *That's* concrete.'

'No, that's *coincidence*. You are being seduced by coincidence.'

'And you by speculation.'

'That you live now near Toulouse and he lived in Toulouse does not mean that you are relatives. And the name Tournier is not so unusual. And that you dream of his blue — well, it is a blue easy to remember from a dream because it is so vivid. It would be harder to remember a dark blue, no?'

'Look, why are you trying so hard to prove he's *not* my relative?'

'Because you are basing all your proof on coincidence and your guts rather than on concrete evidence. You are struck by a painting, by a certain blue, and because of that and the painter's name is yours you decide he is an ancestor? No. No, I shouldn't have to convince you that Nicolas Tournier isn't your relative; you should be convincing me that he *is*.'

I've got to stop him, I thought. Soon I won't have any hope left.

Maybe my face reflected this thought, because when Jean-Paul spoke again his tone was kinder. 'I think maybe this Nicolas Tournier is no help to you. That maybe he is, what is it you say, a red fish.'

'What?' I laughed. 'A red *herring*, you mean. Maybe you're right.' I paused. 'He's taken over, though. I can't even remember what I was going to do about this ancestry business before he appeared.'

'You were going to find lost-long relatives in the Cévennes.'

'I might still do that.' The look on his face made me laugh. 'Yes, I *will*. You know, all your arguing just makes me want to prove you wrong. I want to find out proof – yes, concrete proof that even you'd agree with – about my "lost-long" ancestors. Just to show you that hunches aren't always wrong.'

We were both quiet then. I shifted from one hip to the other; Jean-Paul narrowed his eyes at the evening sun. I became very aware of him standing with me on this little street in France. We're only separated by two feet of air, I thought. I could just –

'And your dream?' he asked. 'You still see it?'

'Uh, no. No, it seems to have gone away.'

'So, you want me to call the archives at Mende and warn them you are coming?'

'No!' My shout made commuters' heads turn. 'That's exactly what I *don't* want you to do,' I hissed. 'Stay out of it unless I ask for help, OK? If I need help I'll ask you.'

Jean-Paul raised his hands as if he had a gun pointed at him. 'Fine, Ella Tournier. We draw a line here and I stay on my side, OK?' He took a step back from the imaginary line, and the distance between us increased.

The next night while we were eating dinner on the patio I told Rick I wanted to go to the Cévennes to look up family records.

'You remember I wrote to Jacob Tournier in Switzerland?' I explained. 'He wrote back and said the Tourniers were from the Cévennes originally. Probably.' I smiled to myself: I was learning to qualify my statements. 'I want to have a look around.'

'But I thought you found out about your family already, with the painter and all.'

'Well, that's not definite, actually. Not yet,' I added quickly. 'Maybe I'll find something there to prove it.'

To my surprise he frowned. 'I suppose this is something Jean-Pierre cooked up.'

'Jean-*Paul*. No, not at all. The opposite, if anything. He thinks I won't find anything.'

'Do you want me to come with you?'

'I have to go during the week, when the archives are open.'

'I could take a couple days off, come with you.'

'I was thinking of going next week.'

'Nope, can't go then. It's crazy at the office now with the German contract. Maybe later in the summer when it's quieter. In August.'

'I can't wait till August!'

'Ella, why are you so interested in your ancestors now? You never were before.'

'I never lived in France before.'

'Yeah, but you seem to be investing a lot in it. What do you expect to get out of it?'

I intended to say something about being accepted by the French, about feeling like I belonged to the country. 'I want to make the blue nightmare go away,' I found myself saying instead.

'You think by finding out about your family you'll get rid of a bad dream?'

'Yes.' I leaned back and gazed at the vines. Tiny green clusters of grapes were just beginning to appear. I knew it made no sense, that there was no link between the dream and my ancestors. But my mind had made the connection anyway, and I stubbornly decided to stick with it.

'Is Jean-Pierre going with you?'

'No! Look, why are you being so negative? It's not like you. This is something I'm *interested* in. It's the first thing I've really wanted to do since we got here. The least you could do is be supportive about it.'

'I thought the thing you really wanted to do was have a baby. I've been supportive about that.'

'Yes, but —' You shouldn't just be supportive about something like that, I thought. You should want to have it too.

Lately I'd been having a lot of thoughts that I censored.

Rick stared at me, frowning, then made a conscious effort to relax. 'You're right. Of course go, babe. If it makes you happy then that's what you should do.'

'Oh, Rick, don't —' I stopped. There was no point criticizing him. He was trying to be supportive without understanding. At least he was trying.

'Look, I'll go for a few days, that's all. If I find out something, great. If I don't, it's no big deal. All right?'

'Ella, if you don't find anything, I'll take you to the best restaurant in Toulouse.'

'Gee, thanks. That makes me feel a lot better.'

Sarcasm was the cheapest form of humor, according to my mother. My remark was made even cheaper by the hurt look in his eyes.

The morning I left it was crisp and bright; there had been thunderstorms the night before, clearing the tension from the air. I kissed Rick goodbye as he left for the train station, then got in the car and drove off in the opposite direction. It was a relief to go. I celebrated by playing loud music and opening both windows and the sun roof to let the wind whip through me.

The road followed the Tarn up to Albi, a cathedral town full of June tourists, then headed north away from the river. I would meet up with the Tarn again in the Cévennes, climbing backwards to its source. Beyond Albi the landscape began to change, the horizon first expanding as I climbed, then narrowing as the hills closed in around me and the sky turned from blue to grey. The poppies and Queen Anne's lace along the road were joined by new flowers, pink Jack-in-the-pulpit and daisies and especially broom, with its sharp, moldy smell. The trees grew darker. Fields were no longer cultivated but left as meadows and grazed by tan goats and cows. Rivers got smaller and faster and louder. Abruptly the houses changed: light chalk stone became hard brown-grey granite, and roofs were more angular, tiled with flat slate rather than curved terracotta. Everything became smaller, darker, more serious.

I closed the windows and sun roof, turned off the music. My mood seemed to be linked with the landscape. I didn't like it, looking out at this beautiful, sad land. It reminded me of the blue.

Mende crowned both the landscape and my mood. Its narrow streets were surrounded by a busy ring road that made the town feel hemmed in. A cathedral squatted in the center, two different spires giving it an awkward, unplanned look. Inside it was dark and grim. I escaped and, standing on its steps, stared at the grey stone buildings around me. *This* is the Cévennes? I thought. Then I smiled at myself: of course I'd assumed Tournier country would be beautiful.

It had been a long drive from Lisle; even the bigger roads curved and climbed, requiring more concentration than straight American highways. I was tired and in an uncharitable mood, which wasn't improved by a dark, narrow hotel room and a lonely supper in a pizzeria where the only other customers were couples or old men. I thought about calling Rick, but knew that instead of cheering me up he would make me feel worse, reminding me of the gap that was growing between us.

The departmental archives were in a brand-new building made of salmon and white stone, and metal painted blue, green and red. The research room was large and airy, the tables three-quarters full of people scrutinizing documents. Everyone looked as if they knew exactly what they were doing. I felt the way I often did in Lisle: as a foreigner my place was on the edge, where I could watch and admire the natives but never take part myself.

A tall woman standing at the main desk looked over and smiled at me. She was about my age, with short blond hair and yellow glasses. I thought, Ah, thank God, *not* another Madame. I went up to the desk and set down my bag. 'I don't know what I'm doing here,' I said. 'Please can you help me?'

Her laugh was the most unlikely shriek for such a quiet place.

'*Alors*, what are you looking for?' she asked, still laughing, her blue eyes magnified through thick lenses. I'd never seen someone wear thick glasses so stylishly.

'I have an ancestor named Etienne Tournier who may have lived in the Cévennes in the sixteenth century. I want to find out more about him.'

'Do you know when he was born or died?'

'No. I know that the family moved to Switzerland at some point but I don't know when exactly. It would have been before 1576.'

'You know no birth or death dates? What about for his children? Or grandchildren, even?'

'Well, he had a son, Jean, who had a child in 1590.'

She nodded. 'So the son Jean was born between, let's say, 1550 and 1575, and the father Etienne twenty to forty years before that, say, from 1510. So you're searching between 1510 and 1575, something like that, yes?'

She spoke French so fast that I couldn't answer right away: I was wading through her calculations. 'I guess so,' I replied finally, wondering if I should mention the painter Tourniers as well, Nicolas and André and Claude.

She didn't give me the chance. 'You want to look for records of baptism and marriage and death,' she declared. 'And maybe *compoix* also, tax records. Now, what village did they come from?'

'I don't know.'

'Ah, that's a problem. The Cévennes is big, you know. Of course there are not so many records from that time. Back then they were kept by the church, but many were burned or lost during the religious wars. So maybe you will not have too much to look through. If you knew the village I could tell you immediately what we have, but never mind, we'll see what we can find.'

She ran through an inventory of documents held there and in other records offices in the *département*. She was right: for the whole region there were only a handful of documents from the sixteenth century. The few records left must have survived arbitrarily. It was clear that the likelihood of a Tournier turning up in the books would be entirely down to luck.

I ordered the relevant sets of records held in the building that fell between the dates she mentioned. I wasn't sure what would appear: I'd been using the term 'record' loosely, expecting some sixteenth-century equivalent to my own neatly typed birth certificate or marriage license. Five minutes later the woman brought over a few boxes of microfiche, a book covered with protective brown paper, and a huge box. She smiled encouragingly and left me to it. I glanced at her as she went back to the desk and grinned to myself at her platform shoes and short leather skirt.

I began with the book. It was bound in greasy off-white calfskin, its cover painted with ancient music and Latin text. The first letter of each line was enlarged and colored red and blue. I opened it to the first page and smoothed it out; it was thrilling to touch something so old. The handwriting was in brown ink, and though it was very neat, it seemed to have been written to be admired rather than read: I couldn't read a word. Several letters were virtually identical, and when I finally began to make out a few words here and there, I realized it didn't make any difference – it was all in a foreign language.

Then I began to sneeze.

The woman came over twenty minutes later to see how I was doing. I had gotten through ten pages, finding dates and little by little picking out what seemed to be names.

I looked up at her. 'Is this document in French?'

'Old French.'

'Oh.' I hadn't thought of that.

She glanced down at the page and ran a pink fingernail over a few lines. 'A pregnant woman drowned in the River Lot, May 1574. *Un inconnu, la pauvre*,' she murmured. 'These deaths are not so useful to you, are they?'

'I suppose not,' I said, and sneezed on the book.

The woman laughed as I apologized. 'Everyone sneezes. Look around you, handkerchiefs everywhere!' We heard a tiny sneeze from an old man on the other side of the room and giggled.

'Take a break from the dust,' she said. 'Come for a coffee with me. My name is Mathilde.' She held out her hand and grinned. 'This is what Americans do, yes? Shake hands when they meet?'

We sat in a café around the corner and were soon chatting like old friends. Despite her rapid-fire delivery, Mathilde was easy to talk to. I hadn't realized how much I'd missed female company. She asked me a million questions about the States, California in particular.

'What are you doing here?' she sighed at last. 'I'd go to California in an instant!'

I tensed, trying to think of an answer that would make it clear I hadn't simply followed Rick to France, as Jean-Paul had implied. But Mathilde went on before I could answer and I realized she wasn't expecting me to explain myself.

She wasn't at all surprised that I was interested in distant ancestors. 'People look into family history all the time,' she said.

'I feel a little silly doing it,' I confessed. 'It's so unlikely I'll find anything.'

'True,' she admitted. 'To be honest, most people don't when they're searching that far back. But don't be discouraged. Anyway the records are interesting, aren't they?'

'Yes, but it takes me so long to understand what they say! All I can really find are dates and sometimes names.'

Mathilde smiled. 'If you think that book is hard to read, wait till you see the microfiche!' She laughed when she saw my face. 'I'm not so busy today,' she continued. 'You keep reading your book and I'll look through the microfiche for you. I'm used to that old handwriting!'

I was grateful for her offer. While she sat at the microfiche machine I tackled the box, which Mathilde explained was a book of *compoix*, records of taxes on crops. It was all in the same handwriting and almost incomprehensible. It took the rest of the day to look through. By the end I was exhausted, but Mathilde seemed disappointed that there wasn't anything else to look at.

'Is that really all?' she asked, flicking through the inventory once more. '*Attends*, there's a book of *compoix* from 1570 at the *mairie* in Le Pont de Montvert. Of course, Monsieur Jourdain! I helped him take inventory of those records a year ago.'

'Who's Monsieur Jourdain?'

'The secretary of the *mairie*.'

'You think it's worth the trouble?'

'*Bien sûr*. Even if you don't find anything, Le Pont de Montvert is a beautiful place. It's a little village at the bottom of Mont Lozère.' She glanced at her watch. '*Mon Dieu* – I must pick up Sylvie!' She grabbed her bag and pushed me out, chuckling as she locked the door behind me. 'You'll have fun with Monsieur Jourdain. If he doesn't eat you alive, of course!'

The next morning I started early and took the picturesque route to Le Pont de Montvert. As I began to climb the road up Mont Lozère the landscape opened out and brightened while also growing more barren. I passed through tiny, dusty villages where the buildings were made entirely of granite, even down to the tiles on the roofs, with hardly a touch of paint to distinguish them from the surrounding land. Many houses were abandoned, roofs gone, chimneys crumbling, shutters askew. I saw few people, and once I got above a certain point, no cars. Soon there were just granite boulders, broom and heather, and the occasional clump of pines.

This is more like it, I thought.

I pulled over near the summit at a place called the Col de Finiels and sat on the hood of the car. After a few minutes the automatic fan cut out and it was wonderfully quiet; I listened and could hear a few birds and the dull roar of the wind. According to my map, to the east across a small pine forest and over a hill was the source of the Tarn. I was tempted to go and look for it.

Instead I drove down the other side of the mountain, zigzagging back and forth, until one last turn brought me coasting into Le Pont de Montvert, passing a hotel, a school, a restaurant, a few shops and bars on one side of the road. Paths branched off the main road, winding among the houses built up the hill. Above the tops of the houses I could see the roof of a church; a bell hung in the stone belfry.

I caught a glimpse of water on the other side of the road, where the Tarn ran, hidden by a low stone wall. I parked by an old stone bridge, walked onto it and looked down at the river.

The Tarn had changed completely. No longer wide and slow, it was twenty feet across at most and racing like a stream. I studied the pebbles in deep reds and yellows gleaming under the water. I could hardly tear my eyes away.

This water will flow all the way to Lisle, I thought. All the way to me.

It was Wednesday, ten a.m. Jean-Paul could be sitting at the café, watching the river too.

Stop it, Ella, I thought sharply. Think of Rick, or don't think at all.

From the outside the *mairie* – a grey building with brown shutters and a French flag hanging limply over one of the windows – was presentable enough. Inside, though, it looked like a junk shop; the sun streamed through a fog of dust. Monsieur Jourdain was reading a newspaper at a desk in the far corner. He was short and plump, with bulging eyes, olive skin and one of those scraggly beards that peters out halfway down the neck and blurs the jaw line. He eyed me suspiciously as I picked my way through battered old furniture and stacks of paper.

'*Bonjour, Monsieur Jourdain*,' I said briskly.

He grunted and glanced down at his paper.

'My name is Ella Turner – Tournier,' I continued carefully in French. 'I would like to look at some records you keep here at the *mairie*. There's a *compoix* from 1570. May I see it?'

He looked up at me briefly, then continued reading the paper.

'Monsieur? You are Monsieur Jourdain, yes? They told me in Mende that I should speak to you.'

Monsieur Jourdain ran his tongue around his teeth. I looked down. He was reading a sports newspaper, the pages open to the racing form.

He said something I didn't understand. '*Pardon?*' I asked. Again he spoke incomprehensibly and I wondered if he was drunk. When

94

I asked him once more to repeat himself, he waved his hands and flecked spit at me, unleashing a torrent of words. I took a step back.

'Jesus, what a stereotype!' I muttered in English.

He narrowed his eyes and snarled, and I turned and left. I sat fuming over a coffee in a café, then found the number of the Mende archives and called Mathilde from a pay phone.

She shrieked when I explained what had happened. 'Leave it to me,' she counselled. 'Go back in half an hour.'

Whatever Mathilde said to Monsieur Jourdain over the phone worked, because although he glared at me he led me down a hall to a cramped room containing a desk overflowing with papers. '*Attendez*,' he mumbled, and left. I seemed to be in a storage room; while waiting I poked around. There were boxes of books everywhere, some very old. Stacks of papers that looked like government documents lay on the floor, and a big pile of unopened envelopes was scattered on the desk, all addressed to Abraham Jourdain.

After ten minutes he reappeared with a large box and dumped it onto the desk. Then without a word or glance he walked out.

The box held a book similar to the *compoix* in Mende, but even bigger and in worse shape. The calfskin binding was so ragged it no longer held the pages together. I handled the book as carefully as I could, but even so bits of corners crumbled and broke off. I hid the fragments furtively in my pockets, worried that Monsieur Jourdain might find them and yell at me.

At noon he threw me out. I'd only been working an hour when he appeared in the doorway, glared down at me and growled something. I could only work out what he meant because he tapped his watch. He stumped down the hall to open the front door, shutting it behind me with a thud and drawing the bolt. I stood blinking in the sunlight, dazed after the dark, dusty room.

Then I was surrounded by children, streaming out from a play-ground next door.

I breathed in. Thank God, I thought.

I bought things for lunch in the shops just as they were closing:

cheese and peaches and some dark red bread the shopkeeper told me was a local specialty, made from chestnuts. I took a path up through granite houses to the church at the top of the village.

It was a simple stone building, almost as wide as it was high. What I took to be the front door was locked, but around the side I found an open door, the date 1828 carved over it, and stepped inside. The room was full of empty wooden pews. Balconies skirted the two long walls. There was a wooden organ, a lectern and a table with a large Bible lying open on it. That was all. No ornamentation, no statues or crosses, no stained glass. I'd never seen such a bare church. There wasn't even an altar to distinguish the minister's place from the people's.

I went over to the Bible, the only thing there with a use beyond the purely functional. It looked old, though not as old as the *compoix* I'd been looking at. I began to leaf through it. It took awhile – I didn't know the order of the books in the Bible – but at last I found what I was looking for. I began to read the thirty-first psalm: *J'ai mis en toi mon espérance: Garde-moi donc, Seigneur*. By the time I reached the first line of the third verse, *Tu es ma tour et forteresse*, my eyes were full of tears. I stopped abruptly and fled.

Silly girl, I scolded myself as I sat on the wall around the church and wiped my eyes. I made myself eat, blinking in the bright sun. The chestnut bread was sweet and dry, and stuck in the back of my throat. I could feel it there for the rest of the day.

When I got back Monsieur Jourdain was sitting behind his desk, hands clasped in front of him. He wasn't reading his paper; in fact it looked like he was waiting for me. I said carefully, '*Bonjour, Monsieur*. May I have the *compoix*, please?'

He opened a filing cabinet next to his desk, pulled out the box and handed it to me. Then he looked closely at my face.

'What is your name?' he asked in a puzzled voice.

'Tournier. Ella Tournier.'

'Tournier,' he repeated, still scrutinizing me. He twisted his mouth to one side, chewing the inside of his cheek. He was staring at my hair. '*La Rousse*,' he murmured.

'What?' I snapped loudly. A wave of goosebumps swept over me.

Monsieur Jourdain widened his eyes, then reached over and touched a lock of my hair. '*C'est rouge. Alors, La Rousse.*'

'But my hair is brown, Monsieur.'

'*Rouge,*' he repeated firmly.

'Of course it's not. It's —' I pulled a clump of hair in front of my eyes and caught my breath. He was right: it *was* shot through with coppery highlights. But it had been brown when I'd looked at myself in the mirror that morning. The sun had brought out highlights in my hair before, but never so fast or so dramatically.

'What is La Rousse?' I asked accusingly.

'It's a Cevenol nickname for a girl with red hair. It's not an insult,' he added quickly. 'They used to call the Virgin La Rousse because they thought she had red hair.'

'Oh.' I felt dizzy and nauseous and thirsty all at once.

'Listen, Madame.' He rolled his tongue over his teeth. 'If you want to use that desk there —' He gestured toward an empty desk across from his.

'No thank you,' I said shakily. 'The other office is fine.'

Monsieur Jourdain nodded, looking relieved that he wouldn't have to share a room with me.

I began where I'd left off, but kept stopping to inspect my hair. Finally I shook myself. Nothing you can do about it right now, Ella, I thought. Just get on with the job.

I worked quickly, aware that Monsieur Jourdain's new tolerance could only be relied on for so long. I stopped trying to work out what the taxes were being levied for and concentrated on names and dates. As I got toward the end of the book I became more and more despondent, and began making small bets to keep myself going: there'll be a Tournier in one of the next twenty sections; I'll find one in the next five minutes.

I glared at the last page: it was a record for a Jean Marcel, and there was only one entry, for *châtaignes*, a word I'd seen often in the *compoix*. Chestnuts. The new color of my hair.

I heaved the book into its box and walked slowly down the hall to Monsieur Jourdain's office. He was still sitting at his desk, typing fast with two fingers on an old manual typewriter. As he leaned forward a silver chain swung out of the V in his shirt; the pendant at the end of it clanked against the keys. He looked up and caught me staring at it. His hand moved to the pendant; he rubbed it with his thumb.

'The Huguenot cross,' he said. 'You know it?'

I shook my head. He held it up for me to see. It was a square cross with a dove with outspread wings attached to the bottom arm.

I set the box on the empty desk opposite him. '*Voilà*,' I said. 'Thank you for letting me look at it.'

'You found anything?'

'No.' I held out my hand. '*Merci beaucoup, Monsieur.*'

He shook hands with me hesitantly.

'*Au revoir, La Rousse*,' he called as I left.

It was too late to go back to Lisle, so I spent the night at one of the two hotels in the village. After supper I tried calling Rick but there was no answer. Then I called Mathilde, who had given me her number and made me promise to give her an update. She was disappointed that I hadn't found anything, even though she knew the odds were against me.

I asked her how she got Monsieur Jourdain to be nicer to me.

'Oh, I just made him feel guilty. I reminded him you were looking for Huguenots. He's from a Huguenot family himself, a descendant of one of the Camisard rebellion leaders, in fact. René Laporte, I think.'

'So that's a Huguenot.'

'Sure. What were you expecting? You mustn't be too hard on him, Ella. He's had a difficult time lately. His daughter ran off with an American three years ago. A tourist. Not only that, a Catholic too! I don't know which made him angrier, being American or being Catholic. You can see how it's affected him. He was a good worker before, a smart man. They sent me over last year to help him sort things out.'

I thought of the room full of books and papers I'd worked in and chuckled.

'Why are you laughing?'

'Did you ever see the back office?'

'No, he said he'd lost the key and there was nothing in it anyway.'

I described it to her.

'*Merde*, I knew he was hiding something! I should have been more persistent.'

'Anyway, thanks for helping me.'

'Bah, it's nothing.' She paused. 'So, who's Jean-Paul?'

I turned red. 'A librarian in Lisle, where I live. How do you know him?'

'He called me this afternoon.'

'He called *you*?'

'Sure. He wanted to know if you had found what you were looking for.'

'He did?'

'Is that such a surprise?'

'Yes. No. I don't know. What did you tell him?'

'I told him he should ask *you*. But what a flirt!'

I flinched.

I took the scenic route back to Lisle, following the Tarn through winding gorges. It was an overcast day and my heart wasn't in the drive. I began to feel carsick from all the curves. By the end I was wondering why I'd bothered with the trip at all.

Rick wasn't in when I got home and there was no answer at his office. The house felt lifeless, and I moved from room to room, unable to read or watch television. I spent a long time examining my hair in the bathroom mirror. My hairdresser in San Francisco had always tried to get me to dye my hair auburn because he thought it would go well with my brown eyes. I'd always dismissed the suggestion, but now he had his way: my hair was definitely going red.

By midnight I was worried: Rick had missed the last train from

Toulouse. I didn't have the home phone numbers of any of his colleagues, the only people I could imagine him being out with. There was no one else I could call nearby, no sympathetic friend to listen and reassure me. I briefly considered phoning Mathilde, but it was late and I didn't know her well enough to inflict distressed calls at midnight on her.

Instead I called my mother in Boston. 'Are you *sure* he didn't tell you where he was going?' she kept saying. '*Where* were you again? Ella, have you been paying enough attention to him?' She wasn't interested in my research into the Tournier family. It wasn't her family anymore; the Cévennes and French painters meant nothing to her.

I changed the subject. 'Mom,' I said, 'my hair's turned red.'

'What? Have you hennaed it? Does it look good?'

'I didn't –' I couldn't tell her it had just turned that way. It made no sense. 'It looks OK,' I said finally. 'Actually it *does* look good. Kind of natural.'

I went to bed but lay awake for hours, listening for Rick's key in the door, fretting about whether or not to be worried, reminding myself that he was a grown-up but also that he always told me where he would be.

I got up early and sat drinking coffee until seven-thirty when a receptionist answered the phone at Rick's firm. She didn't know where he was, but promised to get his secretary to call the moment she got in. By the time she called at eight-thirty I was wired with coffee and slightly dizzy.

'*Bonjour, Madame Middleton*,' she sang. 'How are you?'

I'd given up explaining to her that I hadn't taken Rick's name.

'Do you know where Rick is?' I asked.

'But he is in Paris, on business,' she said. 'He had to go suddenly the day before yesterday. He'll be back tonight. Didn't he tell you?'

'No. No, he didn't.'

'I'll give you his hotel number if you want to call him there.'

When I reached the hotel Rick had already checked out. For some reason that made me angrier than anything else.

By the time he got home that night I could barely speak to him. He looked surprised to see me, but pleased too.

I didn't even say hello. 'Why didn't you tell me where you were?' I demanded.

'I didn't know where *you* were.'

I frowned. 'You knew I was going to the archives in Mende to look up records. You could've gotten in touch with me there.'

'Ella, to be honest I haven't been sure *what* you've been doing for the past few days —'

'What do you mean by that?'

'— Where you've been, where you were going. You haven't called me at all. You weren't clear about where you were going or how long you'd be away. I didn't know you'd be back today. For all I knew you wouldn't come back for weeks.'

'Oh, don't exaggerate.'

'I'm not exaggerating. Give me a break here, Ella. You can't expect me to tell you where I am if you don't tell me where *you* are.'

I scowled at the ground. He was so reasonable and so right that I wanted to hit him. I sighed and said, 'Right. Sorry. I'm sorry. It's just that I didn't find anything and then I came back and you weren't here and oh, I've drunk too much coffee today. It's made me queasy.'

Rick laughed and put his arms around me. 'Tell me about what you didn't find.'

I buried my face in his shoulder. 'A whole lot of nothing. Except I met a nice woman and a crotchety old man.'

I felt Rick's cheek shift against my head. I pulled my head back so I could see his face. He was frowning.

'Did you dye your hair?'

The next day Rick and I strolled through the Saturday market, his arm draped around my shoulders. I felt more relaxed than I had in two months. To celebrate the feeling and the fact that my psoriasis seemed to be receding, I wore my favorite dress, a pale yellow sleeveless shift.

The market had been getting bigger and bigger each weekend as summer approached. Now it was the busiest I'd ever seen it, filling the square completely. Farmers had come with truckloads of fruit and vegetables, cheese, honey, bacon, bread, pâté, chickens, rabbits, goats. I could buy candy in bulk, a housecoat like Madame's, even a tractor.

Everyone was there: our neighbors, the woman from the library, Madame on a bench across the square with a couple of her cronies, women from a yoga class I was taking, the woman with the choking baby and everyone I'd ever bought anything from.

Even with so many people around I spotted him immediately. He seemed to be arguing ferociously with a man selling tomatoes; then they grinned and slapped each other on the back. Jean-Paul picked up a bag of tomatoes, turned around and almost ran into me. I jumped back to avoid getting tomato all over my dress and stumbled. Rick and Jean-Paul each grabbed an elbow and as I regained my balance they both stood holding me for a second before Jean-Paul dropped his hand.

'*Bonjour*, Ella Tournier,' he said, nodding at me and raising his eyebrows slightly. He was wearing a pale blue shirt; I felt a sudden urge to reach out and touch it.

'Hello, Jean-Paul,' I replied calmly. I remembered reading somewhere that the person you address first and introduce to the other is the more important person. I turned deliberately to Rick and said, 'Rick, this is Jean-Paul. Jean-Paul, this is Rick, my husband.'

The two men shook hands, Rick saying *Bonjour* and Jean-Paul Hello. I wanted to laugh, they were so different: Rick tall, broad, golden and open, Jean-Paul small, wiry, dark and calculating. A lion and a wolf, I thought. And how they distrust each other.

There was an awkward silence. Jean-Paul turned to me and said in English, 'How was your researches in Mende?'

I shrugged nonchalantly. 'Not too good. Nothing useful. Nothing at all, in fact.' I wasn't feeling nonchalant, though: I was thinking with guilt and pleasure that Jean-Paul had called Mathilde and I hadn't called him back; that Jean-Paul's awkward English was the only thing that revealed inner turmoil; that he and Rick were so different from each other; that both were watching me closely.

'So, you go to other towns for doing this work?'

I tried not to look at Rick. 'I went to Le Pont de Montvert too but there wasn't anything. There isn't much left from that time. But anyway it's not so important. It doesn't really matter.'

Jean-Paul's sardonic smile said three things: you're lying, you thought it was going to be easy and I told you so.

But he didn't say any of this; instead he looked intently at my hair. 'Your hair is turning red,' he stated.

'Yes.' I smiled at him. He had put it just the right way: no questioning, no blame. For a moment Rick and the market disappeared.

Rick slid his hand up my back to settle on my shoulder. I laughed nervously and said, 'Anyway, we have to go. Nice to see you.'

'*Au revoir*, Ella Tournier,' Jean-Paul said.

Rick and I didn't speak for a few minutes. I pretended to be absorbed in buying honey and Rick weighed eggplants in his hands. Finally he said, 'So that's him, eh?'

I shot him a look. 'That's the librarian, Rick. That's all.'

'Promise?'

'Yes.' It had been a long time since I'd lied to him.

I was coming back from a yoga class one afternoon when I heard the phone ringing from the street. Running to answer it, I managed an out-of-breath 'Hello?' before a high, excited voice spoke so rapidly that I had to sit down and wait for it to finish. At last I interjected in French, 'Who is this?'

'Mathilde, it's Mathilde. Listen, it's wonderful, you must see it!'

'Mathilde, slow down! I can't understand what you're saying. What's wonderful?'

Mathilde took a deep breath. 'We've found something about your family, about the Tourniers.'

'Wait a minute. Who's "we"?'

'Monsieur Jourdain and me. You remember I mentioned working with him before, in Le Pont de Montvert?'

'Yes.'

'Well, I wasn't working at the main desk today, so I thought I'd drive out and visit, see that room you told me about. What a garbage can! So Monsieur Jourdain and I began going through things. And in one of the boxes of books he found your family!'

'What do you mean? A book about my family?'

'No, no, written in the book. It's a Bible. The front page of a Bible. That's where families wrote down births and deaths and marriages, in their Bibles, if they had them.'

'But what was it doing there?'

'That's a good question. He's been terrible, Monsieur Jourdain. Imagine letting valuable old things like that lie around! Apparently someone brought in a whole box of old books. There's all sorts of things, old records from the parish, old deeds, but the Bible is the most valuable. Well, maybe not so valuable, given its condition.'

'What's wrong with it?'

'It's burnt. Most of the pages are black. But it lists many Tourniers. They're your Tourniers, Monsieur Jourdain is sure of it.'

I was silent, taking it in.

'So can you come up and see it?'

'Of course. Where are you?'

'Still in Le Pont de Montvert. But I can meet you somewhere in between. Let's meet in Rodez, in, let's see, three hours.' She thought for a moment. 'I know. We can meet at Crazy Joe's Bar. It's right around the corner from the cathedral, in the old quarter. It's American so you can have a martini!' She shrieked with laughter and hung up.

As I drove out of Lisle I passed the *hôtel de ville*. Keep going, Ella, I thought. He has nothing to do with this.

I stopped, jumped out, ran into the building and up the stairs. I opened the library door and poked my head inside. Jean-Paul sat alone behind his desk, reading a book. He glanced up at me but otherwise didn't move.

I stayed in the doorway. 'Are you busy?' I asked.

He shrugged. After the scene in the market a few days before, his distance wasn't surprising.

'I've found something,' I said quietly. 'Or I should say, someone else has found something for me. Concrete evidence. Something you'll like.'

'Is this about your painter?'

'I don't think so. Come with me to see it.'

'Where?'

'They found it in Le Pont de Montvert, but I'm meeting them in Rodez.' I looked at the floor. 'I want you to come with me.'

Jean-Paul regarded me for a moment, then nodded. 'OK. I'll close early here. Can you meet me at the Fina station up the Albi road in fifteen minutes?'

'The gas station? Why? How will you get there?'

'I'll drive there. I'll meet you and then we can take one car.'

'Why can't you just come with me now? I'll wait for you outside.'

Jean-Paul sighed. 'Tell me, Ella Tournier, you have never lived in a small town before you live in Lisle?'

'No. But –'

'I tell you when we drive.'

Jean-Paul pulled up to the gas station in a battered white Citroën Deux Chevaux, one of those cars that looks like a flimsy Volkswagen Beetle and has a soft roof that can be rolled back like a sardine can. Its engine makes an unmistakable sound, a friendly churning whine that always made me smile when I heard it. I thought Jean-Paul would have a sports car, but a Deux Chevaux made sense.

He looked so furtive getting out of his car and into mine that I laughed. 'So, you think people will talk about us?' I remarked as I pulled onto the Albi road.

'It is a small town. Many old women there have nothing to do but watch and discuss what they see.'

'Surely they don't mean anything by it.'

'Ella, I will describe to you the day of one of these women. She gets up in the morning and has her breakfast out on her terrace, so she watches everyone who goes by. Then she does her shopping; she goes to all the shops every day and talks to the other women and watches what other people do. She comes back and stands in front of her door and talks to her neighbors and watches. She sleeps for an hour in the afternoon when she knows everyone else will be asleep and she will not miss anything. She sits on her terrace for the rest of the afternoon, reading the newspaper but really watching all that passes in the street. In the evening she goes for another walk and talks to all her friends. There is a lot of talking and watching in her day. That is what she does.'

'But I haven't done anything in public for them to talk about.'

'They will take anything and twist it.'

I took a curve wide. 'There's nothing I've done in that town that anyone could possibly find interesting or scandalous or whatever it is you're implying.'

Jean-Paul was quiet for a moment. Then he said, 'You are enjoying your onion quiches, yes?'

I stiffened for a second, then laughed. 'Yeah, quite an addiction, really. I bet the old gossips are really shocked.'

'They thought that you were, that you were —' He stopped. I glanced at him; he looked embarrassed. 'Pregnant,' he finished finally.

'What?'

'That you were having a craving.'

I began to titter. 'But that's ludicrous! Why would they think that? And why would they care?'

'In a small place everyone knows everyone else's business. They believe it is their right to know if you are having a baby. But anyway they know now that you're not pregnant.'

'Good,' I muttered. Then I glared at him. 'How do they know I'm not pregnant?'

To my surprise Jean-Paul looked even more embarrassed. 'Nothing, nothing, they just —' He trailed off and fumbled with his shirt pocket.

'What?' I began to feel sick with disgust at what they might know. Jean-Paul pulled a pack of cigarettes from his pocket. 'Do you know the machine for selling Durex just off the square?' he asked at last.

'Ah.' Someone must have seen Rick buying them that night. God, I thought, what haven't they sniffed out? Does the doctor broadcast every visit? Do they go through our garbage?

'What else have they said?'

'You do not need to know.'

'What else have they said?'

Jean-Paul gazed out the window. 'They notice everything you buy in the shops. The postman tells them about every letter you receive. They know when you go out during the day, and they notice how much you go out with your husband. And, well, if you do not use your shutters they look inside, too.' He sounded more disapproving of me not closing my shutters than of their looking in.

I shivered, thinking of the choking baby, of all those shoulders turned against me.

'What have they said specifically?'

'You want to know?'

'Yes.'

'There was the quiches and the craving. Then they think you are pretentious because you bought a washing machine.'

'But why?'

'They think that you should wash by hand the way they do. That only people with children should have machines. And they think the color you painted your shutters is vulgar and not right for Lisle. They think you lack finesse. That you should not wear dresses without sleeves. That you are rude to speak English to people. That you are a liar because you told Madame Rodin at the *boulangerie* that you lived here when you didn't yet. And you picked the lavender in the square, and no one does that. In fact that was their first impression of you. It is hard to change that.'

We drove in silence for a few minutes. I felt tearful but wanted to laugh too. I had only spoken English once in public, but that counted for much more than all the times I spoke French. Jean-Paul lit a cigarette and opened his window a crack.

'Do you think I'm rude and lack finesse?'

'No.' He smiled. 'And I think you should wear dresses without sleeves more often.'

I blushed. 'So did they have anything nice to say about me?'

He thought for a moment. 'They think your husband is very handsome, even with the –' He gestured at the back of his head.

'Ponytail.'

'Yes. But they do not understand why he runs and they think his shorts are too short.'

I smiled to myself. Jogging did seem out of place in a French village, but Rick was impervious to people's stares. Then my smile faded.

'Why do *you* know all this about me?' I asked. 'About quiches and being pregnant and shutters and washing machines? You act like you're above all this gossip, but you seem to know as much as everybody else.'

'I am not a gossip,' Jean-Paul replied firmly, blowing smoke at the top of the window. 'Someone repeated it to me as a warning.'

'A warning of what?'

'Ella, it is a public event every time you and I meet. It is not right for you to meet me. I was told that they are gossiping about us. I should have been more careful. It does not matter about me, but you are a woman, and it is always worse for a woman. Now you will say that it is wrong,' he continued as I tried to interrupt, 'but whether right or wrong, it's true. And you are married. And you are a stranger. All these things make it worse.'

'But it's insulting that you feel their judgment comes before mine. What's wrong with seeing you? I'm not doing anything wrong, for God's sake. I'm married to Rick, but that doesn't mean I can't ever talk to another man!'

Jean-Paul didn't say anything.

'How do you live with this?' I said impatiently. 'With this gossipy village life? Do they know everything about you?'

'No. Of course it was a shock after big cities, but I learned to be discreet.'

'And you call this discreet, sneaking off to meet me like this? Now we really *do* look guilty.'

'It's not exactly like that. What offends them most is when it's in front of them, under their nostrils.'

'Noses.' I smiled in spite of everything.

'Noses, under their noses.' He smiled back grimly. 'It is a different psychology.'

'Well anyway, the warning hasn't worked. Here we are, after all.'

We were silent for the rest of the journey.

The cover was burned half off, the pages charred and unreadable, except for the first. Written in a spidery hand, in faded brown ink, was the following:

> Jean Tournier n. 16 août 1507
> m. Hannah Tournier 18 juin 1535
>> Jacques n. 28 août 1536
>> Etienne n. 29 mai 1538
>> m. Isabelle du Moulin 28 mai 1563
>>> Jean n. 1 janvier 1563
>>> Jacob n. 2 juillet 1565
>>> Marie n. 9 octobre 1567
>> Susanne n. 12 mars 1540
>> m. Bertrand Bouleaux 29 novembre 1565
>>> Deborah n. 16 octobre 1567

Four pairs of eyes rested on me: those of Jean-Paul, Mathilde, Monsieur Jourdain – who to my surprise was sitting next to Mathilde drinking a highball when we walked in – and a small blond girl perched on a stool with a Coke in her hand, eyes wide with excitement, introduced as Mathilde's daughter, Sylvie.

I felt a little sick, but I clutched the Bible to my chest and smiled at them.

'*Oui*,' I said simply. '*Oui*.'

5. *The Secrets*

The mountains were the most obvious difference.

Isabelle gazed at the surrounding slopes; the bare slice of rock near the summit looked as if it might tumble down at any moment. The trees were foreign, bunched together like moss, allowing here and there a bright flash of meadow.

The Cevenol mountains are like a woman's belly, she thought. These mountains of the Jura are like her shoulders. Sharper, more defined, less welcoming. My life will be different in mountains like these. She shivered.

They were standing by a river at the edge of Moutier, part of a group travelling from Geneva in search of a place to settle. Isabelle wanted to beg them not to stop here, to keep going until they found a gentler home. No one else shared her uneasiness. Etienne and two other men left them by the river and went to the village inn to ask about work.

The river running through the valley was small and dark and lined with silver birches. Except for the trees, the Birse was not so different from the Tarn, but looked unfriendly. Though low now, it would triple in size in the spring. While the adults debated, the children ran down to the water, Petit Jean and Marie dipping their hands in it while Jacob crouched by the edge, staring at the pebbles on the bottom. He reached in carefully and pulled out a black stone in the shape of a lopsided heart, holding it up between two fingers for them to see.

— *Eh, bravo, mon petit!* shouted Gaspard, a jovial man blinded in one eye. He and his daughter, Pascale, had run an inn in Lyons and escaped with a cart of food they shared with anyone who needed it. The Tourniers met them on the road from Geneva when their chestnuts were gone and they had only enough potatoes to last another day. Gaspard and Pascale fed them, refusing all thanks or offers of repayment.

— God wills it, Gaspard said, and laughed as if he had just told a joke. Pascale simply smiled, reminding Isabelle of Susanne, with her quiet face and gentle ways.

The men came back from the inn, a puzzled look on Etienne's face, his eyes wide and wild without lashes or brows to anchor them.

— There is no Duc de l'Aigle here, he said, shaking his head. No estate to lease land from or work for.

— Who do they work for? Isabelle demanded.

— Themselves. He sounded dubious. Some of the farmers need help with their hemp crop. We could stay for a time.

— What's hemp, Papa? Petit Jean asked.

Etienne shrugged.

He doesn't want to admit he doesn't know, Isabelle thought.

They stopped in Moutier. In the time left before the snow came, the Tourniers were hired by one farmer after another. On the first day they were led into a field of hemp that they were to cut and leave to dry. They stared at the tough, fibrous plants as tall as Etienne.

Finally Marie said what they had all been thinking.

— Maman, how do you eat those plants?

The farmer laughed.

— *Non, non, ma petite fleur*, he said, this plant is not for eating. We spin thread from it, for cloth and rope. Do you see this shirt? He pointed to the grey shirt he wore. This is made from hemp. Go on, touch it!

Isabelle and Marie rubbed the cloth between their fingers. It was thick and scratchy.

— This shirt will last until my grandson has children!

He explained that they would cut and dry the hemp, soak it in a pit of water to soften and separate the fiber from the wood, and dry it again before beating the plants to separate the fiber completely. Then the fiber would be carded and spun.

— That is what you will do all winter. He nodded at Isabelle and Hannah. Makes your hands strong.

— But what do you *eat*? Marie persisted.

– Plenty! We trade hemp at the market in Bienne for wheat and goats and pigs and other things. Fear not, *fleurette*, you won't go hungry.

Etienne and Isabelle were silent. In the Cévennes they had rarely traded at market: they sold their surplus to the Duc de l'Aigle. Isabelle clutched her neck. It didn't seem right, growing things that could not be eaten.

– We have kitchen gardens, the farmer assured them. And some grow winter wheat. Don't worry, there is plenty here. Look at this village – do you see hunger? Are there poor people here? God provides. We work hard and He provides.

It was true that Moutier was wealthier than their old village. Isabelle picked up a scythe and stepped into the field. She felt as if she were lying on her back in the river and had to trust that she would float.

East of Moutier the Birse turned north, cutting through the mountain range, leaving behind a towering gorge of yellow-grey rock, solid in places, crumbling at the edges. The first time Isabelle saw it she wanted to drop to her knees; it reminded her of a church.

The farm they moved to was not by the Birse, but by a stream further east. They passed the gorge whenever they walked to or from Moutier. When Isabelle passed it alone she crossed herself.

Their house was built of stone they did not recognize, lighter and softer than Cevenol granite. There were gaps where mortar had crumbled away, making the house drafty and damp. The window and door frames were made of wood, as was the low ceiling, and Isabelle feared the house would catch fire. The Tournier farm had been built entirely of stone.

Strangest of all, it had no chimney; nor did any of the farms in the valley. Instead the low wood ceiling was false, and smoke gathered in the space between it and the roof, dispersing through small holes cut under the eaves. Meat was hung there to smoke, but that seemed to be its only benefit. Everything in the house was covered with a layer of soot and the air became dark and stuffy whenever windows and doors were closed.

Sometimes during that first winter, when Isabelle wrapped her hair in greasy, grey linen, or spun endlessly, trying to keep her bloody fingers from staining the coarse hemp thread, or sat at the table in the dim smoke, coughing and gasping, knowing the sky outside was low and heavy with snow and would remain so for months, she thought she would go mad. She missed the sun on the rocks, the frozen broom, the clear cold days, the huge Tournier hearth that had radiated warmth and sent the smoke outside. She said nothing. They were lucky to have a house at all.

— Someday I will build a chimney, Etienne promised on a dark winter day when the children could not stop coughing. He glanced at Hannah, who nodded.

— A house needs a chimney and a proper hearth, he continued. But first we must grow crops. When I can I will build it, and the house will be complete. And safe. He stared into the corner, not meeting Isabelle's eye.

She left the room, entering the *devant-huis*, an open area between the house, barn and stable, all covered by the same roof. There she could stand and look outside without being buffeted by the wind or swept with snow. She took a deep breath of fresh air and sighed. The door faced south but there was no brightening, warming sun. She gazed across at the white slopes opposite and saw a grey figure crouched in the snow. Stepping back into the darker shadows of the *devant-huis*, she watched as it loped into the woods.

— I feel safe now, she said under her breath to Etienne and Hannah. And it has nothing to do with *your* magic.

Every few days Isabelle walked the frozen path past the yellow gorge to Moutier's communal oven. At home she had always baked bread in the Tournier chimney or at her father's house, but here it was baked in one place. She waited for the oven door to open, for the wave of heat to reach her as she slid her loaves inside. Around her women wearing round wool caps talked quietly. One smiled at her.

— How are Petit Jean and Jacob and Marie? she asked.

Isabelle smiled back.

— They want to be outside. They don't like staying in so much. Back at home it wasn't so cold. Now they fight more.

— *This* is your home now, the woman corrected gently. God will look after you here. He has given you a mild winter, this winter.

— Of course, Isabelle agreed.

— God keep you, Madame, the woman said as she stepped away, loaves tucked under her arms.

— And you.

Here they call me Madame, she thought. No one sees my red hair. No one knows about it. Here is a village of 300 people who never call me La Rousse. Who know nothing about the Tourniers other than that we are followers of the Truth. When I walk away they won't talk about me behind my back.

For that she was grateful. For that she could live with the rough, steep mountains, the strange crops, the hard winters. Perhaps she could even manage without a chimney.

Isabelle often met Pascale at the communal oven and at church. At first Pascale said very little, but slowly she became more talkative, until eventually she was able to describe her past life in detail to Isabelle.

— In Lyons I worked in the kitchen as much as I could, she said as they stood among the crowd outside church one Sunday. But when Maman died from the plague I had to start serving. I didn't like being around so many strange men, touching me everywhere. She shuddered. And then to serve so much wine when we are not meant to drink it, it seemed wrong. I preferred to stay hidden. When I could. She was silent for a moment.

— But Papa, he loves it, she continued. You know he hopes to take over running the Cheval-Blanc if the owners leave. He stays friendly with them, just in case. In Lyons the inn was called the Cheval-Blanc too. He sees it as a sign.

— And you don't miss your old life?

Pascale shook her head.

– I like it here. I feel safer than in Lyons. It was so crowded and full of people you couldn't trust.

– Safe, yes. But I miss the sky, Isabelle said. The wide sky you can see all the way to the edge of the world. Here the mountains close up the sky. At home they opened it.

– I miss chestnuts, Marie announced, leaning against her mother.

Isabelle nodded.

– When we always had them, I didn't think about them. Like water. You don't think about water until you are thirsty and there is none.

– But there was danger back home too, yes?

– Yes. She swallowed, remembering the smell of burning flesh. She did not share this memory.

– Their round caps are funny, don't you think? she said instead, gesturing at a group of women. Can you imagine wearing one on top of your headcloth?

They laughed.

– Maybe one day we will wear them, and new arrivals will laugh at us, Isabelle added.

From the crowd Gaspard's voice boomed out: – Soldiers! I can tell you two or three things about Catholic soldiers that will make your hair stand up!

Pascale's smile faded. She looked down, body rigid, hands clenched. She never talked about their escape, but Isabelle had already heard Gaspard describe it in detail several times, as he was repeating it now for a new friend.

– When the Catholics heard of the massacre in Paris they went crazy and came to the inn ready to tear us apart, Gaspard explained. Soldiers burst in and I thought: The only way to save ourselves is to sacrifice the wine. So quick as that I offered them all free wine. *Aux frais de la maison!* I kept shouting. Well, that stopped them. You know Catholics, they love their cups! That's what gave us good business. Soon they were so drunk they had forgotten why they came, and while Pascale kept them busy I just packed up everything we had, right under their noses!

Abruptly Pascale left Isabelle's side and disappeared behind the church. How can Gaspard not see that something is wrong with his daughter? Isabelle thought as Gaspard continued to talk and laugh.

After a moment she went to find her. Pascale had been sick and was leaning against the wall, wiping her mouth shakily. Isabelle noted her paleness and pinched eyes and nodded to herself. Three months along, she said to herself. And she has no husband.

– Isabelle, you were a midwife, yes? Pascale said at last.

Isabelle shook her head.

– My mother taught me, but Etienne – his family would not let me continue when we married.

– But you know about – about babies, and –

– Yes.

– What if – what if the baby vanishes, do you know about that too?

– You mean if God wills the baby to disappear?

– I – yes, that is what I mean. If God wills it.

– Yes, I know about that.

– Is there something – a special prayer?

Isabelle thought for a moment.

– Meet me in two days at the gorge and we will pray together.

Pascale hesitated.

– It was in Lyons, she blurted out. When we tried to leave. They had drunk so much. Papa doesn't know about –

– And he won't know.

Isabelle went deep into the woods to find the juniper and rue. When Pascale met her two days later, among the rocks at the top of the gorge, Isabelle gave her a paste to eat, then knelt on the ground with her and prayed to Saint Margaret until the ground was red with blood.

That was the first secret of her new life.

Their first Christmas in Moutier Isabelle discovered that the Virgin had been waiting for her.

There were two churches. Followers of Calvin had taken over the Catholic church of Saint Pierre, burned the images of the saints and reversed the altar. The canons had fled, closing the abbey that had been there for hundreds of years, witness of many miracles. The chapel attached to the abbey, l'Eglise de Chalières, was now used for the parish of Perrefitte, the tiny hamlet next to Moutier. Four times a year, on the festival days, the Moutier villagers attended morning services at Saint Pierre and afternoon services at Chalières.

That first Christmas, dressed in black clothes lent to them by Pascale and Gaspard, the Tourniers pushed into the tiny chapel. It was so crowded that Isabelle stood on her toes to try to see the minister. She soon gave up and looked above him at the murals in green and red and yellow and brown covering the choir walls, of Christ holding the Book of Life on the curved ceiling, the twelve Apostles in panels below him. She had not seen decoration in a church since the colored glass and the statue of the Virgin and Child of her childhood.

On her toes again to look at the figures painted at eye level, she stifled a gasp. To the minister's right was a faint image of the Virgin, staring sadly into the distance. Though Isabelle's eyes filled with tears, she kept her expression dull. She watched the minister, now and then her glance darting to the mural.

The Virgin looked at her and smiled for a moment before resuming her mournful expression. No one saw but Isabelle.

That was the second secret.

After that she always hurried to Chalières on festival days to stand as near to the Virgin as possible.

Spring sun brought the third secret. Overnight the snow melted, forming waterfalls that plummeted from the surrounding mountains and flooded the river. The sun reappeared, the sky turned blue, grass sprang up. They could leave the door and windows open, the children and the smoke escaping outside, Etienne stretching in the sun like a cat and smiling briefly at Isabelle. His grey hair made him look old.

Isabelle welcomed the sun, but it also made her vigilant. Every day she took Marie to the woods and inspected her hair, pulling out any red strands. Marie stood patiently and never cried out at each spark of pain. She asked her mother to let her keep the hair, hiding the growing ball in a hole in a nearby tree.

One day Marie ran to Isabelle and buried her head in her lap.

— My hair is gone, she whispered through tears, even then understanding that she should say nothing to the others. Isabelle glanced at Etienne, Hannah and the boys. Except for Hannah's sour expression, nothing in their faces suggested suspicion.

She was helping Marie search the tree again when she looked up and saw a bird's nest glinting in the sun.

— There! she pointed. Marie laughed and began to clap her hands.

— Take it! she cried to the birds, holding her hair up by the ends and letting it drop in a slow cascade. Take it, it's yours! Now I will always know where it is.

She spun in a circle and fell to the ground laughing.

The high-pitched whistle rose and fell before ending in a bird-like trill. It was heard all the way along the valley. After a time the rattles and jingles and creaks of a cart could be heard, bouncing off the rocks high above to reach them in the fields they were planting with flax. Etienne sent Jacob to find out what was coming. When he returned he took Isabelle's hand and led her, the rest of the family following, along the path to the edge of the village. There the cart had stopped, surrounded by a crowd.

The peddler was short and dark, with a beard and a long mustache curled into elaborate whorls, and a red and yellow striped cap shaped like an upside-down bucket pulled over his ears. He perched high above them on a cart heaped with goods, swinging and climbing over it with the assuredness of a man who knows every toehold and hand-grip. As he climbed he talked non-stop over his shoulder in a strange singing accent that made Isabelle smile and Etienne stare.

— Oranges! Oranges! I show you oranges, olives, lemons from Sevilla! Here is your beautiful copper pot. And here your leather bag. And here your buckles. You want buckles on those shoes, fair lady? Yes, you do! And I give you buttons to match! And your thread, and your lace here, yes, your finest lace. Come, come! Come look, come touch, don't be afraid. *Ah, Jacques La Barbe, bonjour encore!* Your brother says he comes from Geneva soon, but your sister he says stays near Lyons. Why she does not join you here in this lovely place? Never mind. And Abraham Rougemont, there is a horse for you ready in Bienne. A good buy, I saw it with these my eyes. You give that pretty daughter of yours a ride around the village. And *Monsieur le régent*, I meet your son —

On and on he talked, passing on messages while selling his goods. People laughed and teased him; he was a familiar and welcome sight, arriving every year after the worst of the winter and again during the harvest festival.

In the middle of the excitement he leaned over to Isabelle.

— *Que bella*, I have not seen you before! he cried. You come and look at my things? He patted the rolls of cloth next to him. Come look!

Isabelle smiled shyly and bowed her head; Etienne frowned. They had nothing to trade with, less than nothing, for they owed favors to everyone in Moutier. On their arrival they had been given two goats, a small sack each of flax and hemp seeds, blankets, clothes. There was no need to pay anyone back, but they were expected to be as generous when the next refugees arrived with nothing. They stood for a long time watching the purchases, admiring the lace, the new harness, the white linen smocks.

Isabelle heard the peddler mention Alès.

— He might know, she whispered to Etienne.

— Don't ask, he hissed.

He doesn't want to know, she thought. But I do.

She waited until Etienne and Hannah had left, and Petit Jean and Marie had tired of running round and round the cart and had gone off to the river, before she approached him.

— Please, Monsieur, she whispered.

— Ah, *Bella*, you want to look! Come, come!

She shook her head.

— No, I want to ask — you have been to Alès?

— At Christmas, yes. Why, you have a message for me?

— My sister-in-law and her husband are there – might be there. Susanne Tournier and Bertrand Bouleaux. They have a daughter, Deborah, and maybe a baby, if God wills.

For the first time the peddler was quiet, thinking. He seemed to be searching through all the faces and names he had seen and heard in his travels and stored in his memory.

— No, he said at last, I have not seen them. But I look for them for you. In Alès. And your name?

— Isabelle. Isabelle du Moulin. And my husband, Etienne Tournier.

— Isabella, *que bella*. A perfect name I will not forget! He smiled at her. And for you I show you the perfect thing I have, the special thing. He lowered his voice. *Très cher* – I do not show this to most people.

He led Isabelle around his cart and began to dig among bundles of cloth until he pulled out a bale of white linen. Jacob appeared at Isabelle's side and the peddler motioned to him.

— Come, come, you like to look at things! I see your eyes looking. Now look at this.

He stood over them and shook out the white cloth. Out fell the fourth secret, the color Isabelle had thought she would never see again. She cried out, then reached over and rubbed the cloth between her fingers. It was a soft wool, dyed very deep. She bowed her head and touched the cloth to her cheek.

The peddler nodded.

— You know this blue, he said with satisfaction. I knew you know this blue. The blue of the Virgin of Saint Zaccaria.

— Where is that? Isabelle smoothed the cloth.

— Ah, a beautiful church in Venezia. There is a story to this blue, you know. The weaver who made this cloth modelled it after the robe of the Virgin who is in a painting in Saint Zaccaria. This was so to thank her for the miracle.

— What miracle? Jacob stared at the peddler with wide brown eyes.

— The weaver had a little daughter he loved, and one day she disappeared, as children often do in Venezia. They fall into the canals, you see, and they drown. The peddler crossed himself.

— So the little daughter did not come home and the weaver, he went to Saint Zaccaria to pray for her soul. He prayed to the Virgin for hours. And when he goes home he finds his daughter there, all alive! And in thanks he makes this cloth, this special blue, you see, for his daughter to wear and live safely forever in the Virgin's care. Others have tried to copy it but no one can. There is a secret in the dye, you see, and only his son knows now. A family secret.

Isabelle stared at the cloth, then looked up at the peddler, tears in her eyes.

— I have nothing, she said.

— For you, then, *Bella*, I give you a little something. A gift of blue.

He bent over the cloth and from a frayed end pulled off a piece of thread the length of her finger. With a deep bow he presented it to her.

Isabelle often thought about the blue cloth. She had no way of buying it; even if she did Etienne and Hannah would not allow it in the house.

— Catholic cloth! Hannah would mutter if she could speak.

She hid the thread in the hem of her dress and brought it out only when she was alone or with Jacob, who used words sparingly and would say nothing about the bit of color they shared.

Then one of their goats had a hidden kid and Isabelle had one last secret to keep.

The goat had given birth to two kids, licked them clean, nursed them, slept with them pushed against her swollen udder. When Isabelle left the fields to check on her she noticed the red membrane of another head pushing out. She pulled out the tiny body, saw that it was alive and set it in front of the goat to clean. As the new kid fed Isabelle sat and watched it and thought. Her secrets were making her bold.

The woods around Moutier were so big that she knew of places where no one went. She took the kid to one of these spots, built a shelter of wood and hay, fed it and looked after it for a whole summer without anyone knowing.

Except for one. She was letting the kid suck at a sack filled with its mother's milk one day when Jacob stepped out from behind a beech tree. Squatting beside her, he put his hand on the kid's back.

— Papa wants to know where you are, he said as he stroked the kid.

— How long have you known I come here?

He shrugged and played with the kid's hair, flattening it one way and then the other.

— Will you help me look after it?

He looked up at her.

— Of course, Maman.

His smile was so rare that to see it was like receiving a gift.

This time she was ready when she heard the peddler's whistle. The peddler smiled broadly when he saw Isabelle. She smiled back. While she and Hannah looked at his linen Jacob climbed up and began to show him his pebbles, passing on her message in a low voice. The peddler nodded, all the while admiring the strange shapes and colors of the stones.

— You have a good eye, *mio bambino*, he said. Good colors, good shapes. You look and you say not much, not like me! I love my words, me, but you, you like to look and see things, yes? Yes.

When he began to recite messages his eyes lit on Isabelle and he snapped his fingers.

— Ah, yes, I remember now! Yes, I find your family in Alès!

Despite themselves, even Etienne and Hannah looked up at him expectantly. He warmed to his audience.

— Yes, yes, he said, waving his hands elaborately. There I see them in the market of Alès, ah, *bella famiglia*! And I tell them of you and they are happy you are well.

— And they are well? Isabelle asked. And there is a baby?

— Yes, yes, a baby. Bertrand and Deborah and Isabella, now I remember.

— No, *I'm* Isabelle. You mean to say Susanne. Isabelle had not thought the peddler could make a mistake.

— No, no, it is Bertrand and the two girls, Deborah and Isabella, just a baby, Isabella.

— But what about Susanne? The mother?

— Ah. The peddler paused, looking down at them and stroking his mustache nervously. Ah, well. She died giving birth to the baby, you see. To Isabella.

He turned away then, uncomfortable at passing on bad news, and busied himself in sorting through leather harness straps for a customer. Isabelle hung her head, eyes blurred with tears. Etienne and Hannah left the crowd and stood silently at a distance, heads bowed.

Marie took Isabelle's hand.

— Maman, she whispered. Some day I will see Deborah. Won't I?

The peddler met Jacob later, further down the road. In the dark the exchange was made, goat for blue. The boy hid the cloth in the woods. The next day he and Isabelle shook it out and stared for a long time at the block of rippling color. Then they wrapped the cloth inside a piece of linen and hid it in the straw mattress Jacob shared with Marie and Petit Jean.

— We will do something with it, Isabelle promised him. God must tell me what.

In the autumn they harvested their own hemp crop. One day Etienne sent Petit Jean to the woods to cut thick sticks of oak which they would use to beat the hemp. The others set up trestles and began bringing out armfuls of hemp from the barn to lay across them.

Petit Jean returned with five sticks over his shoulder and the nest of Marie's hair.

— Look what I've found, Mémé, he said, holding out the nest to Hannah, the red catching in the light as he turned it.

– Oh! Marie cried out before she could stop herself. Isabelle flinched.

Etienne glanced from Marie to Isabelle. Hannah studied the nest, then Marie's hair. She glared at Isabelle and handed the nest to Etienne.

– Go to the river, Etienne ordered the children.

Petit Jean set down the sticks, then reached over and pulled Marie's hair as hard as he could. She began to sob and Petit Jean smiled, with a look that reminded Isabelle of Etienne when she first knew him. As he walked away he held his knife by its point and flicked it away. It lodged neatly in a tree trunk.

He is ten years old, she thought, but already he acts and thinks like a man.

Jacob took Marie's hand and led her away, looking back at Isabelle with wide eyes.

Etienne said nothing until the children were gone. Then he gestured at the nest.

– What is this?

Isabelle glanced at it, then looked at the ground. She did not know enough about keeping secrets to know what to do when they were revealed.

So she told the truth.

– It is Marie's hair, she whispered. She has been growing red hair and I pull it out in the woods. The birds took it to make a nest. She swallowed. I didn't want her to be teased. To be – judged.

When she saw the look that passed between Etienne and Hannah her stomach felt as if she had swallowed stones. She wished she had lied to them.

– I was helping her! she cried. It was to help us! I didn't mean any harm!

Etienne fixed his eyes on the horizon.

– There have been rumors, he said slowly. I have heard things.

– What things?

– The woodcutter Jacques La Barbe said he thought he saw you with a kid in the woods. And another found a patch of blood on the ground. They are talking about you, La Rousse. Is that what you want?

They are talking about me, she thought. Even here. My secrets are not to be secrets after all. And they lead to other secrets. Will they find out about them too?

– There is one more thing. You were with a man when we left Mont Lozère. A shepherd.

– Who says that? This was a secret she had kept even from herself, not allowing herself to think about him. Her secret secret.

She looked at Hannah and suddenly knew. She can talk, Isabelle thought. She can talk and she is talking to Etienne. She saw us on Mont Lozère. The thought made her shiver violently.

– What do you have to say, La Rousse?

She kept silent, knowing words could not help her, fearing more secrets would fly out if she opened her mouth.

– What are you hiding? What did you do with that goat? Kill it? Sacrifice it to the devil? Or did you trade it with that Catholic peddler looking at you like that?

He picked up one of the sticks, grabbed her wrist and dragged her into the house. He made her stand in a corner while he searched everywhere, throwing down pots, stirring the fire, pulling apart their straw mattress, then Hannah's. When he reached the children's mattress Isabelle held her breath.

Now the end has come, she thought. Holy Mother, help me.

He turned the mattress over and pulled out all the straw.

The cloth was not there.

The blow was a surprise; he had never hit her before. His fist knocked her halfway across the room.

– You won't drag us down with your witchery, La Rousse, he said softly. Then he picked up the stick Petit Jean had cut and beat her till the room went black.

6. The Bible

Either the smoke or the cold air from the open window woke me. When I opened my eyes I saw the orange button of a lit cigarette, then the hand holding it, draped over the steering wheel. Without moving my head I followed the arm up to the shoulders and then to his profile. He was looking out over the steering wheel as if he were still driving, but the car was stationary, the engine dead, not even ticking the way it does when it's first switched off. I had no idea how long we'd been sitting there.

I was curled sideways in the passenger seat, facing him, my cheek crushed against the coarse weave of the head rest; my hair had fallen over my face and stuck to my mouth. I glanced between the gap in the seats; the Bible was on the back seat, wrapped in a plastic bag.

Though I hadn't moved or spoken, Jean-Paul turned his head and looked at me. We held each other's gaze for a long time without saying anything. The silence was comfortable, though I couldn't tell what he was thinking: his face wasn't blank, but it wasn't open either.

How long does it take to overcome two years of marriage, two more of a relationship? I had never been tempted before; once I'd found Rick I'd considered the search over. I had listened to my friends' stories about their quest for the right man, their disastrous dates, their heartbreaks, and never put myself in their place. It was like watching a travel show about a place you knew you'd never go to, Albania or Finland or Panama. Yet now I seemed to have a plane ticket to Helsinki in my hand.

I reached over and placed my hand on his arm. His skin was warm. I moved my hand up over the crease of his elbow and the ring of cloth where the sleeve was rolled up. When I was halfway along his upper arm and not sure what to do next, he reached over and covered my hand with his, stopping it on the curve of his biceps.

Keeping a firm grip on his arm, I sat up in my seat and brushed the hair from my face. My mouth tasted of olives from the martinis Mathilde had ordered for me earlier in the evening. Jean-Paul's black jacket was draped around my shoulders; it was soft and smelled of cigarettes, leaves and warm skin. I never wore Rick's jackets: he was so much taller and broader than me that his jackets made me look like a box and the sleeves immobilized my arms. Now I felt I was wearing something that had been mine for years.

Earlier, when we were with the others at the bar, Jean-Paul and I had spoken to each other in French the whole evening, and I'd vowed to continue to do so. Now I said, '*Nous sommes arrivés chez nous?*' and immediately regretted it. What I had said was grammatically correct, but the *chez nous* made it sound like we lived together. As was so often the case with my French, I was only in control of the literal meaning, not the words' connotations.

If Jean-Paul sensed this implication in the grammar, he didn't let on. '*Non, le Fina,*' he said.

'Thank you for driving,' I continued in French.

'It's nothing. You can drive now?'

'Yes.' I felt sober all of a sudden, and focussed on the pressure of his hand on mine. 'Jean-Paul,' I began, wanting to say something, not knowing what else to say.

He didn't respond for a moment. Then he said, 'You never wear bright colors.'

I cleared my throat. 'No, I guess not. Not since I was a teenager.'

'Ah. Goethe said only children and simple people like bright colors.'

'Is that supposed to be a compliment? I just like natural cloth, that's all. Cotton and wool and especially — what's this called in French?' I gestured at my sleeve; Jean-Paul took his hand off mine to rub the cloth between his finger and thumb, his other fingers brushing my bare skin.

'*Le lin.* And in English?'

'Linen. I've always worn linen, especially in the summer. It looks better in natural colors, white and brown and –' I trailed off. The vocabulary of clothes colors was way beyond my French; what were the words for pumice, caramel, rust, ecru, sepia, ochre?

Jean-Paul let go of my sleeve and rested his hand on the steering wheel. I looked at my own hand adrift on his arm, having overcome so many inhibitions to get there, and felt like weeping. Reluctantly I lifted it off and tucked it under my arm, shrugging Jean-Paul's jacket over my shoulders and turning to face forwards. Why were we sitting here talking about my clothes? I was cold; I wanted to go home.

'Goethe,' I snorted, digging my heels into the floor and pushing my back impatiently against the seat.

'What about Goethe?'

I lapsed into English. 'You would bring up someone like Goethe right now.'

Jean-Paul flicked the stub of his cigarette outside and rolled up the window. He opened the door, climbed out of the car and shook the stiffness from his legs. I handed him his jacket and climbed into the driver's seat. He slipped on the jacket, then leaned into the car, one hand on the top of the door, the other on the roof. He looked at me, shook his head and sighed, an exasperated hiss through gritted teeth.

'I do not like to break into a couple,' he muttered in English. 'Not even if I can't stop looking at her and she argues with me always and makes me angry and wanting her at both the same time.' He leaned in and kissed me brusquely on both cheeks. He began to straighten up when my hand, my bold, treacherous hand, darted up, hooked around his neck, and pulled his face down to mine.

It had been years since I'd kissed anyone besides Rick. I'd forgotten how different each person can be. Jean-Paul's lips were soft but firm, giving only an indication of what lay beyond them. His smell was intoxicating; I pulled away from his mouth, rubbed my cheek along the sandpaper of his jaw, buried my nose in the base of his neck and inhaled. He knelt down and pulled my head back, running his fingers through my hair like combs. He smiled at me. 'You look more French with your red hair, Ella Tournier.'

'I haven't dyed it, really.'

'I never say you did.'

'It was Ri –' We both stiffened; Jean-Paul stopped his fingers.

'I'm sorry,' I said. 'I didn't mean to –' I sighed and plunged ahead. 'You know, I never thought I was unhappy with Rick, but now it feels like something isn't – like we were a jigsaw puzzle with every piece in place, but the puzzle frames the wrong picture.' My throat began to tighten and I stopped.

Jean-Paul dropped his hands from my hair. 'Ella, we have a kiss. That does not mean your marriage falls apart.'

'No, but –' I stopped. If I had doubts about me and Rick I should be voicing them to Rick.

'I want to keep seeing you,' I said. 'Can I still see you?'

'At the library, yes. Not at the Fina station.' He raised my hand and kissed its palm. '*Au revoir, Ella Tournier. Bonne nuit.*'

'*Bonne nuit.*'

He stood up. I shut the door and watched him walk over to his tin-can car and get in. He started it, beeped the horn lightly and drove away. I was relieved he didn't insist on waiting until I left first. I watched till his tail-lights winked out of sight at the end of the long tree-lined road. Then I let out a long breath, reached to the back seat for the Tournier Bible and sat with it in my lap, staring up the road.

I was shocked at how easy it was to lie to Rick. I had always thought he would know right away if I cheated on him, that I could never hide my guilt, that he knew me too well. But people see what they look for; Rick expected me to be a certain way, so that was how I was to him. When I walked in with the Bible under my arm, having been with Jean-Paul only half an hour before, Rick glanced up from his newspaper, said cheerfully, 'Hey, babe,' and it was as if nothing had happened. That was how it felt, at home with Rick clean and golden under the light of the reading lamp, far away from the dark car, the smoke, Jean-Paul's jacket. His face was open and guileless; he hid nothing from me. Yes, I could almost say it hadn't happened. Life could be surprisingly compartmentalized.

This would be so much easier if Rick were a jerk, I thought. But then I'd never have married a jerk. I kissed his forehead. 'I have something to show you,' I said.

He threw his newspaper down and sat up. I knelt beside him, pulled the Bible out of the bag and dropped it in his lap.

'Hey, now. This is something,' he said, running his hand down the front cover. 'Where'd you get it? You weren't clear on the phone about where you were going.'

'The old man who helped me in Le Pont de Montvert, Monsieur Jourdain, found it in the archives. He gave it to me.'

'It's *yours*?'

'Yeah. Look at the front page. See? My ancestors. That's them.'

Rick glanced down the list, nodded and smiled at me.

'You did it. You found them!'

'Yes. With a lot of help and luck. But yes.' I couldn't help noticing that he didn't inspect the Bible as closely and lovingly as Jean-Paul had. The thought made my stomach knot with guilt: these comparisons were completely unfair. No more of this, I thought sternly. No more of this with Jean-Paul. That's it.

'You know this is worth a lot of money,' Rick said. 'Are you sure he *gave* it to you? Did you ask for a receipt?'

I stared at him, incredulous. 'No, I didn't ask for a receipt! Do you ask for a receipt every time I give you a present?'

'C'mon, Ella, I'm just trying to be helpful. You don't want him changing his mind and asking for it back. You get it in writing, you won't have that problem. Now, we should put this in a safe deposit box. Probably in Toulouse. I doubt the bank here has one.'

'I'm not putting it in a safe deposit box! I'm keeping it here, with me!' I glared at him. Then it happened: like one of those one-cell creatures under the microscope that for no apparent reason suddenly divides into two, I felt us pulling apart into distinct entities with separate perspectives. It was strange: I hadn't realized how together we'd been until we were far apart.

Rick didn't seem to notice the change. I stared at him until he frowned. 'What's the matter?' he asked.

'I – well, I'm not going to put it in a safe deposit box, that's for sure. It's too valuable for that.' I picked it up and hugged it to me.

To my relief Rick had to go on his German trip the next day. I was so shaken by the new space between us that I needed some time alone. He kissed me goodbye, oblivious to my inner turmoil, and I wondered if I was as blind to his internal life as he seemed to be to mine.

It was a Wednesday and I badly wanted to go over to the café by the river to see Jean-Paul. Head won over heart: I knew it would be better to leave things awhile. I deliberately waited until I knew he'd be safely buried in his paper at the café before I left the house on my daily rounds. A chance encounter on the street around so many people fascinated with our every move was distinctly unappealing. I had no intention of playing out this drama in front of the town. As I approached the central square Jean-Paul's depiction of Lisle and what it thought of me came flooding back; it was almost enough to make me run back to the privacy of my house, and even use the shutters.

I made myself keep going. When I bought the *Herald Tribune* and *Le Monde*, the woman who sold them was perfectly pleasant, giving me no strange looks, even remarking on the weather. She didn't seem to be thinking about my washing machine, shutters or sleeveless dresses.

The real test was Madame. I headed resolutely to the *boulangerie*. '*Bonjour, Madame!*' I sang out as I entered. She was in the middle of talking to someone and frowned slightly. I glanced at her audience and found myself face to face with Jean-Paul. He hid his surprise, but not quickly enough for Madame, who eyed us with triumphant disgust and glee.

Oh, for Christ's sake, I thought, enough's enough. '*Bonjour*, *Monsieur*,' I said in a bright voice.

'*Bonjour*, *Madame*,' he replied. Though his face didn't move his voice sounded as if he had raised his eyebrows.

I turned to Madame. 'Madame, I would like twenty of your quiches, please. You know, I adore them. I eat them every day, breakfast, lunch, dinner.'

'*Twenty* quiches,' she repeated, leaving her mouth ajar.

'Yes, please.'

Madame snapped her mouth shut, pressing her lips together so hard they disappeared, and, eyes on me, reached behind her for a paper bag. I heard Jean-Paul quietly clear his throat. When Madame bent down to shovel the quiches in the bag I glanced at him. He was staring into the corner at a display of sugared almonds. His mouth had tightened and he was rubbing his jaw line with his index finger and thumb. I looked back at Madame and smiled. She straightened up from the glass case and twisted the corners of the bag shut. 'There are only fifteen,' she muttered, glaring at me.

'Oh, that's too bad. I'll have to go to the *pâtisserie* to see if they have any.' I suspected Madame wouldn't like the *pâtisserie*; what they sold would seem too frivolous to her, a serious bread woman. I was right: her eyes widened and she sucked in her breath, shook her head, and made a rude noise. 'They don't have quiches!' she exclaimed. 'I'm the only one who makes quiches in Lisle-sur-Tarn!'

'Ah,' I replied. 'Well, maybe at the Intermarché.'

At this Jean-Paul made a garbled sound and Madame nearly dropped the bag of quiches. I'd committed the sin of mentioning her arch rival and the worst threat to her business: the supermarket on the edge of town, with no history, no dignity, no finesse. Kind of like me. I smiled. 'What do I owe you?' I asked.

Madame didn't answer for a moment; she looked like she needed to sit down. Jean-Paul took this opportunity to murmur '*Au revoir*, *Mesdames*' and slip away.

The moment he was gone I lost interest in struggling with her. When she demanded 150 francs I handed it over meekly. She took every centime I had, but it was worth it.

Outside Jean-Paul fell in step with me.

'You are very wicked, Ella Tournier,' he murmured in French.

'Would you like some of these quiches?' We laughed.

'I thought we mustn't see each other in public. This –' I waved my hand around the square – 'is very public.'

'Ah, but I have a professional reason to talk to you. Tell me, have you looked carefully at your Bible?'

'Not yet. Look, don't you ever stop? Don't you sleep?'

He smiled. 'I have never needed much sleep. Bring the Bible over to the library tomorrow. I've discovered some interesting things about your family.'

The Bible was an odd size, long and unexpectedly narrow. But it wasn't too heavy and it felt comfortable in my arms. The cover was made of worn, cracked leather, rubbed dull and soft and mottled in shades of chestnut brown. The leather was cracked and wrinkled, and an insect had bored tiny holes in several places. The back cover was blackened and burned half away, but on the front an intricate design of lines and leaves and dots stamped in gold was intact. Gold flowers had been stamped down the spine, and a modified pattern of the design had been tapped with a hammer and a pin into the sides of the pages.

I turned to the beginning of Genesis: '*Dieu crea av commencement le ciel & la terre.*' The text was in two columns, the typeface clear, and though the spelling was peculiar I could understand the French – what was left of it. The back of the book had been burned away, the middle pages scorched beyond recognition.

At Crazy Joe's Bar Mathilde and Monsieur Jourdain had a long discussion about the Bible's origins, Jean-Paul chipping in now and then. I could only partly follow what they said because Monsieur Jourdain's accent was so hard to decipher and Mathilde's delivery so fast. It was always harder to follow a conversation in French when people weren't speaking directly to me. From what I could gather they agreed that it had probably been published in Geneva, and possibly translated by someone named Lefèvre d'Etaples. Monsieur Jourdain was particularly emphatic about the name.

'Who was he?' I asked hesitantly.

Monsieur Jourdain began to chuckle. 'La Rousse wants to know who Lefèvre was,' he kept repeating, shaking his head. By then he'd downed three highballs. I nodded patiently, letting him have his little joke; the martinis had made me more tolerant about being teased.

Eventually he explained that Lefèvre d'Etaples had been the first to translate the Bible from Latin into the French vernacular so that people other than priests could read it. 'That was the beginning,' he declared. 'That was the beginning of everything. The world split apart!' With that pronouncement he pitched forward on his stool and landed halfway across the bar.

I tried not to grin, but Mathilde covered her hand with her mouth, Sylvie laughed outright and Jean-Paul smiled as he leafed through the Bible. Now I remembered that he had studied the page with the Tourniers on it for a long time and scribbled something on the back of an envelope. I'd been too tipsy to ask what he was doing.

To Mathilde's disgust and my disappointment, Monsieur Jourdain had not been able to remember exactly who turned in the Bible to him. 'It's for this that you must keep records!' she scolded. 'Important questions, for someone like Ella!' Monsieur looked suitably hangdoggish and wrote down the names of all the family members listed in the Bible, promising to see if he could find out anything about them, including those with last names other than Tournier.

I was assuming the Bible had come from around Le Pont de Montvert, but I knew it could have been brought from anywhere, with people moving to the area and bringing things with them. When I suggested this, however, Mathilde and Monsieur Jourdain both shook their heads.

'They would not have brought it to the *mairie* if they were outsiders,' Mathilde explained. 'Only a true Cevenol family would have given it to Monsieur Jourdain. There is a strong sense of history here, and family things like this Bible don't leave the Cévennes.'

'But families leave. My family left.'

'That was religion,' she replied with a dismissive wave of her hand. 'Of course they left then, and many more families after 1685. You know, it's funny that your family left when it did. It was much worse for Cevenol Protestants 100 years later. The Massacre of Saint Bartholomew was a –' She stopped and shrugged, then waved a hand at Jean-Paul. 'You explain, Jean-Paul.' She was wearing a pink leotard and plaid miniskirt.

'A bourgeois event, more or less,' he continued smoothly, smiling at her. 'It destroyed the Protestant nobility. But the Cevenol Huguenots were peasants and the Cévennes too isolated to be threatened. There could have been tensions with the few local Catholics, I suppose. The cathedral in Mende remained Catholic, for example. They could have decided to go terrorize a few Huguenots. What do you think, Mademoiselle?' he addressed Sylvie. She regarded him with a level gaze, then stuck her legs out, wiggled her toes and said, 'Look, Maman painted my toenails white!'

Now I turned back to the list of Tourniers and studied it. Here was the family that must have ended up in Moutier: Etienne Tournier, Isabelle du Moulin and their children Jean, Jacob and Marie. According to my cousin's note, Etienne had been on a military list in 1576 and Jean married in 1590. I checked the dates; they made sense. And this Jacob was one of the Jacobs in the long line that ended with my cousin. He should know about this, I thought. I'll write and tell him.

My eye was drawn to writing on the inside cover that no one had noticed before. It was dirty and faint, but I managed to make out 'Mas de la Baume du Monsieur'. Farm of the Balm of the Gentleman, clumsily translated. I got out the detailed map I'd bought of the area around Le Pont de Montvert and began looking. I searched in concentric rings out from the village for a similar name. After only five minutes I found it, about two kilometers northeast of Le Pont de Montvert. It was a hill just north of the Tarn, half covered with forest. I nodded. Here was something for Jean-Paul.

But he couldn't have seen the name of the farm the night before or he would have pointed it out. What was he talking about when he said he knew something about my family? I stared at the names and dates, but could only find two things unusual about the list: a Tournier had married a Tournier, and one of the Jeans had been born on New Year's Day.

When I arrived at the library the next afternoon with the Bible in a carrier bag, Jean-Paul made a show of presenting me to the other librarian. Once she clapped eyes on the Bible she stopped looking suspicious.

'Monsieur Piquemal is an expert in old books, in history,' she said in a singsong voice. 'That's his domain. But I know more about novels, romance, things like that. The more popular books.'

I sensed a dig at Jean-Paul, but I simply nodded and smiled. Jean-Paul waited for us to finish, then led me to a table in the other room. I opened the Bible while he pulled out his scrap of envelope.

'So,' he said expectantly. 'What did you discover?'

'Your last name is Piquemal.'

'So?'

'"Bad sting." Perfect.' I grinned at him and he frowned.

'*Pique* can also mean lance,' he muttered.

'Even better!'

'So,' he repeated. 'What did you find?'

I pointed to the name of the farm on the inside cover, then spread out my map and pinpointed the spot. Jean-Paul nodded. 'Good,' he said, scrutinizing the map. 'No buildings there now, but at least we are sure that the Bible is from the area. What else?'

'Two Tourniers married each other.'

'Yes, probably cousins. It was not so uncommon then. What else?'

'Um, one of them was born on New Year's Day.'

He raised his eyebrows; I wished I hadn't said anything. 'Anything else?' he persisted.

'No.' He was being irritating again, yet I found it hard to sit next to him and talk as if nothing had happened the other night.

His arm was so near mine on the table that I could easily brush against it. This is the closest we're going to get, I thought. This is as far as it goes. Sitting next to him seemed a sad, futile act.

'You found nothing else interesting?' Jean-Paul snorted. 'Bah, American education. You would make a bad detective, Ella Tournier.' When he saw my face he stopped and looked embarrassed. 'I'm sorry,' he said, switching to English as if that would soothe me. 'You do not like my teasing.'

I shook my head and kept my eyes on the Bible. 'It's not that. If I didn't want you to tease me I could never talk to you. No, it's just –' I waved my hand as if to chase the subject away – 'the other night,' I explained quietly. 'It's hard to sit here like this.'

'Ah.' We sat side by side, staring at the family list, very aware of each other.

'Funny,' I broke the silence. 'I've just noticed. Etienne and Isabelle married the day before his birthday. May 28th, May 29th.'

'Yes.' Jean-Paul tapped a finger lightly against my hand. 'Yes. That is what I noticed first. Strange. So I asked was it a coincidence? Then I saw how old he was. He had twenty-five the next day after his marriage.'

'He *turned* twenty-five.'

'Yes. Now, among the Huguenots then, when a man *turned* twenty-five he did not any longer need permission from his parents to marry.'

'But he was twenty-four when he married, so he must have had their permission.'

'Yes, but it seemed strange to marry so close to twenty-five. To give anyone doubt about what his parents thought. Then I looked more.' He gestured at the page. 'Look at the birth date of their first son.'

'Yes, New Year's Day, like I said. So what?'

He frowned at me. 'Look again, Ella Tournier. Use the brain.'

I stared at the page. When I figured out what he meant I couldn't believe I hadn't noticed it before, me of all people. I began to calculate rapidly, counting back on my fingers.

'You understand now.'

I nodded, working out the final days, and announced, 'She would've conceived around April 10th, more or less.'

Jean-Paul looked amused. 'April 10th, eh? What is all this?' He pretend-counted on his fingers.

'Birth is calculated at roughly 266 days from conception. More or less. Gestation varies from woman to woman, of course, and it was probably a little different back then. Different diet, different physique. But in April, anyway. A good seven weeks before they married.'

'And how do you know this 266 days, Ella Tournier? You have no children, no? Have you hidden them somewhere?'

'I'm a midwife. I know things like that.'

He looked puzzled, so I said it in French. '*Une sage-femme. Je suis une sage-femme.*'

'*Toi? Une sage-femme?*'

'Yes. You never even asked what I did for a living.'

He looked crestfallen, an unusual expression for him, and I felt triumphant; for once I'd gained the upper hand.

'You always surprise me, Ella,' he said, shaking his head and smiling.

'Come, come, no flirting or your colleague will tell the whole town.'

We both instinctively glanced at the doorway and sat up straighter. I leaned away from him.

'So it was a shotgun wedding,' I declared to get us back on track.

'A gun wedding?'

'*Shot*gun. It's like a rifle. Her parents forced him to marry her once they found out she was pregnant. In the States there's this stereotypical image of the father holding a shotgun to the man to get him to the altar.'

Jean-Paul thought for a moment. 'Maybe that is what happened.' He didn't sound convinced.

'But?'

'But that – a rifle wedding, you say – does not explain why they married so close to his birthday.'

'Well, so it was a coincidence that they married the day before his birthday. So what?'

'You and your coincidences, Ella Tournier. You choose which ones you want to believe are more than coincidences. So this is a coincidence and Nicolas Tournier is not.'

I tensed up. We hadn't discussed the painter since disagreeing so strongly about him.

'I could say the same thing about you!' I retorted. 'We just choose different coincidences to be interested in, that's all.'

'I was interested in Nicolas Tournier, until I found out he was not your relative. I gave him a chance. And I give this coincidence a chance too.'

'OK, so why is this more than a coincidence?'

'It's the date and the day of the wedding. Both are bad.'

'What do you mean, bad?'

'There was a belief in the Languedoc, never to marry in May or November.'

'Why not?'

'May is the month of rain, of tears, November the month of the dead.'

'But that's just superstition. I thought Huguenots were trying not to be superstitious. That was supposed to be a Catholic vice.'

That stopped him for a moment. He wasn't the only one who'd been reading books.

'Nevertheless it is true there were fewer weddings in those months. And then the 28th of May 1563 was a Monday, and most weddings were on Tuesday or Saturday. They were the favorite days.'

'Wait a minute. How could you possibly know it was a Monday?'

'I have a friend nearby with a computer connected to the university. I went over yesterday and we found a calendar on it.'

The most unlikely nerd. I sighed. 'So you obviously have a theory about what happened. I don't know why I bother to think I have any say in all this.'

He looked at me. '*Pardon.* I've stolen your search from you, yes?'

'Yes. Look, I appreciate your help, but I feel like when you do it, it's all in the head, not the heart. Do you understand that?'

He pushed his lips out in a kind of pout and nodded.

'Still, I'd like to hear your theory. But it's just a theory, right? I can still keep my idea that it was a shotgun wedding.'

'Yes. So, maybe his parents were opposed to the marriage until they found out about the child. Then they hurried with the marriage so their neighbors would believe the parents had always consented.'

'But wouldn't people have suspected that, given the dates?' I could easily imagine a sixteenth-century version of Madame working that one out.

'Maybe, but it would still be better to be seen to consent.'

'For appearance's sake.'

'Yes.'

'So nothing's changed much over 400 years, really.'

'Did you expect it to?'

The other librarian appeared in the doorway. We must have looked deep in consultation, for she just smiled at us and disappeared again.

'There is one thing more,' Jean-Paul said. 'Just a little thing. The name Marie. That's a strange name for a Huguenot family to give to a child.'

'Why?'

'Calvin wanted people to stop worshipping the Virgin Mary. He believed in direct contact with God rather than through a figure like her. She was seen as a distraction from God. And she is a part of Catholicism. It is odd that they named her after the Virgin.'

'Marie,' I repeated.

Jean-Paul closed the Bible. I watched him touch the cover, trace the gold leaf.

'Jean-Paul.'

He turned to me, his eyes bright.

'Come home with me.' I hadn't even realized I was going to say it.

Outwardly his face didn't change, but the shift between us was like the wind switching direction.

'Ella. I'm working.'

'After work.'

'What about your husband?'

'He's away.' I was beginning to feel humiliated. 'Forget it,' I muttered. 'Forget I even asked.' I started to get up, but he put his hand on mine and stopped me. As I sank back into my seat, he glanced at the doorway and removed his hand.

'Will you come somewhere tonight?' he asked.

'Where?'

Jean-Paul wrote something on a scrap of paper. 'It is a good time to come around eleven.'

'But what is it?'

He shook his head. 'A surprise. Just come. You'll see.'

I took a shower and spent more time on my appearance than I had in a long while, even though I had no idea where I was going: Jean-Paul had simply scribbled down an address in Lavaur, a town about twelve miles away. It could be a restaurant or a friend's house or a bowling alley, for all I knew.

His comment the night before about my clothes had lingered in my mind. Though I wasn't sure he meant it as a criticism, I looked through my wardrobe for something with color in it. In the end I wore the pale yellow sleeveless dress again, the closest I could get to a bright color. At least I felt comfortable in it, and with brown slingbacks and a little lipstick I didn't look too bad. I couldn't begin to compete with French women, who looked stylish wearing just jeans and a T-shirt, but I would pass.

I had just shut the front door behind me when the phone rang. I had to scramble to get to it before the answering machine did.

'Hey, Ella, did I get you out of bed?'

'Rick. No, actually I was, just, uh, going for a walk. Out to the bridge.'

'A walk at eleven at night?'

'Yeah, it's hot and I was bored. Where are you?'

'At the hotel.'

I tried to remember: was it Hamburg or Frankfurt? 'Did the meeting go well?'

'Great!' He told me about his day, giving me time to compose myself. When he asked me what I'd been up to, though, I couldn't think of a thing to say that he would want to hear.

'Not much,' I answered hurriedly. 'So when are you coming back?'

'Sunday. I have to stop in Paris first on my way back. Hey, babe, what are you wearing?' This was an old game we used to play on the phone: one of us described what we were wearing and the other described stripping it off. I looked down at my dress and shoes. I couldn't tell him what I was wearing, or why I didn't want to play.

Luckily I was saved by Rick himself, who said, 'Hang on, I have a call waiting. I'd better take it.'

'Sure. See you in a few days.'

'Love you, Ella.' He hung up.

I waited a few minutes, feeling sick, to make sure he didn't call back.

In the car I kept saying to myself every few minutes, You can turn back, Ella. You don't have to do this. You can drive all the way there, park, get to the door of wherever and turn back. You can even see him and spend time with him and it'll be perfectly innocent and you can come back pure and unadulterated. Literally.

Lavaur was a cathedral town about three times the size of Lisle-sur-Tarn, with an old quarter and some semblance of night-life: a cinema, a choice of restaurants, a couple of bars. I checked a map, parked next to the cathedral, a lumbering brick building with an octagonal tower, and walked into the old town. Even with tantalizing night-time activities there was no one around; every shutter was shut, every light dark.

I found the address easily: it was hard to miss, marked by a startling neon sign announcing a tavern. The entrance was in a side alley, the shutters of the window next to the door painted with what looked like faceless soldiers guarding a woman in a long robe. I stopped and studied the shutters. The image unnerved me; I hurried inside.

The contrast between outside and inside couldn't have been greater. It was a small bar, dimly lit, loud and crowded and smoky. The few bars I'd been to in small French towns were generally grim affairs, male and unwelcoming. This was like a chink of light in the middle of darkness. It was so unexpected that I stood in the doorway and stared.

Directly in front of me a striking woman wearing jeans and a maroon silk blouse was singing 'Every Time We Say Goodbye' in a heavy French accent. And though his back was to me, I knew immediately that it was Jean-Paul hunched over the white upright, wearing his soft blue shirt. He kept his eyes on his hands, occasionally glancing at the singer, his expression concentrated but also serene.

People came in behind me and I was forced to slip into the crowd. I couldn't take my eyes off Jean-Paul. When they finished the song there were shouts and prolonged clapping. Jean-Paul looked around, noticed me and smiled. A man to my right patted my shoulder. 'Better watch out – that's a wolf, that one!' he shouted, laughing and nodding toward the piano. I turned red and moved away. When Jean-Paul and the woman began another song, I squeezed my way to the bar and miraculously found a stool free.

The singer's olive skin seemed to be lit from within, her dark eyebrows perfectly shaped. Her long brown hair was wavy and dishevelled, and she drew attention to it as she sang, pulling her fingers through it, tossing her head, holding her wrists to her temples when she hit a high note. Jean-Paul was less flamboyant, his calm presence balancing her theatrics, his playing underlining her sparkling voice. They were very good together – relaxed, confident enough to play around and tease each other. I felt a pang of jealousy.

Two songs later they took a break and Jean-Paul started toward me, stopping first to speak to every second person. I pulled nervously at my dress, wishing now that it covered my knees.

When he arrived at my side he said, '*Salut*, Ella,' and kissed my cheeks the way he had ten other people. I grew calmer, relieved but vaguely disconcerted that I wasn't given special attention. What do you *want*, Ella? I asked myself furiously. Jean-Paul must have seen the confusion in my face. 'Come, I'll introduce you to some friends,' he said simply.

I slid off the stool and picked up my beer, then waited while he got a whiskey from the barman. He gestured toward a table across the room and put his hand on the middle of my back to guide me, keeping his hand there as we pushed through the crowd, dropping it when we reached his friends.

Six people, including the singer, were sitting on benches on either side of a long table. They squeezed together to make room for us. I ended up next to the singer with Jean-Paul across from me, our knees touching in the cramped space. I looked down at the table, littered with beer bottles and glasses of wine, and smiled to myself.

The group was discussing music, naming French singers I'd never heard of, laughing uproariously at cultural references that meant nothing to me. It was so loud and they spoke so fast that after a while I gave up listening. Jean-Paul lit a cigarette and chuckled at jokes, but otherwise was quiet. I could feel his eyes rest on me occasionally; once when I returned his gaze he said, '*Ça va?*'

I nodded. Janine the singer turned to me and said, 'So, do you prefer Ella Fitzgerald or Billie Holiday?'

'Oh, I don't listen to either very much.' This sounded ungracious; she was after all giving me an opening to the conversation. I also wanted to convince myself that I wasn't jealous of her, her beauty and effortless style, her link to Jean-Paul. 'I like Frank Sinatra,' I added quickly.

A balding man with a baby face and two-day stubble sitting next to Jean-Paul snorted. 'Too sentimental. Too much "show-biz." He used the English phrase and fluttered his hands next to his ears while putting on a cheesy smile. 'Now, Nat King Cole, that's different!'

'Yes, but –' I began. The table looked at me expectantly. I

was remembering something my father had said about Sinatra's technique and trying desperately to translate it quickly in my head: exactly what Madame Sentier had told me never to do.

'Frank Sinatra sings without breathing,' I said, and stopped. That wasn't what I meant: I was trying to say he sang so smoothly that you couldn't hear him breathe, but my French failed me. 'His —'

But the conversation had gone on; I hadn't been fast enough. I frowned and shook my head slightly, annoyed at myself and embarrassed the way you are when you start telling a story and realize no one's listening.

Jean-Paul reached over and touched my hand. 'You remind me of being in New York,' he said in English. 'Sometimes in a bar I could hear nothing and everyone yelled and used words I didn't know.'

'I can't think quickly enough in French yet. Not complicated thoughts.'

'You will. If you stay here long enough you will.'

The baby-faced man heard our English and looked me up and down. '*Tu es américaine?*' he demanded.

'*Oui.*'

My response had a strange effect: it was like an electric current raced around the table. Everyone sat up and glanced from me to Jean-Paul. I looked at him too, puzzled by the reaction. Jean-Paul reached for his glass and with a jerk of his wrist finished the whiskey, a gesture laced with defiance.

The man smiled sarcastically. 'Ah, but you're not fat. Why aren't you like every other American?' He puffed out his cheeks and cupped his hands around an imaginary paunch.

One thing I discovered about my French — when I was mad it came out like a jet stream. 'There are fat Americans but at least they don't have huge mouths like the French!'

The table erupted in laughter, even the man. In fact he looked ready for more. Dammit, I thought. I've taken the bait and now he'll get at me for hours.

He leaned forward.

C'mon, Ella, the best defense is offense. It was Rick's favorite phrase; I could almost hear him saying it.

I interrupted him before he could get a sentence out. 'Now, America. Of course you will mention, wait, I must get the order right. Vietnam. No, maybe first American films and television, Hollywood, McDonald's on the Champs-Elysées.' I ticked off my fingers. '*Then* Vietnam. And violence and guns. And the CIA, yes, you must mention the CIA several times. And maybe, if you are a Communist – are you a Communist, Monsieur? – maybe you will mention Cuba. But finally you will mention World War II, that the Americans entered late and were never occupied by the Germans like the poor French. That is the *pièce de résistance, n'est-ce pas?*'

Five people were grinning at me while the man pouted and Jean-Paul brought his empty glass to his mouth to hide his laughter.

'Now,' I continued. 'Since you are French, maybe I should ask you if the French treated the Vietnamese better as colonizers. And are you proud of what happened in Algeria? And that Le Pen is so popular now? And the racism here against North Africans? And the nuclear-testing in the Pacific? You see, you are French, so of course you are a representation of your government, you agree with everything it does, don't you? You little shit,' I added under my breath in English. Only Jean-Paul caught it; he looked at me in astonishment. I smiled. Not so ladylike, then.

The man put his fingertips to his chest and flung them outwards in a gesture of defeat.

'Now, we were discussing Frank Sinatra and Nat King Cole. You must excuse my French, sometimes it takes me a little while to say what I mean. What I wanted to say was that one cannot hear his – what do you call it?' I put my hand on my chest and breathed in.

'*Respiration,*' Janine suggested.

'Yes. It is impossible to hear it when he sings.'

'They say that's because of a technique of circular breathing he learned from —' A man at the other end of the table was off and running, to my relief.

Jean-Paul stood up. 'I must play now,' he said quietly to me. 'You will stay?'

'Yes.'

'Good. You are good at fighting your angle, yes?'

'What?'

'You know, fighting your —' He pointed to the back of the room.

'Starting a bar-room brawl?'

'No, no.' He ran his finger around a corner edge of the table.

'Oh, fighting my *corner*. Yes, I'll be OK. I'll be fine.'

And it was fine. No one brought up other American stereotypes, I managed to contribute occasionally, and when I couldn't understand what they were talking about I just listened to the music.

Jean-Paul played some honky-tonk; then Janine joined him. They ran through a range of songs: Gershwin, Cole Porter, several French songs. At one point they briefly conferred; then with a glance at me Janine began singing Gershwin's 'Let's Call The Whole Thing Off', while Jean-Paul smiled into his keys.

Later the crowd thinned and Janine came to sit across from me. There were only three of us left at the table and we'd fallen into that late-night comfortable silence when everything has been said. Even the balding man was quiet.

Jean-Paul continued to play — quiet, contemplative music, a few chords underlying simple lines of melody. It veered between classical and jazz, a combination of Erik Satie and Keith Jarrett.

I leaned across to Janine. 'What's he playing?'

She smiled. 'It's his own music. He composes it himself.'

'It's beautiful.'

'Yes. He only plays it when it is late.'

'What time is it?'

She looked at her watch. It was almost two.

'I didn't know that it was so late!'

'You have no watch?'

I held out my wrists. 'I left it at home.' Our eyes lit on my wedding ring at the same time; instinctively I drew my hands in. It was so much a part of me that I'd forgotten all about it. If I had remembered it I probably still wouldn't have taken it off: that would have been too calculated.

I met her eyes and blushed, making things even worse. For a moment I considered going to the bathroom and removing the ring, but I knew she would notice, so I hid my hands in my lap and changed the subject, pointedly asking her where she got her blouse. She took the hint.

A few minutes later the rest of the table got up to go. To my surprise Janine left with the balding man. They waved cheerily at me, Janine blew a kiss at Jean-Paul and they were gone with the last of the crowd. We were alone except for the barman, who was collecting glasses and wiping down tables.

Jean-Paul finished the piece he was playing and sat silent for a moment. The barman whistled tunelessly as he stacked chairs on tables. 'Eh, François, two whiskeys here if you're not being cheap.' François smirked but went behind the bar and poured out three glasses. He placed one before me with a brief bow and set another on top of the piano. Then he removed the cash register and, balancing it in one hand and his glass in another, disappeared into a back room.

We raised our glasses and drank at the same time.

'There is nice light on your head, Ella Tournier.' I glanced up at the soft yellow spotlight above me: it was touching my hair with copper and gold. I looked back at him; he played a low soft chord.

'Did you have classical training?'

'Yes, when I was young.'

'Do you know any Erik Satie?'

He set his glass down and began to play a piece I recognized, in five-four time with an even, stark melody. It fit the room, the light, the hour perfectly. While he played I rested my hands in my lap and removed my ring, dropping it into my dress pocket.

When he finished he left his hands on the keys for a moment, then picked up his glass and drained it. 'We must go,' he said, standing up. 'François needs his sleep.'

Going outside was like re-entering the world after having had flu for a week: the world felt big and strange and I wasn't sure of my bearings. It was cooler now and there were stars overhead. We passed by the shutters with the painting of the woman and soldiers on them. 'Who was she?' I asked.

'That's La Dame du Plô. She was a Cathar martyr in the thirteenth century. Soldiers raped her, then threw her down a well and filled it with stones.'

I shuddered and he put his arm around me. 'Come,' he said, 'or you'll accuse me of talking about the wrong things at the wrong time.'

I laughed. 'Like Goethe.'

'Yes, like Goethe.'

Earlier I'd wondered if there would be a moment when we'd have to decide something, discuss it, analyze it. Now that the moment had arrived it was clear we had been silently negotiating all evening and a decision had already been made. It was a relief not to say anything, just to walk to his car and get in. In fact we hardly spoke on the drive back. When we passed Lavaur cathedral he noted my car alone in the parking lot. 'Your car,' he said, a statement rather than a question.

'I'll take the train here tomorrow.' That was it; no fuss.

When we reached the countryside I asked him to roll back the Deux Chevaux's. He flipped it over without stopping. I rested my head on his shoulder; he put his arm around me and ran his hand up and down my bare arm while I leaned back and watched the sycamores whipping by overhead.

When we crossed the bridge over the Tarn into town I sat up. Even at three in the morning some decorum seemed necessary. Jean-Paul lived in an apartment on the other side of town from me, close to where the countryside began. Even so it was only a ten-minute walk from my house, a fact I was working hard to push from my mind.

We parked and got out, then snapped the roof back on together.

The surrounding houses were dark and shuttered. I followed him up a set of stairs on the outside of a house to his door. I stood just inside while he switched on a lamp, illuminating a neat room lined with books.

He turned around and held his hand out to me. I swallowed; my throat was tight. When it came down to the final deciding moment, I was terrified.

When at last I reached out, took his hand and pulled him to me, put my arms around him and clung to his back, my nose in his neck, the fear vanished.

The bedroom was spare but contained the largest bed I'd ever seen. A window looked out over fields; I stopped him from closing the shutters.

It felt like one long movement. There was no point when I thought, Now I'm doing this, now he's doing that. There was no thought, just two bodies recognizing each other, making themselves whole together.

We didn't sleep until the sun rose.

I woke to bright sunlight and an empty bed. I sat up and looked around. There were two bedside tables, one covered with books, a framed black and purple poster for a jazz piano concert on the wall over the bed, a coarse woven mat the color of wheat on the floor. Outside the fields behind the house were bright green and extended far back to a row of sycamores and a road. It all had the same air of simplicity as Jean-Paul's clothes.

The door opened and Jean-Paul entered, dressed in black and white, carrying a small cup of black coffee. He set it down on the bedside table and sat on the edge of the bed next to me.

'Thank you for the coffee.'

He nodded. 'Ella, I must go to work now.'

'Are you sure?'

He smiled in reply.

'I feel like I didn't get any sleep,' I said.

'Three hours. You can sleep more here if you want.'

'That would be strange, being in this bed without you.'

He ran a hand up and down my leg. 'If you want you maybe wait until there are not so many people in the street.'

'I guess so.' For the first time I heard the shouts of children passing; it was like kicking down a barrier, the first intrusion of the outside world. With it came the unwelcome furtiveness, the need to be cautious. I wasn't sure I was ready for that yet, or to have him be so sensible.

Pre-empting my thoughts, he held my gaze and said, 'It's you I think of. Not me. It's different for me. It's always different for a man here.'

It was sobering, such straight talk. It forced me to think.

'This bed –' I paused. 'It's way too big for one person. And you wouldn't have two tables and lamps like this if it was just you sleeping here.'

Jean-Paul scanned my face. Then he shrugged; with that gesture we really did re-enter the world.

'I lived with a woman for a while. She left about a year and a half ago. The bed was her idea.'

'Were you married?'

'No.'

I put my hand on his knee and squeezed it. 'I'm sorry,' I said in French. 'I should not have mentioned it.'

He shrugged again, then looked at me and smiled. 'You know, Ella Tournier, all that talk in French last night has made your mouth bigger. I am sure of it!'

He kissed me, his lashes glittering in the sun.

When the front door shut behind him everything seemed to change. I had never felt so strange being in someone else's house before. I sat up stiffly, sipped the coffee, set it down. I listened to the children outside, the cars passing, the occasional Vespa. I missed him terribly and wanted to leave as soon as possible, but felt trapped by the sounds outside.

Finally I got up and took a shower. My yellow dress was crumpled and smelled of smoke and sweat. When I put it on I felt like a tramp. I wanted to go home but forced myself to wait until the streets were quieter. While I waited I looked at his books in the living room. He had a lot on French history, many novels, a few books in English: John Updike, Virginia Woolf, Edgar Allan Poe. A strange combination. I was surprised that the books weren't in any order: fiction and non-fiction were mixed up and not even alphabetized. Apparently he didn't bring his work habits home with him.

Once I was sure the street was clear, I felt reluctant to leave, knowing that after I'd left I couldn't come back. I looked around the rooms once more. In the bedroom I went to the closet and got out the pale blue shirt Jean-Paul had worn the night before, rolled it into a ball and stuffed it in my bag.

When I stepped outside I felt like I was making a big stage entrance, though as far as I could see I had no audience. I ran down the stairs and walked quickly toward the center of town, breathing a little easier when I reached the part I often walked in during the morning, but still feeling exposed. I was sure everyone was staring at me, at the wrinkles in my dress, the rings under my eyes. C'mon, Ella, they always stare at you, I tried to reassure myself. It's because you're still a stranger, not because you've just – I couldn't bring myself to finish the thought.

Only when I reached our street did it strike me that I didn't want to go home: I saw our house and a wave of nausea hit me. I stopped and leaned against my neighbor's house. When I go inside, I thought, I'll have to face my guilt.

I remained there for a long time. Then I turned around and headed toward the train station. At least I could get the car first; it gave me a concrete excuse to put off the rest of my life.

I sat on the train in a daze, half sweet, half sour, barely remembering to change at the next stop for the Lavaur train. Around me sat businessmen, women with their shopping, teenagers flirting. It seemed so strange to me that something extraordinary had happened, yet no one around me knew. 'Do you have any idea what I've just done?' I wanted to say to the grim woman knitting across from me. 'Would you have done it too?'

But the events of my life made no difference to the train or the rest of the world. Bread was still being baked, gas pumped, quiches made, and the trains were running on time. Even Jean-Paul was at work, advising old ladies on romance novels. And Rick was at his German meetings in a state of ignorance. I drew in my breath sharply: it was only me who was out of step, who had nothing else to do but pick up a car and feel guilty.

I had an espresso at a café in Lavaur before returning to my car. As I was swinging the car door open I heard '*Eh, l'américaine!* to my left and turned to find the balding man I'd fought with the night before coming toward me. He now had three-day stubble. I pulled the door open wide and leaned against it, a shield between him and me. '*Salut*,' I said.

'*Salut, Madame.*' His use of Madame was not lost on me.

'*Je m'appelle Ella*,' I said coldly.

'Claude.' He held out his hand and we shook formally. I felt a little ridiculous. All the clues of what I'd just done were set out for him like a window display: the car still here, my rumpled dress from the night before, my tired face, even my damp hair would all lead him to one conclusion. The question was whether he'd have the tact not to mention it. Somehow I doubted it.

'Would you like a coffee?'

'No, thank you, I've had one already.'

He smiled. 'Come, you will have a coffee with me.' He made a gesture like he was rounding me up and began to walk away. I didn't move. He looked around, stopped and began to laugh. 'Oh, you, you are difficult! Like a little cat with its claws like this –' he mimed claws with stiff, bent fingers – 'and its fur all ruffled. All right, you don't want a coffee. Look, come sit with me on this bench for a moment, OK? That's all. I have something to say to you.'

'What?'

'I want to help you. No, that's not right. I want to help Jean-Paul. So, sit. Just for a second.' He sat on a nearby bench and looked at me expectantly. Finally I shut the car door, walked over and sat down next to him. I didn't look at him, but kept my eyes on the garden in front of us, where careful arrangements of flowers were just beginning to bloom.

'What do you want to say?' I made sure I used the formal address with him to counter his familiar tone with me. It had no effect.

'You know, Jean-Paul, he is a good friend of Janine and me. Of all of us at La Taverne.' He pulled out a pack of cigarettes and offered it to me. I shook my head; he lit one and sat back, crossing his legs at the ankle and stretching.

'You know he lived with a woman for a year,' he continued.

'Yes. So?'

'Did he tell you anything about her?'

'No.'

'She was American.'

I glanced at Claude to see what reaction he was expecting from me, but he was following the traffic with his eyes and gave away nothing.

'And was *she* fat?'

Claude roared with laughter. 'You!' he shouted. 'You are – I understand why Jean-Paul likes you. A little cat!'

'Why did she leave?'

He shrugged, his laughter finally subsiding. 'She missed her country and felt she didn't fit in here. She said people weren't friendly. She was alienated.'

'Jesus,' I muttered in English before I could stop myself. Claude leaned forward, his legs apart, elbows on his knees, hands dangling. I glanced at him. 'Does he still love her?'

He shrugged. 'She's married now.'

That's no answer – look at me, I thought, but didn't say it.

'You see,' he said, 'we protect Jean-Paul a little. We meet a pretty American woman, with much spirit, like a little cat, with her eyes on Jean-Paul but married, and we think –' he shrugged again – 'maybe this is not so good for him, but we know he won't see that. Or he sees it but she is a temptation anyway.'

'But –' I couldn't argue back. If I countered that every American doesn't run home with her tail between her legs – not that I hadn't considered that option myself in my more alienated moments – Claude would just bring up my being married. I couldn't tell which he was emphasizing more; perhaps that was part of his strategy. I disliked him too much to probe.

What he was unarguably saying was that I wasn't good for Jean-Paul.

With that thought – combined with my lack of sleep and the absurdity of sitting on this bench with this man telling me things I already knew – I finally cracked. I leaned over, elbows on my knees, and cupped my hands around my eyes as if shielding them from strong sunlight. Then I began to cry silently.

Claude sat up straight. 'I am sorry, Ella. I did not say these things to make you unhappy.'

'How else did you expect me to respond?' I replied sharply. He made the same gesture of defeat with his hands as he had the night before.

I wiped my damp hands on my dress and stood. 'I have to go,' I muttered, brushing my hair back from my face. I couldn't bring myself to thank him or say goodbye.

I cried all the way home.

The Bible sat like a reproach on my desk. I couldn't stand being in a room by myself, not that I had much choice. What I needed was to talk to a female friend; it was women who usually saw me through moments of crisis. But it was the middle of the night in the States; besides, it was never the same on the phone. Here I had no one I could confide in. The closest I'd come to a kindred spirit was Mathilde, but she had enjoyed flirting with Jean-Paul so much that she might not be too pleased to hear what had happened.

Late in the morning I remembered I had a French lesson in Toulouse in the afternoon. I called Madame Sentier and cancelled, telling her I was ill. When she asked, I said it was a summer fever.

'Ah, you must get someone to take care of you!' she cried. Her words made me think of my father, his concern that I'd be stranded out here without help. 'Call Jacob Tournier if you have any problems,' he'd said. 'When there are problems it's good to have family close by.'

★

Jean-Paul –

I'm going to my family. It seemed the best thing to do. If I stayed here I would drown in my guilt.

I've taken your blue shirt.

Forgive me.

Ella

Rick didn't get a note; I called his secretary and left the briefest of messages.

7. *The Dress*

She was never alone. Someone always remained with her, Etienne or Hannah or Petit Jean. Usually it was Hannah, which Isabelle preferred: Hannah could not or would not speak to her, and was too old and small to hurt her. Etienne's arms were now loose with rage, and Petit Jean she no longer trusted, with his knife and the smile in his eyes.

How has this happened? she thought, linking her hands behind her neck and pressing her elbows to her chest. That I can't even trust my own little son? She stood in the *devant-huis* and looked out across the dull white fields to the dark mountains and the grey sky.

Hannah hovered in the door behind her. Etienne always knew what Isabelle had been doing, yet she had not been able to catch Hannah speaking to him.

– Mémé, close the door! Petit Jean called from within.

Isabelle looked over her shoulder into the dim, smoky room and shivered. They had covered the windows and were keeping the door shut; the smoke had built up into a thick, choking cloud. Her eyes and throat stung and she had begun to walk around the room ponderously, slowed down as if she were moving through water. Only in the *devant-huis* could she breathe normally, despite the cold.

Hannah touched Isabelle's arm, jerked her head toward the fire and stood aside to usher her back in.

There was spinning all day during the winter, endless piles of hemp waiting in the barn. As she worked, Isabelle thought of the softness of the blue cloth, pretending she was holding it rather than the coarse fiber that raked at her skin and left a web of tiny cuts on her fingers. She could never spin the hemp as fine as she had wool in the Cévennes.

She knew Jacob must have hidden the cloth somewhere, in the woods or the barn, but she never asked. She never had a chance to; yet even if they had been left alone for a moment she would have let him keep the secret. Otherwise Etienne might have beaten it out of her.

She found it hard to think in the smoke, faced with the endless hemp, the dark, the muffled silence of the room. Etienne often stared at her and did not look away when she stared back. His eyes were harder without eyelashes and she could not meet his gaze without feeling threatened and guilty.

She began to speak less, silent now by the fire at night, no longer telling the children stories or singing or laughing. She felt she was shrinking, that if she kept quiet she might become less visible, and be able to escape the suspicion entrapping her, the nameless threat hanging in the air.

First she dreamed of the shepherd in a field of broom. He was pulling off the yellow flowers and squeezing them between his fingers. Put these in hot water and drink it, he said. Then you will be well. His scar was gone, and when she asked him where it was, he said it had moved to another part of his body.

Next she dreamed that her father was poking through the ashes of a broken chimney, the ruins of a house smoking around him. She called out to him; intent on his search, he did not look up.

Then a woman appeared. Isabelle was never able to look directly at her. She stood in doorways, next to trees and once by a river that looked like the Tarn. Her presence was a comfort, though she never said anything or came near enough for Isabelle to see her clearly.

After Christmas these dreams stopped.

Christmas morning the family dressed in the customary black, their own clothes this time that they had made from their hemp crop. The cloth was hard and coarse but it would last a long time.

The children complained that it scratched and itched. Isabelle silently agreed but said nothing.

Outside the Eglise Saint Pierre they saw Gaspard among the crowd gathered in front of the church and went over to greet him.

— *Ecoute, Etienne,* Gaspard said, I saw a man at the inn who can get you granite for your chimney. Back in France, a day's ride, there is a granite quarry, near Montbéliard. He can bring you a big slab for the hearth in the spring. You tell me the size and I will give a message to the next person going that way.

Etienne nodded.

— You told him I would pay in hemp?

— *Bien sûr.*

Etienne turned to the women.

— We will build a chimney in the spring, he said softly so that their Swiss neighbors would not hear and take offense.

— God be thanked, Isabelle replied automatically.

He glanced at her, tightened his lips, and turned away as Pascale joined them. She nodded at Hannah, smiled uncertainly at Isabelle. They had seen each other at church several times but had never been able to talk.

The minister, Abraham Rougemont, approached. As he was greeting Hannah, Isabelle took the opportunity to speak softly to Pascale.

— I'm sorry I have not come to see you. It is — difficult now.

— Do they know about — about —

— No. Don't worry.

— Isabelle, I have the —

She stopped, flustered, for Hannah had appeared at Isabelle's side, her mouth set, eyes fixed on Pascale's face.

Pascale struggled for a moment, then said simply: — May God watch over you this winter.

Isabelle smiled wanly.

— And you as well.

— You will come to our house between the services?

— *Bien sûr.*

— Good. Now, Jacob, what do you have for me this time, *chéri?*

He pulled from his pocket a dull green stone shaped like a pyramid and handed it to her.

Isabelle turned to go in. When she glanced back she saw Jacob whispering to Pascale.

After the morning service Etienne turned to her.

— You and Maman will go home now, he muttered.

— But the service at Chalières —

— You're not going to it, La Rousse.

Isabelle opened her mouth but stopped when she saw the set of his shoulders and the look in his eyes. Now I won't see Pascale, she thought. Now I won't see the Virgin. She closed her eyes and pressed her arms against the sides of her head, as if expecting a blow.

Etienne grabbed her elbow and pulled her roughly from the crowd.

— Go, he said, pushing her in the direction of home. Hannah stepped to her side.

Isabelle held out her hand stiffly.

— Marie, she called. Her daughter jumped to her side.

— Maman, she said, taking the outstretched hand.

— No. Marie will go to church with us. Come here, Marie.

Marie looked up at her mother, then over to her father. She let go of Isabelle's hand and went to stand halfway between them.

— Here. Etienne pointed to a spot next to him.

Marie looked at him with wide blue eyes.

— Papa, she said in a loud voice, if you hit me the way you do Maman, I'll bleed!

Etienne's anger made him taller. He took a step toward her but stopped when Hannah put a warning hand out and shook her head. He glanced at the crowd: it had gone quiet. Glaring at Marie, he turned and strode away in the direction of Gaspard's house.

Hannah turned down the path that led toward their farm. Isabelle didn't move.

— Marie, she said, come with us.

Marie remained standing in the same spot until Jacob came up to her and took her hand.

— Let's go to the river, he said. Marie let him lead her away. Neither looked back.

Jacob played with Marie while the cold trapped them indoors, inventing new games with his pebbles. He taught her to count, and to sort them in various ways: by color, size, origin. They began outlining objects with the pebbles. They laid a scythe on the floor and placed pebbles all the way around it, then picked up the tool and left behind its outline in stone. They did this with rakes, spades, pots, the bench, smocks, breeches, their hands.

— Let me outline you, he suggested one evening.

Marie clapped her hands and laughed. She lay on her back on the floor and he carefully pulled at her dress so that the pebbles would outline its full shape. He chose the pebbles carefully: Cevenol granite around her head and neck, white around the dress, dark green for her legs, feet and hands. He was meticulous, following the lines of the dress, even marking the cut of the waist, the tapering of the arms. When he was done he helped Marie up without disturbing the pebbles. They all admired the outline of the girl, arms and legs spread on the dirt floor. Isabelle glanced up and noticed that both Jacob and Etienne were looking at it intently. Etienne's lips were moving slightly.

He's counting, she thought. Why is he counting? A wave of fear swept over her.

— Stop it! she shouted, rushing into the outline and kicking at the stones.

The dark months after Christmas were the hardest. It was so cold that they opened the door only once a day, to get wood and hemp. Often the sky was grey, full of snow, and it was almost as dark outside as in the house. Isabelle would look out, hoping to escape for a moment, but found no comfort in the heavy sky, the smooth surface of the snow broken here and there in the distance by the black tops of firs or scabs of rock. When the cold touched her it felt like a metal bar pressed into her skin.

She began to taste metal as well, in the hard rye bread Hannah baked once a week in the communal oven, in the mushy vegetable stew they ate day after day. She had to force herself to eat, try to ignore the taste of blood, hide her gagging. Often she let Marie finish her food for her.

Then her arms and legs began to itch, in the creases on the inside of the elbow and behind the knee. At first she scratched at her skin through the layers of cloth: it was too cold to undress and pick off the lice. But one day she discovered blood seeping through the cloth, pulled up her sleeves and studied the sores: dry, silvery skin flaking away, rough patches of red, no trace of lice. She hid the rusty stains, fearful of what Etienne would accuse her of if he saw the blood.

She lay in bed at night, staring up at the dark and scratching with as little movement as possible so that Etienne would not notice. She listened to his even breathing, fearful of his waking, preferring to stay awake so that she would be ready – she did not know what for, but she waited in the dark for something, scarcely breathing.

She thought she was being careful, but one night he grabbed her hand and discovered the blood. He beat her and afterwards took her violently from behind. It was a relief not to have to look at his face.

One evening Gaspard came to sit at their fire.

– The granite is ordered, he told Etienne, pulling his pipe from his pocket and taking up his flint. The price is agreed and he has the measurements you gave me. He will bring it before Easter. Now, do you want more? For the chimney itself?

Etienne shook his head.

– I cannot pay for it. And anyway, the limestone here will be good enough for the chimney itself. It is the hearth that gets the hottest and needs the hardest stone.

Gaspard chuckled.

– They think you are crazy, down at the inn. *Why does he want a chimney?* they ask. *He lives in a fine house as it is!*

There was a silence; Isabelle knew what they were all thinking: they were remembering the Tournier chimney.

Marie hung at Gaspard's elbow, waiting for him to tickle her. He reached out, chucked her under the chin, pulled her ears.

— Eh, you want a chimney, *mon petit souris*, is that what you want? You don't like this smoke?

— It's Maman who hates it the most, Marie replied, giggling.

— Ah, Isabelle. Gaspard turned to her. You don't look well. Are you eating enough?

Hannah frowned. Etienne spoke for her.

— There is plenty to eat in this house for those who want it, he said gruffly.

— *Bien sûr, bien sûr*. Gaspard swept his hands in front of him as if smoothing ruffled cloth. You have had a good hemp crop, you have goats, all is well. Except you lack a chimney for Madame. He nodded at Isabelle. And Madame gets what she wants.

Isabelle blinked and peered at him through the smoke. Again there was silence until Gaspard laughed uncertainly.

— I joke! he cried. I'm teasing you, that's all.

After he left Etienne paced around the room, looking at the fire from every angle.

— The hearth will go here, against this wall, he explained to Petit Jean, patting the wall furthest from the door. We can build through the roof there. You see? There will be four pillars here — he pointed — holding up a stone roof that will lead the smoke up and out the hole we cut at the top.

How big will the hearth be, Papa? Petit Jean asked. As big as the one at the old farm?

Etienne glanced around before his eyes rested on Marie.

— Yes, he said, it will be a big hearth. You think so, Marie?

He rarely spoke her name. Isabelle knew he hated it. She had threatened to put a curse on their crops if he didn't let her name the baby Marie. In all the years she had been with the Tourniers it had been the only time she dared use their fear of her. Now that fear was gone; instead there was anger.

Marie frowned at Etienne. When he continued to look at her

with his cold wide eyes she burst into tears. Isabelle put her arm around her daughter.

– It's nothing, *chérie*, don't cry, she whispered, stroking her hair. You'll make it worse. Don't cry.

Over Marie's head she saw Hannah perched in the far corner of the room. For a moment she thought something was wrong with her. Her face looked different, the web of wrinkles more pronounced. Then she realized it was because the old woman was smiling.

Isabelle began to keep Marie close to her, teaching her to spin, having her roll up balls of thread, knitting little dresses for her doll. Isabelle touched her often, gripping her arm, stroking her hair, as if to reassure herself that the girl was still there. She kept Marie's face clean, scrubbing it with a cloth every day so that it shone through the gloom of the smoke.

– I need to be able to see you, *ma petite*, she explained, though Marie never asked for an explanation.

Isabelle kept Hannah away from the girl as much as she could, placing herself physically between them.

She did not always succeed. One day Marie came to Isabelle with shiny lips.

– Mémé spread pig fat on my bread! she cried.

Isabelle frowned.

– Maybe she will give you some tomorrow, her daughter continued, to fatten you too. You are becoming so thin, Maman. And so tired.

– Why does Mémé want you to be fat?

– Perhaps I'm special.

– No one is special in the eyes of God, Isabelle said sternly.

– But the pig fat was good, Maman. So good that I want more.

One morning she woke up to the sound of water and knew it was finally over.

Etienne opened the door to let in sunlight and a warmth that lifted her body. Everywhere the snow was melting and forming rivulets that ran down to the stream. The children burst outside as if they had been tied up, running and laughing, dragging clods of mud around on their shoes.

Isabelle knelt in the kitchen garden and let the mud soak her knees. She was alone for the first time in months, all of them so busy with spring's arrival that they left her unguarded. She bowed her head and began to pray out loud.

— Holy Mother, I cannot live through another winter here, she murmured. One winter like this is all I can survive. Please, dear Virgin, do not let this happen again. She pressed her arms across her stomach. Keep me and this baby safe. You are the only one who knows.

Isabelle had not been to Moutier since Christmas. All winter Hannah had taken the bread to be baked. When the weather was fair Etienne had taken the children to church, but Isabelle was always left behind with Hannah. When they heard the peddler's whistle for his spring visit, Isabelle expected to be told she could not go, to be beaten even for asking. She remained in the garden, planting herbs.

Marie came to find her.

— Maman, she said. Are you coming?

— No, *ma petite*. You see I am busy here.

— But Papa sent me to find you, to say you can come.

— Your father wants me to come to town?

— Yes. Marie lowered her voice. Please come, Maman. Don't say anything. Just come.

Isabelle looked at her face, blue eyes bright and level, blond hair light on top and dark underneath as her father's had once been. The red hairs had begun to appear again, one per day that Hannah herself now pulled out.

— You are too young to be so wise.

Marie twirled around, plucked at the new lavender bush and ran away laughing.

— We are going to town, all of us! she shouted.

Isabelle tried to smile when they reached the crowd gathered at the peddler's cart. She could feel people staring at her. She had no idea what the town thought of her, whether or not Etienne had encouraged or stifled the rumors about her, or if people talked of her at all.

Monsieur Rougemont approached.

– It is a pleasure to see you again, Isabelle, he said stiffly, taking her hand. We will see you on Sunday as well, I hope?

– Yes, she replied. He would not treat a witch like this, she thought uncertainly.

Pascale came up to her, face tight with concern.

– Isabelle, have you been ill?

Isabelle glanced at Hannah, standing next to her, uncomfortable.

– Yes, she said. Ill with the winter. But better now, I think.

– *Bella!* she heard behind her and turned to see the peddler hanging over her on his cart. He reached over, took her hand and kissed it. Ah, a joy to see you, Madame! A joy. He held on to her hand and, scrambling among his things, led her around the cart, away from Etienne and Hannah and the children, who watched them but did not follow. It was as if the peddler had placed a spell on them that froze them in place.

He let go of her hand, squatted on the edge of his cart and looked at her closely.

– But you are so sad, *Bella*, he said softly. What has happened to you? How can you be so sad with such beautiful blue cloth to look at?

Isabelle shook her head, unable to explain. She closed her eyes to hide her tears.

– Listen, *Bella*, he said, still quietly. Listen. I must ask you something.

She opened her eyes.

– You trust me, yes?

She looked deep into his dark eyes.

– Yes, I trust you, she whispered.

– You must tell me what color is your hair.

Isabelle's hand moved automatically to her headcloth.

– Why?

– I have a message maybe for you but I know only for sure when you tell me the color.

Isabelle shook her head slowly.

– The last news you gave me was that my sister-in-law is dead. Why would I want to hear more from you?

The peddler leaned closer.

– Because you are sad now and this message may make you happy, no more sad. I promise you, *Bella*. No bad news. Besides – he paused, looking at her face. It has been bad, this winter for you, yes? You hear no worse than what you have lived.

Isabelle looked down at the mud outlining her shoes. She took a deep breath.

– Red, she said. It's red.

He smiled.

– But that is beautiful, no? The color of the Virgin's hair, may we bless her. Why to be ashamed? And it is the good answer too! Now you can have the message. It is from a shepherd I meet in Alès in the winter. He describes you and asks me to watch for you. He has black hair and a scar on his cheek. You know?

Isabelle froze. Out of the smoke, the exhaustion, the fear clogging her thoughts, came a glimmer.

– Paul, she whispered.

– *Si, si*, that is his name! He says to tell you – the peddler closed his eyes and thought – he still looks for you in summer near the source of the Tarn. He looks for you always.

Isabelle began to weep. Luckily it was Marie rather than Etienne or Hannah who came to her side and took her hand.

– What's wrong, Maman? What did that bad man say to you? She scowled at the peddler.

– He is not a bad man, Isabelle said through her tears.

The peddler laughed and tousled Marie's hair.

– You, *bambina*, are like a little boat, a gondola. You rock up and down and hold to the water and you are brave but very small.

He continued to run his fingers through her hair until he found a red strand that Hannah had missed.

– You see, he said to Isabelle, not shameful. Is beautiful.

– Tell him I am there always in my mind, Isabelle said.

Marie looked between them.

– Tell who?

– It is nothing, Marie. We were just talking. Thank you, she said to the peddler.

– Be happy, *Bella*.

– I will try.

The day before Good Friday the hearth arrived.

Etienne and the boys were plowing while Isabelle and Hannah cleaned the house, ridding it of the winter smoke and darkness. They scrubbed the floors and walls, scalded the pots, washed the clothes, changed the straw in the bedding, mucked out the barn. They did not whitewash the walls yet. All the houses in the valley whitewashed their rooms once a year in the spring, but the Tourniers were waiting until after the chimney was built.

Isabelle was stirring a vat full of steaming clothes when she saw the cart approaching, the horse straining against the load.

– Marie, go tell Papa the granite has arrived, she said. Marie dropped the stick she had been pushing among the sodden cloth and ran toward the fields.

By the time Etienne and the boys arrived the man was sitting over a bowl of stew at the newly scrubbed table. He ate quickly, mouth close to the bowl. When he finished he raised his head.

– We will need two more men to lift it.

Etienne nodded at Petit Jean.

– Go and find Gaspard, he said.

While they waited Etienne explained how he would build the chimney.

– First I will dig a bed for it to lie in so it will be even with the floor, he said.

Hannah, who had been standing behind Etienne, took the man's bowl and refilled it, then set it in front of him with a bang.

– Why don't you dig it now? he asked. Then we can set the stone right away.

– It would take too long, Etienne replied uneasily. The ground is still frozen, you see. I don't want to make you wait.

The man kicked at the floor.

– It doesn't feel frozen to me.

– It's still very hard. I have been in the fields and not had the time to dig. Besides, I thought you were coming later. After Easter.

That's not true, Isabelle thought, staring hard at Etienne, who kept his eyes on the floor where the man had kicked a small hole with his toe. Gaspard had told them to expect it before Easter. It was rare to hear him lie so blatantly.

The granite man finished the second bowl. – Your women have no problem cooking on this fire here, he said, jerking his head at the flames in the corner. Why change it?

Etienne shrugged.

– We are accustomed to having a chimney.

– But you are in a new country now. With new customs. They should become yours too.

– Some old ways stay with us always, wherever we go, Isabelle said. They are a part of us. Nothing can replace them completely.

They all stared at her, an ugly look crossing Etienne's face.

Why did I speak? she thought. I know keeping silent is the best way. Why did I say such a thing? Now he will beat me, just like during the winter. And he may hurt the baby. She touched her belly.

When the men arrived Etienne became too busy to act on his anger. It took four of them, all strong men, to lift the slab from the cart and stagger inside with it, where they leaned it against the wall just inside the door. Jacob ran his hands up and down it. Marie spread herself against it as if it were a bed.

– It's warm, Maman, she said. Like home.

Easter was a time of redemption, when the hardship of the winter was explained. Isabelle got out their black clothes for the church service and changed with an easiness she thought she had lost.

This is called hope, she thought. This is what I had forgotten.

She had wondered if Etienne would forbid her to go to church for saying what she had to the granite man, but he did not mention it. Her boldness in speaking was balanced by his lie.

She helped Marie into her dress. Her daughter was fidgety, jumping around the room, laughing to herself. When it was time to go she took Isabelle's hand, Jacob the other, and the three walked down the narrow path side by side, following Etienne and Hannah, Petit Jean running ahead.

Isabelle dared not think about the Virgin at Chalières. It is enough that I go to the first service and see others, that I walk in the sunshine, she thought. I will not expect more.

At the end of the morning service at Saint Pierre Etienne simply turned toward Gaspard's house without speaking to Isabelle; the rest of the family fell in behind him. Pascale came up and walked beside her, smiling.

– I am glad you are coming to the second service, she whispered. It is good that you are here today.

At the house Isabelle sat next to Pascale by the fire and listened to gossip from the winter that she had known nothing about.

– But surely you know all this! Gaspard cried each time he told a new story. Hannah must have heard about this when she came to bake bread – surely she told you! Oh! He put a hand to his mouth, too late to stop the words, and glanced at Hannah, who was sitting next to Etienne on the other bench, her eyes closed. She opened them and looked at Gaspard, who laughed nervously.

– Eh, Hannah, he said quickly, you know all the gossip, *n'est-ce pas*? You can hear, even if you can't talk.

Hannah shrugged and closed her eyes again.

She is getting old, Isabelle thought. Old and tired. But she can still speak, I am sure of it.

Petit Jean soon disappeared with a neighbor's sons, but Jacob and Marie hung around restlessly, both with shiny, expectant eyes. At last Pascale said in a high voice: – Come, I'll show you the new kids. Not you, Isabelle. Just these two. She led the two children to the barn.

When they reappeared they were giggling, Marie in particular. She walked around the room, head held high as if she were wearing a crown.

— What were the kids like? Isabelle asked.

— Soft, Jacob replied, and he and Marie burst into laughter.

— Come here, *petit souris*, Gaspard said, or I'll throw you in the river!

Marie shrieked as he chased her around the room and, catching her, began to tickle her.

— She'll never keep quiet during the service if you do that, Etienne said stiffly.

Gaspard abruptly let Marie go.

Pascale returned to sit next to Isabelle. She had a smile on her face that Isabelle did not understand. She did not ask. She had learned not to ask.

— So you will have a chimney soon, Pascale said.

— Yes. Etienne will set the hearth after planting, with Gaspard's help, of course. The granite is so heavy. Then he will build the chimney.

— No more smoke. Pascale sounded envious and Isabelle smiled.

— No, no more smoke.

Pascale lowered her voice.

— You look better than when I saw you last.

Isabelle glanced around. Etienne and Gaspard were deep in conversation; Hannah appeared to be asleep.

— Yes, I've been outside more, she replied cautiously. I've had fresh air.

— It's not just that. You look happier. As if someone has told you a secret.

Isabelle thought of the shepherd.

— Maybe someone has.

Pascale widened her eyes and Isabelle laughed.

— It's nothing, she said. Just the spring and a chimney.

— So the children have said nothing to you.

Isabelle sat up straight.

— What would they say?

– Nothing. We should eat now. It will be time to go to Chalières soon. Pascale got up before Isabelle could say anything.

After eating they walked in an informal procession to the chapel: Etienne and Gaspard leading with Hannah at Etienne's elbow, then the women with Marie holding Isabelle's hand, and Petit Jean and his friends following in a rough pack, pushing and shouting. Behind them all Jacob followed alone, hands in his pockets, smiling.

They arrived early; the chapel was only half full and they were able to stand close enough to see the minister without difficulty. Isabelle kept her eyes lowered but positioned herself so that she could see the Virgin when she dared to look up. Marie stayed at her side, hugging herself and giggling.

– Maman, she whispered. Do you like my dress?

Isabelle glanced down at her.

– Your dress is the proper thing to wear, *ma fille*. Black for the Holy Days.

Marie giggled, then bit her lip when Jacob frowned at her.

– You are playing a game, you two, Isabelle declared.

– Yes, Maman, Jacob replied.

– No games here – this is the house of God.

During the service Isabelle was able to glance several times at the Virgin. She felt Etienne's eyes on her occasionally, but kept her face solemn, her joy hidden.

Monsieur Rougemont spoke for a long time about Christ's sacrifice and the need to live a pure life.

– God has already chosen who among you will follow His son to heaven, he stated baldly. Your behavior here indicates His decision. If you choose to sin, to persist in old habits when you have been shown the Truth, to worship false idols – Isabelle dropped her eyes to the ground – to carry evil thoughts, you will have no chance of gaining God's forgiveness. But if you lead lives of purity, of hard work and simple worship, you may yet prove to be one of God's chosen and be worthy of His son's sacrifice. Let us pray.

Isabelle's cheeks burned. He is speaking to me, she thought. Without moving her head she glanced nervously at Etienne and

Hannah; to her surprise she saw on their faces looks of fear. She looked the other way and, except for the serene faces of the children, saw the same expression all around her.

Perhaps none of us is chosen, she thought. And we know it.

She looked up at the Virgin.

– Help me, she prayed. Help me to be forgiven.

Monsieur Rougemont ended the service by bringing out the cup of wine and thin wafers for Communion.

– The children first, he said. Blessed are the innocent.

– Go. Isabelle gave Marie a push and she, Jacob and Petit Jean joined the other children kneeling before the minister.

While they waited, Isabelle rested her eyes on the Virgin again. Look at me, she pleaded silently. Show me my sins have been forgiven.

The Virgin's eyes were cast down, focussed on something below her. Isabelle followed her gaze to Marie. Her daughter was kneeling patiently, waiting her turn, her black dress pushed up around her legs where she knelt. Underneath, though, there was no white undercloth. It was blue. Marie was wearing the cloth.

Isabelle gasped, turning the heads of her neighbors and of Etienne and Hannah. She tried but couldn't take her eyes off the blue.

Others began to see it too. Nudges and whispers spread quickly through the chapel. Jacob, kneeling next to Marie, glanced back, then down at Marie's legs. He made a move as if to tug Marie's black dress back down, then stopped himself.

When Etienne finally saw it his face went white, then red. He pushed his way through the crowd to the front and pulled Marie to her feet. She looked up at him and her smile disappeared. She seemed to crawl inside herself. Etienne dragged her through the congregation to the door, where they disappeared outside.

Jacob had gotten off his knees and stood motionless in front of the kneeling children, his eyes fixed on the church door. As Isabelle turned to follow she caught sight of Pascale: she had begun to weep.

She pushed her way to the door. Outside Etienne had lifted Marie's black skirt high to reveal the blue one underneath.

— Who gave this to you? Who dressed you? he demanded. Marie said nothing. Etienne pushed her to her knees.

— Who gave it to you? Who?

When Marie still didn't tell him he hit her hard on the back of her head. She fell forward onto her face.

— I gave it to her, Isabelle lied.

Etienne turned.

— I should have guessed you would trick us, La Rousse. But not anymore. You won't be able to hurt us. Get up, he said to Marie.

She sat up slowly. Blood had run from her nose to her chin.

— Maman, she whispered.

Etienne stepped between them.

— Don't touch her, he hissed at Isabelle. He yanked Marie up and looked around. Petit Jean, *viens*, he said as their son appeared at the door.

Petit Jean walked over to him.

— Pascale, he announced to Etienne. It was Pascale, Papa. He took Marie's other arm. They began to march her away between them. She turned her head and looked back at Isabelle.

— Please, Maman, she said. She stumbled; Etienne and Petit Jean grabbed her arms more tightly.

Hannah and Jacob had appeared in the doorway. Jacob came now to stand next to Isabelle.

— The pebbles on the ground, she said without looking at him. They were the outline for the dress.

— Yes, he answered quietly. It was meant to protect her. Like the peddler said. From drowning.

— Why was your father counting those pebbles too? Why would he want to know how big Marie is?

Jacob stared at her with wide eyes.

— I don't know.

8. The Farm

I flew from Toulouse to Geneva, then caught a train to Moutier. It all happened fast and easily: there was a flight, there was a train, and Jacob sounded more pleased than surprised that I wanted to come on such short notice. Very short notice: I called him at noon; at six the train pulled into Moutier.

On the train from Geneva my mind began working again. I'd sat in a daze on the flight from Toulouse, but now the rhythm of the train, more natural than a plane's, shook me awake. I began to look around.

Across from me sat a sturdy middle-aged couple, he in a chocolate blazer and striped tie, reading a carefully folded newspaper, she wearing a grey wool dress and darker grey jacket, gold bows clipped to her ears, Italian shoes. Her hair had just been done, puffed out and newly colored a reddish-brown that wasn't so far from my own except that it looked synthetic. She held a sleek leather handbag on her lap and was writing what looked like a list in a tiny notebook.

Probably doing her Christmas card list already, I thought, self-conscious in my limp, wrinkled linen.

They didn't say a word to each other the whole hour I sat across from them. When I got up to change trains at Neuchâtel the man raised his eyes briefly and nodded. '*Bonne journée, Madame*', he said with a politeness only people over fifty manage gracefully. I smiled and nodded to him and his companion. It was that kind of place.

The trains were quiet, clean and punctual. The passengers were also quiet and clean, soberly dressed, purposeful in their reading, deliberate in their movements. There were no couples making out, no men staring, no skimpy dresses or barely covered breasts, no drunks lolling over two seats — all common sights on the train from Lisle to Toulouse. This was not a lolling country; the Swiss never took up two seats if they'd only paid for one.

Maybe I was looking for such order after the chaos I'd left. It was typical for me to pinpoint national character traits after only an hour in a country, to come up with an opinion I could tinker with as I went, altering it to encompass the people I met. If I really wanted I could probably have found sordidness somewhere on those trains, torn clothes and raised voices, romance novels, someone shooting up in the toilet, some passion, some fear. Instead I looked around and clung to the perceived normality.

The new landscape fascinated me: the solid mountains of the Jura rising steeply away from the train tracks, the banks of dark green firs, the sharp lines of the houses, the crisp order of the fields and farms. I was surprised that it was so different from France, though logically I shouldn't have been. It was a different country, after all, as I had pointed out to my father. The real surprise was realizing that the French landscape I'd left behind – the gentle hills, the bright green vineyards, the rust color of the earth, the silver light – was no longer strange to me.

Jacob had said over the phone that he would meet me at the station. I knew nothing about him, not even how old he was, though I suspected he was closer to my father's age than to mine. When I stepped onto the Moutier platform I spotted him immediately: he reminded me of my father, though his hair wasn't grey but brown, the same color mine had been. He was very tall and wore a cream sweater stretched out of shape across shoulders that sloped down like a bow. His face was long and thin, almost gaunt, with a delicate chin and bright brown eyes. He had the energetic look of a man in his late fifties, still driven by work, not yet part of that group who have relaxed into retirement, but knowing he would join them soon and wondering how he would cope with so much freedom.

He strode up to me, took my head in his large hands and kissed my cheeks three times.

'Ella, you look just like your father,' he said, using the familiar form, in clear French.

I grinned up at him. 'Ah, then I must look like you, because *you* look just like my father!'

He picked up my bag, put his arm around me and led me down a flight of stairs and out to the street. He swung my bag in a wide semicircle as he gestured with his whole arm. '*Bienvenue à Moutier!*' he cried.

I took a step forward and just managed to say '*C'est très –*' before I fell to the ground.

I woke up in a white room, small and rectangular and plain, like a monk's cell, with a bed, table, chair and bureau. Behind my head was a window; when I rolled my eyes back to look out, I could see upside-down the white steeple of a church, the black clock face on it partially obscured by a tree.

Jacob was sitting in the chair next to the bed; a strange man with a round face hovered in the doorway. I lay looking at them, unable to speak. Jacob said gently, '*Ella, tu t'es évanouiée.*' I'd never heard the word he used, but I understood immediately what he meant. 'Lucien –' he gestured behind him at the man – 'was passing in his truck just then and he brought you here. We were worried because you were unconscious for a long time.'

'How long?' I struggled to sit up and Jacob gripped my shoulders to help me.

'Ten minutes. All the way in the car and into the house.'

I shook my head slowly. 'I don't remember a thing.'

Lucien stepped forward with a glass of water and handed it to me.

'*Merci*,' I murmured. He smiled in reply, barely moving his lips. I sipped it, then felt my face; it was wet and sticky. 'Why is my face wet?'

Jacob and Lucien glanced at each other. 'You were crying,' Jacob replied.

'While I was unconscious?'

He nodded and I became aware of my sore, runny nose, my hoarse throat, my exhaustion.

'Was I talking?'

'You were reciting something.'

'*J'ai mis en toi mon espérance: Garde-moi, donc, Seigneur.* Yes?'

'Yes,' Lucien replied. 'That was –'

'You need to sleep,' Jacob interrupted. 'Just rest. We'll talk later.' He pulled a thin blanket over me. Lucien raised his hand in a motionless wave. I nodded and he disappeared.

I closed my eyes, then opened them just as Jacob was closing the door. 'Jacob, does this house have shutters?'

He paused and tipped his head into the room. 'Yes, but I don't like them. I never use them.' He smiled and shut the door.

It was dark when I next woke, sweaty and disoriented. Outside there were windows lit up all around; it seemed that no one used their shutters here. The church steeple was spotlit. At that moment the bells in the tower began to chime and I automatically followed them, counting to ten: I'd been asleep four hours. It felt like days.

I reached over and switched on the bedside lamp. The shade was yellow and cast a soft golden light around the room. I had never been in a room with no decoration whatsoever; the spareness was oddly comforting. I lay for a while, studying the way the light fell, not sure that I wanted to get up. But I did finally, leaving the room and feeling my way down the dark stairs. At the bottom I stood in a square hallway facing three closed doors. I chose one with a string of light along the bottom and opened it into a bright kitchen painted yellow, with a polished wood floor and a bank of windows along one wall. Jacob was sitting at a round wooden table reading a newspaper propped against a bowl of peaches. A woman younger than me with dark frizzy hair leaned into the kitchen sink, scrubbing at a pan. When she turned at my entrance I knew she must be related to Jacob: she had the same gaunt face and pointed chin, softened by wisps of hair on her forehead and long lashes around the same brown eyes. She was taller than me and very slight, with long thin hands and small wrists.

'Ah, Ella, there you are,' Jacob said as the woman kissed me three times. 'This is my daughter, Susanne.'

I smiled at her. 'I'm sorry,' I said to them both. 'I didn't realize it was so late. I don't know what was wrong with me.'

'It's nothing. You needed to sleep. Will you eat something now?' Jacob pulled out a chair for me at the table. Then he and Susanne began to set out cheese and salami, bread, olives and salad. It was exactly what I wanted, something simple. I didn't want them fussing over me.

We said little as we ate. Susanne asked me in French as clear as her father's if I would drink some wine, and Jacob remarked on the cheese, but otherwise we were silent.

When we had pushed our plates aside and Jacob had refilled my glass, Susanne slipped out of the room. 'Do you feel better?' he asked.

'Yes.'

From another room a delicate music began, like a piano but stringier. Jacob listened for a moment. 'Scarlatti,' he said with pleasure. 'Susanne studies harpsichord at the Concertgebouw in Amsterdam, you see.'

'Are you a musician too?'

He nodded. 'I teach at the music school here, just up the hill.' He gestured behind him.

'What do you play?'

'Many things, but I teach mostly piano and flute here. The boys all want to play guitar, the girls flute, all of them violin or recorder. A few piano.'

'Are there good students?'

He shrugged. 'Most take lessons because their parents want them to. They have other interests too, horses or football or skiing. Every winter four or five children break their arms skiing and can't play. There is one boy, a pianist, who plays very good Bach. He may go on to study elsewhere.'

'Did Susanne study with you?'

He shook his head. 'With my wife.'

My father had told me Jacob's wife was dead, but I couldn't remember how long ago or the circumstances.

'Cancer,' he said, as if I'd asked him aloud. 'She died five years ago.'

'I'm sorry,' I said. Feeling the inadequacy of the words, I added, 'You miss her still, yes?'

He smiled sadly. 'Of course. You are married yourself?'

'Yes,' I replied uncomfortably, then changed the subject. 'Would you like to see the Bible now?'

'Let's wait until the morning when the light is better. Now, you look better but you're still pale. Are you pregnant, maybe?'

I flinched, astonished that he asked me so casually. 'No, no, I'm not. I – I don't know why I fainted but it's not that. I haven't been sleeping well for the last few months. And hardly at all last night.' I stopped, remembering Jean-Paul's bed, and shook my head slowly. It was impossible to describe my situation to him.

We'd obviously entered shaky territory; Jacob saved us by pointedly changing the subject.

'What do you do for work?'

'I'm a, well, I *was* a midwife, in America.'

'Really?' His face lit up. 'What a wonderful thing to do!'

I looked at the bowl of peaches and smiled. His response was similar to Madame Sentier's.

'Yes,' I said. 'It was good work.'

'So of course you would know if you were pregnant.'

I chuckled. 'Yes, I guess so.' I usually did know if a woman was pregnant, even in the early days. It was apparent in the deliberate way they carried themselves, their bodies like bubble-wrap around something they didn't even know they held. I saw it in Susanne, for instance: a certain distracted look in her eyes, as if she were listening to a conversation deep inside, in a foreign language, and not necessarily pleased with what she heard even if she didn't understand it.

I looked at Jacob's open face. He doesn't know yet, I thought. It was funny: I was family enough for him to ask me personal questions, but not so close that he would be afraid to hear the answer. He would never ask his own daughter so directly.

I slept badly that night, my mind burdened with thoughts about Rick and Jean-Paul, and harsh thoughts about myself. I got nowhere with them, just worked myself up into a state. When I finally managed to fall asleep, I still woke early.

I brought the Bible downstairs with me. Jacob and Susanne were already at the table reading the paper, along with a pale man with orange-red hair like a carrot rather than chestnut like mine. His eyelashes and brows were red too, giving his face a fuzzy, undefined look. He stood up as I came in and held out his hand.

'Ella, this is Jan, my boyfriend,' Susanne said. She looked tired; her coffee was untouched, its surface beginning to form a wrinkled scum.

Ah, the father-to-be, I thought. His handshake was limp. 'I am sorry I was not here to greet you last evening,' he said in perfect English. 'I was playing at an engagement at Lausanne and arrived back only very late in the evening.'

'What do you play?'

'I play the flute.'

I smiled, partly at his formal English, partly because his body was a bit like a flute: thin, rounded limbs and a certain stiffness in his legs and chest, like the tin man in *The Wizard of Oz*.

'You are not Swiss, no?'

'No, I am Dutch.'

'Oh.' I couldn't think of anything else to say, his formality freezing me. Jan remained standing. I turned awkwardly to Jacob. 'I'll put the Bible in another room for you to look at after breakfast, OK?' I said.

Jacob nodded. I went back to the hall and tried another door. It led into a long sunny room painted cream, with unfinished wood trim and gleaming black tiles on the floor. It was sparsely furnished with a sofa and two battered armchairs; like the bedroom, there was nothing on the walls. At the far end of the room stood a black grand piano, lid closed, and a delicate rosewood harpsichord facing it. I set the Bible down on the grand piano and went to the window to get my first real look at Moutier.

Houses were scattered willy-nilly around us and up the hill behind the house. Each house was grey or cream, with a steep slate roof ending in a lip that jutted out like a flared skirt. The houses were taller and newer than those in Lisle, with freshly painted shutters in sober reds, greens and browns, though just across from Jacob's house there was a surprising electric-blue pair. I opened the window and leaned out to look at Jacob's shutters: they weren't painted at all, but left a natural caramel-colored wood.

I heard a step behind me and pulled myself back inside. Cup of coffee in each hand, Jacob stood laughing at me. 'Ah, you are spying on our neighbors already!' he cried, handing me a cup.

I grinned. 'Actually I was looking at your shutters. I wanted to see what color you painted them.'

'Do you like them?'

I nodded.

'Now, where is this Bible? Ah, there. Good, now you can go home,' he teased.

I sat next to him on the sofa as he opened the book to the front page. He gazed at the names for a long time, a pleased look on his face. Then he reached behind him and from a bookcase pulled a sheaf of papers taped together. He began unfolding and spreading them on the floor. The papers were yellow, the tape brittle.

'This is the family tree my grandfather made,' he explained.

The handwriting was clear, the tree carefully plotted. Even so it was a messy affair: there were tangents, branches shooting off, gaps where lines petered out. When Jacob finished setting up the sheets, they formed not a neat rectangle or pyramid, but an irregular patchwork, with sheets tacked on here and there to hold information.

We crouched next to it. Everywhere I saw the names Susanne, Etienne, Hannah, Jacob, Jean. At the top of the tree it was sketchier, but it began with Etienne and Jean Tournier.

'Where did your grandfather find all this?'

'Various places. Some at the *bourgeoisie* in the *hôtel de ville* here – there are records that go back to the eighteenth century, I think. Before that I don't know. He spent years studying records. And now you've added to his work; you've made the great leap to France! Tell me now how you found this Tournier Bible.'

I recounted an abbreviated version of my search with Mathilde and Monsieur Jourdain, leaving out Jean-Paul.

'What a coincidence! You've been lucky, Ella. And you've come all this way to show it to me.' Jacob ran his hand over the leather cover. A question lurked behind his words, but I didn't answer it. It must have seemed extreme to him, my coming here so suddenly just to show him the Bible, but I didn't feel I could confide in him: he was too much like my father. I wouldn't dream of telling my parents about what I'd just done, the scene I'd left behind.

Later Jacob and I went for a walk around town. The *hôtel de ville*, a deliberate building with grey shutters and a clock tower, stood in the center. Shops were clustered around it, making up what was called the old town, though it seemed very new compared to Lisle: many of the buildings were modern, and all had been modernized, with fresh plaster and paint and new square roof tiles. There was a peculiar building with an onion-shaped dome to one side and a stone monk placed in a niche under it, holding a lantern over the street corner, but otherwise the buildings were uniform and unadorned.

In the last century the town had expanded to 8,000 people, and houses had spread up the hillsides around the old town to accommodate the population. It all had an unplanned feel about it, strange after living in Lisle with its grid of streets and sense of being an organic whole. With a few exceptions the buildings were functional rather than aesthetically pleasing, built for a purpose, with no decorous brickwork or cross-beams or tiling like in Lisle.

A little out of the center we strolled along a path next to the River Birse. It was small, more like a stream than a river, and lined with silver birches. There was something cheering about water running through a town, connecting it with the rest of the world, a reminder that the place was not so static or isolated.

Everywhere we went Jacob introduced me as a Tournier from America. I was greeted with a look of recognition and acceptance I hadn't expected. It was certainly different from my reception in

Lisle. I mentioned this to Jacob, who smiled. 'Maybe it is you who are different,' he said.

'Maybe.' I didn't add that though the people's attitude toward me here was gratifying, I was also slightly suspicious of such wholesale embracing of a family name. If you knew how awful I've been, I thought grimly, you wouldn't think Tourniers were so wonderful.

Jacob had classes to teach. On his way to the school he took me to a chapel in the cemetery on the edge of town and left me to inspect the interior. He told me there'd been monasteries at Moutier from the seventh century; the existing chapel of Chalières dated from the tenth. Inside it was small and simple, with faded Byzantine-style frescos in rust and cream on the choir walls and whitewash everywhere else. I studied the figures obediently – Christ standing with his arms outstretched, a row of Apostles below him, pale circles of halos framing their heads, some of the faces washed out beyond expression – but except for the faint trace of a sad-looking woman off to one side, the frescos left me cold.

When I came out I saw Jacob partway up the hill, standing in front of a headstone, head bowed, eyes closed. I watched him for a moment, ashamed of my own worries when here was real tragedy, a man grieving over his wife's grave. To give him privacy I went back inside the chapel. A cloud had crossed the sun and it was darker inside; the fresco figures hung suspended above me like ghosts. I stood in front of the faint lines of the woman and studied her more closely. There was little left of her: heavy-lidded eyes, large nose, pursed mouth, framed by a robe and a halo. Yet these rudimentary elements captured her misery precisely.

'Of course. The Virgin,' I said softly.

There was something about her expression that made her different from Nicolas Tournier's Virgin. I closed my eyes and tried to remember it: the pain, the resignation, the strange peace in her face. I opened my eyes and looked at the figure in front of me again. Then I saw it: it was in the mouth, the tight little turns at the corners. This Virgin was angry.

★

When I left the chapel again the sun had come back out and Jacob was gone. I walked toward town through the newer houses, ending finally at the Protestant church, the one I'd seen when I first woke up in Jacob's house. It was a big building, made of limestone and surrounded by old trees. In some ways it reminded me of the church in Le Pont de Montvert: both were situated in the same place in relation to the town – not in the center, but still dominant, halfway up the north slope of a hill, with a grassy porch and wall where you could sit and look out over the town. I circled the church and found the front entrance open. Inside there was more decoration than there had been in the church at Le Pont de Montvert, with marble floors and a bit of stained glass in the choir. Still, it felt bare, austere and, after the Chalières chapel, large and impersonal. I didn't stay long.

I sat on the wall in the sun, just as I had before in Le Pont de Montvert. It was warm now and I took off my jacket. Underneath, my arms had broken out with psoriasis again. 'Dammit,' I muttered. I folded my arms to my chest, then straightened them and held them up to the sun. The stretching movement made a patch on my arm fill with blood.

At that moment a black Labrador bounded up to me, scrambled half onto the wall and pushed his head into my side. I laughed and petted him. 'Perfect timing, dog,' I said. 'Don't let me wallow.'

Lucien appeared across the green. As he approached I got a better look at him than I had the night before, at his baby face, dark wiry hair and wide hazel eyes. He must have been about thirty, but he looked like he'd never been touched by worry or tragedy. A Swiss innocent. I glanced down, deliberately keeping my psoriasis exposed. I noticed another patch on my ankle and cursed myself for forgetting to pack my cortisone cream.

'*Salut, Ella*,' he said, standing awkwardly until I invited him to sit down. He was wearing old shorts and a T-shirt, both covered in spots of paint. The Lab looked at us, panting, tail moving; when he was sure we weren't going anywhere, he began nosing around the nearby trees.

'Are you a painter?' I asked to break the silence, wondering if he'd heard of Nicolas Tournier.

'Yes,' he replied. 'I'm working up there.' He gestured behind us up the hill. 'You see the ladder?'

'Ah, yes.' A house painter. This shouldn't make a difference, I said to myself. But my questions dried up; I didn't know what to say.

'I build houses too. I fix things.' Lucien was looking out over the town, but I could see he was also surreptitiously glancing at my arms.

'Where do you live?' I asked.

He pointed out another house up the hill, and glanced at my arms again.

'It's psoriasis,' I said abruptly.

He nodded once; he was not a talkative man. I noticed his hair had streaks of white paint in it and his forearms were covered with a mist of white speckles that comes from using a roller. I was reminded of moving with Rick: the first thing we did when we got a new place was to paint every room white. Rick said it was so he could see the dimensions of the rooms better; for me it was like cleansing them of ghosts. Only after we'd lived in a place for a while, when its character became apparent and we felt comfortable living in it, did we start painting rooms different colors. Our house in Lisle was still white.

The phone call came a day later. I don't know why it caught me off-guard: I'd known my other life would intrude eventually, but had done nothing to prepare myself.

We were eating fondue at the time. Susanne had been amused to learn that after Swiss Army knives, clocks and chocolate, fondue was the fourth thing Americans associate with Switzerland and insisted on making it for me. 'From an old family recipe, *bien sûr*,' she teased. She and Jacob had invited a few people: Jan was there, of course, as well as a German-Swiss couple who turned out to be the neighbors with the blue shutters, and Lucien, who sat next to me and stared at my profile from time to time as we ate. At least

I had covered my arms so he couldn't stare at the psoriasis.

I'd tried fondue only once, when I was young and my grandmother made it. I didn't remember much about it. Susanne's was wonderful and extremely alcoholic. On top of that we'd been drinking wine steadily and were getting louder and sillier. At one point I dipped a piece of bread into the cheese and my fork came up empty. Everyone began to laugh and clap.

'Wait a minute, what is it?' Then I remembered the tradition my grandmother had taught me: whoever loses their bread in the fondue pot first will never marry. I laughed too. 'Oh, no, now I'll never marry! But wait a minute, I *am* married!'

There was more laughter. 'No, no, Ella,' Susanne cried. 'If you drop the bread first it means you *will* marry, and soon!'

'No, in our family it means you *won't* marry.'

'But this *is* your family,' Jacob said, 'and the tradition is that you will marry.'

'Then we must've gotten it wrong somewhere. I'm *sure* my grandmother said –'

'Yes, you got it wrong the way the family's last name is wrong,' Jacob declared. 'Tuurr-nuurr,' he pronounced dolefully, drawing out each syllable. 'Where are the vowels to lift it and make it sound beautiful, like Tour-ni-er? But never mind, *ma cousine*, you know what your real name is. Do you know,' he continued, turning to his neighbors, 'that my cousin is a midwife?'

'Ah, a good profession,' the man replied automatically. I felt Susanne's eyes on me; when I glanced at her she looked down. Her wine glass was still full and she hadn't eaten much.

When the phone rang Jan got up to answer it, glancing around the table, his eyes coming to rest on me. He held the phone out. 'This telephone call is for you, Ella,' he said.

'Me? But –' I hadn't given anyone the number here. I got up and took it, everyone's eyes on me.

'Hello?' I said uncertainly.

'Ella? What the hell are you doing there?'

'Rick?' I turned my back on the table, trying to create a little privacy.

'You sound surprised to hear from me.' I'd never heard him sound so bitter.

'No, it's just – I didn't leave the phone number.'

'No, you didn't. But it's not that hard to get the number of Jacob Tournier of Moutier. There were two listed; when I called the other one first he told me you were here.'

'He knew I was here? Another Jacob Tournier?' I repeated stupidly, surprised that Rick had actually remembered my cousin's name.

'Yeah.'

'Well, it's a small town.' I glanced around. Everyone was eating, trying to look like they weren't listening to me, but listening all the same, except for Susanne, who got up abruptly and went over to the sink, where she took a deep breath by the open window.

They all know my business, I thought. Even a Tournier across town knows my business.

'Ella, why did you go away? What's the matter?'

'Rick, I – Look, can we talk another time? Now's not a good time.'

'I take it you left your wedding ring on the bedroom floor as some kind of statement.'

I spread out my left hand and stared at it, shocked that I hadn't even noticed it was gone. It must have fallen out of my yellow dress when I was changing.

'Are you mad at me? Did I do something?'

'Nothing, you just – Oh, Rick, I – you haven't done anything, I just wanted to meet my family here, that's all.'

'Then why rush off like that? You didn't even leave me a note. You *always* leave me a note. Do you realize how worried I was? And how humiliating it was to find out from my secretary?'

I was silent.

'Who answered the phone just now?'

'What? My cousin's boyfriend. He's Dutch,' I added usefully.

'Is that – guy with you?'

'Who?'

'Jean-Pierre.'

'No, he's not here. What made you think that?'

'You slept with him, didn't you? I can tell from your voice.'

That I hadn't expected from him. I took a deep breath.

'Look, I *really* can't talk right now. There are – people in the room. I'm sorry, Rick, I just – don't know what I want anymore. But I can't talk right now. I just can't.'

'Ella –' Rick sounded slightly strangled.

'Just give me a few days, OK? Then I'll come back and – and we'll talk. All right? Sorry.' I hung up and turned around to face them. Lucien was staring at his plate; the neighbors were chatting deliberately to Jan. Jacob and Susanne looked at me steadily with brown eyes the same color as mine.

'So,' I said brightly. 'What were we just saying about me getting married?'

I got up in the middle of the night, feeling dehydrated from the wine, the fondue sitting like lead in my stomach, and went down to the kitchen to get some mineral water. I left the lights off and sat at the table with the glass, but the room still smelled of cheese and I decided to move to the living room. As I reached the door I heard the faint stringy sound of the harpsichord. I opened the door quietly and saw Susanne sitting at the instrument in the dark, a distant streetlight picking out her profile. She played a few bars, stopped and just sat. When I whispered her name she looked up, then let her shoulders slump. I went over and put my hand on her shoulder. She was wearing a dark silk kimono smooth to the touch.

'You should be in bed,' I said softly. 'You must be tired. You need lots of sleep now.'

Susanne pressed her face into my side and began to cry. I stood still and stroked her frizzy hair, then knelt next to her.

'Does Jan know yet?'

'No,' she replied, wiping her eyes and cheeks. 'Ella, I'm not ready for this. I want to do other things. I've worked so hard and am just beginning to get more concerts.' She placed her hand on the keyboard and played a chord. 'A baby now would ruin my opportunities.'

'How old are you?'

'Twenty-two.'

'And you want to have children?'

She shrugged. 'Someday. Not yet. Not now.'

'And Jan?'

'Oh, he would love to have children. But you know, men don't think in the same way. It wouldn't make any difference to his music, to his career. When he talks about having children it's so abstract that I know I would be the one to look after them.'

That was a familiar refrain.

'Does anyone else know yet?'

'No.'

I hesitated, unaccustomed to talking to women about abortion as an option: in my profession, by the time women consulted me they'd decided to have the baby. Besides, I didn't even know the words for 'abortion' or 'option'.

'What are the things you could do?' I finally asked lamely, taking care at least over the verb tense.

She stared at the keys. Then she shrugged. '*Un avortement,*' she said in a flat voice.

'What do you think about — abortion?' I could have kicked myself for the clumsiness of my question. Susanne didn't seem to notice.

'Oh, I would prefer to do it, even if I don't like the idea. I'm not religious, it would not be offensive like that. But Jan —'

I waited.

'Well, he's Catholic. He doesn't go to church now and he thinks of himself as liberal, but — it's different when it's a real choice. I don't know what he will think. He may be very upset.'

'You know, you have to tell him, it's his right, but you don't have to decide with him. It's for *you* to decide what to do. Of course it's better if you agree, but if you don't agree, it has to be your decision because you carry the baby.' I tried to say this as firmly as possible.

Susanne glanced at me sideways. 'Have you – have you yourself –'

'No.'

'Do you want to have children?'

'Yes, but –' I didn't know what to explain first. Unaccountably I began to giggle. Susanne stared at me, the whites of her eyes gleaming in the streetlight. 'Sorry. I have to sit down,' I said. 'Then I'll tell you.'

I sat in one of the armchairs while Susanne switched on a small lamp on the piano. She curled up in a corner of the sofa, legs tucked under her, green silk pulled tight over her knees, and looked at me expectantly. I think she was relieved the spotlight was no longer on her.

'My husband and I talked about having children,' I began. 'We thought now would be a good time. Well, actually, I suggested it and Rick agreed. So we started to try. But I was – disturbed. By a nightmare. And now, now I think – well, we're having problems now.

'There was also – there is also something else. Someone else.' I felt humiliated putting it like that, but it was also a relief to tell someone.

'Who?'

'A librarian in the town where I live. We've been – flirting for awhile. And then we –' I waved my hands in the air. 'Afterwards I felt bad and had to get away. So I came here.'

'Is he handsome?'

'He – oh, yes. *I* think so. He is kind of – severe.'

'And you like him.'

'Yes.' It was strange talking about him; I actually found it hard to picture him. From this distance, in this room with Susanne curled up in front of me, what had happened with Jean-Paul seemed far away and not as earth-shattering as I'd thought. It was a funny thing: once you tell your story to others it becomes more like fiction and less like truth. A layer of performance is added to it, removing you further from the real thing.

'How long have you and Rick been married?'

'Two years.'

'And the man, what is his name?'

'Jean-Paul.' There was something so definite about his name that saying it made me smile. 'He's helped me look into my family history,' I continued. 'He argues with me a lot, but it's because he is interested in me, in what I do – no, in what I am, really. He listens to me. He sees *me*, not the idea of me. You know?'

Susanne nodded.

'And I can talk to him. I even told him about the nightmare and he was very good, he made me describe it. That helped.'

'What is it about, this nightmare?'

'Oh, I don't know. It doesn't have a story. Just a feeling, like a – like I have no – *respiration*.' I patted my chest. Frank Sinatra, I thought. Ole blue eyes.

'And a blue, a certain color blue,' I added. 'Like in Renaissance paintings. The color they painted the Virgin's robe. There is this painter – tell me, have you heard of Nicolas Tournier?'

Susanne sat up straight and gripped the arm of the sofa. 'Tell me more about this blue.'

At last, a connection with the painter. 'It has two parts: there's a clear blue, the top layer, full of light and –' I struggled for words. 'It moves with the light, the color. But there's also a darkness underneath the light, very somber. The two shades fight against each other. That's what makes the color so alive and memorable. It's a beautiful color, you see, but sad too, maybe to remind us that the Virgin is always mourning the death of her son, even when he's born. Like she knows already what will happen. But then when he's dead the blue is still beautiful, still hopeful. It makes you think that nothing is completely one thing or the other; it can be light and happy but there is always that darkness underneath.'

I stopped. We were both quiet.

Then she said, 'I have had the dream too.'

'I had it only once, about six weeks ago, back in Amsterdam. I woke up terrified and I was crying. I thought I was being smothered in blue, the blue you describe. It was strange because I felt happy and sad at the same time. Jan said I'd been saying something, like reciting something from the Bible. I couldn't sleep afterwards. I had to get up and play, like tonight.'

'Do you have any whiskey?' I asked.

She went to the bookcase and opened the cupboard at the bottom, taking out a half-empty bottle and two small glasses. She sat back in the corner of the sofa and poured us each a shot. I considered saying something about her drinking in her condition, but didn't have to: after handing me my glass she took one sniff of hers and grimaced, then uncorked the bottle and poured the whiskey back.

I gulped mine. It cut through everything: the fondue, the wine, my misery about Rick and Jean-Paul. It gave me what I needed to ask awkward questions.

'How long have you been pregnant?'

'I'm not sure.' She put a hand up each sleeve of the kimono and rubbed her arms.

'When did you miss your, your –' I gestured at her.

'Four weeks ago.'

'How did you get pregnant? You weren't using anything? I'm sorry, but it's important.'

She looked down. 'I forgot to take the pill one day. Usually I take it before I go to bed, but I forgot. I didn't think it would matter.'

I began to say something but Susanne interrupted me. 'You know, I'm not stupid or irresponsible. It's just that –' She pressed her hand against her mouth. 'Sometimes it's difficult to believe there is a connection between a little pill and becoming pregnant. It's like magic, two things that are completely unrelated, that they should have anything to do with each other, it's crazy. Intellectually I can understand it but not truly in my heart.'

I nodded. 'Pregnant women often don't make the connection between their babies and sex. Neither do men. The two are so different, it is like magic.'

We were quiet for a minute.

'When did you miss that pill?' I asked.

'I don't remember.'

I leaned forward. 'Try. Was it around the time of the dream?'

'I don't think so. No, wait a minute, now I remember. Jan was in Brussels at a concert the night I forgot the pill. He came back the next day and that night I had the dream. That's it.'

'And you and Jan – did you – make love that night?'

'Yes.' She looked embarrassed.

I apologized. 'It's just that I only had the dream after Rick and I had sex,' I explained. 'The same as you. But the dream stopped when I began using contraceptives, and for you it stopped once you were pregnant.'

We looked at each other.

'That is very strange,' Susanne said quietly.

'Yes, it is strange.'

Susanne smoothed her kimono over her stomach and sighed.

'You must tell Jan,' I said. 'That is the first thing to do.'

'Yes, I know. And you must tell Rick.'

'It seems he already knows.'

The next day I looked at records in the town hall. Though Jacob's grandfather had done a thorough job on the family tree, I felt the urge to hold the source material in my own hands. I had acquired a taste for it. I sat all afternoon at a table in a meeting room, looking through carefully recorded lists of births and deaths and marriages from the eighteenth and nineteenth centuries. I hadn't realized how established a family the Tourniers were in Moutier: there had been hundreds and hundreds of them.

These brief records told me a lot: the size of families, the age they married – usually in their early twenties – the men's occupations – farmer, teacher, innkeeper, watch engraver. A lot of babies died. I found a Susanne Tournier who between 1751 and 1765 had eight children, and five of them died within a month of birth. She died giving birth to the last. I'd never had a baby or a mother die on me. I'd been lucky.

There were other eye-openers. A lot of illegitimacy and incest were openly recorded. So much for Calvinist principles, I thought, but underneath my cynicism I was shocked that when Judith Tournier gave birth to her father Jean's son in 1796, it was recorded in the official records. Other records baldly stated that children were illegitimate.

It was strange seeing all the first names in use back then, to know that they were still being used. But among all the names – many of them Old Testament names favored by Huguenots like Daniel, Abraham and even a Noah – I noticed there were plenty of Hannahs and Susannes, and later Ruth and Anne and Judith, but not one Isabelle, not one Marie.

When I asked about records earlier than the mid-eighteenth century, the woman in charge told me I would have to look at parish records held at Berne and Porrentruy, advising me to call them first. I wrote down the names and phone numbers and thanked her, smiling to myself: she would have been horrified by my spontaneous trip to the Cévennes and my success despite myself. This was a country where luck wasn't involved; results came from conscientious work and careful planning.

I went to a nearby café to consider my next move. The coffee arrived, presented on a doily, with the spoon, sugar cubes and a square of chocolate arranged on the saucer. I studied the composition: it reminded me of the records I'd just looked at, precisely recorded facts in clear handwriting. Though they were easier to decipher they lacked the charm and haphazardness of the French records. It was like the French themselves: irritating because they weren't accommodating to strangers, but also more interesting as a result. You had to work harder with them, so you got more out of it.

Jacob was at the piano when I got back, playing something slow and sad. I lay down on the sofa and closed my eyes. The music consisted of clear notes, simple lines of melody, like the sound was being picked out with a needle. It reminded me of Jean-Paul.

I was just dozing off when he finished. I opened my eyes and met his gaze across the piano.

'Schubert,' he said.

'Beautiful.'

'Did you find what you were looking for?'

'Not really. Jacob, could you make some phone calls for me?'

'*Bien sûr, ma cousine.* And I've been thinking about what you might want to see. Family things. There's a place where there was a mill that Tourniers owned. There's a restaurant, a pizzeria now, run by Italians, that used to be an inn run by a Tournier in the nineteenth century. And there's a farm about a kilometer outside of Moutier, toward Grand Val. We're not sure it really is a Tournier farm, but family tradition says it is. It's an interesting place anyway because it has an old chimney. Apparently it was one of the first houses in the valley to have one.'

'Don't all houses have chimneys?'

'They do now, but long ago it was unusual. None of the farms in this region had chimneys.'

'What happened to the smoke?'

'There was a false ceiling, and the smoke gathered between that and the roof. The farmers hung their meat up there to dry.'

It sounded appalling. 'Wouldn't the house have been smoky? And dirty?'

Jacob chuckled. 'Probably. There's a farm in Grand Val itself without a chimney. I've been inside and the hearth and the ceiling above the fire are completely black with soot. But the Tournier farm, if it is a Tournier farm, isn't like that. It has a kind of chimney.'

'When was it built?'

'Seventeenth century, I think. Maybe the end of the sixteenth. The chimney, that is. The rest of the farm has been rebuilt several times, but the chimney has remained. In fact, the local historical society bought the farm a few years ago.'

'So it's empty now? Can we go see it?'

'Of course. Tomorrow, if it's a nice day. I don't have any students until late in the afternoon. Now, where are those phone numbers?'

I explained what I wanted, then left him to it while I went for a walk. There wasn't much left to see of Moutier that Jacob hadn't already shown me, but it was nice to walk around and not be stared at. After three days here people even said hello to me first, the way no one ever did in Lisle-sur-Tarn after three months. They seemed to be more polite and less suspicious than the French.

I did find one new thing as I zigzagged through the streets: a plaque announcing that Goethe had slept at the Cheval-Blanc inn on that spot one night in October 1779. He'd mentioned Moutier in a letter, describing the rock formations surrounding it, in particular an impressive gorge just to the east of town. It was a stretch to put up a plaque commemorating one night spent there: that was how little had happened in Moutier.

I turned from the plaque to find Lucien coming toward me, carrying two cans of paint. I had a feeling he'd been watching me and only now picked up the cans and moved.

'*Bonjour*,' I said. He stopped and set down the cans.

'*Bonjour*,' he replied.

'*Ça va?*'

'*Oui, ça va.*'

We stood awkwardly. I found it hard to look straight at him because he was looking so hard at me, searching my eyes for something. His attention was the last thing I needed right now. That was probably why he was drawn to me. He was certainly fascinated by my psoriasis. Even now he kept glancing at it.

'Lucien, it's psoriasis,' I snapped, secretly pleased to be able to embarrass him. 'I told you that the other day. Why do you keep looking at it?'

'I'm sorry.' He looked away. 'It's just that – I get it myself sometimes. In the same place on my arms. I always thought it was an allergic reaction to paint.'

'Oh, I'm sorry!' Now I felt guilty, but still irritated with him, which made me feel even more guilty. A vicious circle.

'Why haven't you seen a doctor?' I asked more gently. 'He'd tell you what it is and give you something to put on it. There's a cream – I left it at home or I'd use it now.'

'I don't like doctors,' Lucien explained. 'They make me feel – maladjusted.'

I laughed. 'I know what you mean. And here – in France, I mean – they prescribe so many things. Too many things.'

'Why do you get it? The psoriasis?'

'Stress, they say. But the cream isn't bad. You could just ask the doctor to –'

'Ella, will you have a drink with me one night?'

I paused. I should nip this in the bud: I wasn't interested and it was inappropriate, particularly now. But I'd always been bad at saying no. I wouldn't be able to bear the look on his face.

'OK,' I said finally. 'In a couple days, all right? But Lucien –'

He looked so happy that I couldn't go on. 'It's nothing. Some night this week, then.'

When I returned Jacob was playing again. He stopped and picked up a scrap of paper. 'Bad news, I'm afraid,' he said. 'The records at Berne go back only to 1750. At Porrentruy the librarian told me the parish records for the sixteenth and early seventeenth centuries were lost in a fire. There are some military lists you could look at, though. That is where my grandfather got his information, I think.'

'Probably your grandfather found everything there was to find. But thanks for calling for me.' Military lists were no use – it was the women I was interested in. I didn't tell him that.

'Jacob, have you heard of a painter named Nicolas Tournier?' I said instead.

He shook his head. I went to my room and got the postcard I'd brought with me.

'See, he came from Montbéliard,' I explained, handing him the card. 'I just thought he could be an ancestor. A part of the family that moved to Montbéliard, maybe.'

Jacob looked at the painting and shook his head. 'I've never heard of there being a painter in the family. Tourniers tended to have practical occupations. Except for me!' He laughed, then turned serious. 'Ah, Ella, Rick called while you were out.'

'Oh.'

He looked embarrassed. 'He asked me to tell you he loves you.'

'Oh. Thank you.' I looked down.

'You know you can stay with us as long as you want. As long as you need to.'

'Yes. Thanks. We have – there are some problems. You know.'

He said nothing, just gazed at me, and for a moment I was reminded of the couple on the train. Jacob was Swiss, after all.

'Anyway, I'm sure everything will be fine soon.'

He nodded. 'Until then you stay with your family.'

'Yes.'

Once I'd said something to Jacob about Rick and me I no longer felt like I had to justify being there. It rained the next day so we put off our trip to the farm, and I felt comfortable sitting around all day reading and listening to Susanne and Jacob play. That night we ate at the pizzeria that had once been a Tournier inn but now felt decidedly Italian.

The next morning we all went to see the farm. Susanne had never been to it, though she'd lived in Moutier most of her life. At the east edge of town we took a path clearly marked with a yellow sign proclaiming it a '*Pédestre tourisme*' and telling us it would take forty-five minutes to walk to Grand Val. Only in Switzerland do they say how long a walk should take rather than how far it is. To our left was the beginning of the limestone gorge Goethe had written about: a dramatic wall of yellow-grey rock extending from mountains on either side, crumbled in the center to allow the Birse to pass through. It was impressive with the sun shining on it; it reminded me of a cathedral.

The valley we followed was gentler, with a nameless stream and a railroad track along the bottom, fields on the lower slopes, then pines and a sudden steep incline into rocks high above us. Horses and cows grazed in the fields; farms appeared at regular intervals. It was all neat, in clean lines and bright, sharp light.

The men walked briskly together while Susanne and I followed. She was wearing a blue-green sleeveless tunic and loose white pants that billowed around her slim legs. She looked pale and tired, her cheerfulness tacked on. I knew from the way she kept a certain distance from Jan and glanced at me guiltily that she hadn't told him yet.

We lagged further and further behind the men, as if we were about to say something private to each other. I shivered, though it was a warm, sunny day, and wrapped Jean-Paul's blue shirt around me. It smelled of smoke and of him.

Jacob and Jan stopped where the path forked, and as we reached them Jacob pointed to a house a little way above us, near the point where the fields stopped and the trees began to climb into the mountains. 'That's the farm,' he said.

I don't want to go, I thought. Why is that? I glanced at Susanne. She was looking at me and I knew she was thinking the same thing. The men started up the hill, while she and I stood looking at their backs.

'C'mon,' I gestured to Susanne, and turned to follow the men. She came slowly behind me.

The farm was a long low structure, the left side a stone house, the right a wooden barn. The two sides were held under one long shallow roof and shared a gaping entrance that led to a dim porch-like area Jacob said was called a *devant-huis*. A kind of porch, it was strewn with straw and bits of lumber and old buckets. I'd thought that the historical society would have done something to preserve it, but the place was slowly falling apart: the shutters were askew, the windows broken, and moss was growing on the roof.

Jacob and Jan stood admiring the farm, while Susanne and I looked at our feet. 'See the chimney?' Jacob pointed to a strange lumpy formation poking up from the roof – nothing like the neat line of stone up one wall that I'd expected. 'It's made of limestone, you see,' Jacob explained. 'Soft stone, so they used a kind of cement to shape and harden it. Most of the chimney is inside rather than up the outside wall. Let's go in and you'll see the rest.'

'Is it open?' I asked reluctantly, wanting there to be a lock on the door, a sign saying '*Propriété privée*'.

'Oh, yes, I've been in before. I know where the key is hidden.'

Damn, I thought. I couldn't explain why I didn't want to go

inside; after all, we had come here for my sake. I could feel Susanne looking at me helplessly, as if I were the one who had to stop everything. It was like we were being dragged inside by a cool male logic we couldn't fight. I held out my hand to her. 'Come,' I said. She put her hand in mine. It was ice-cold.

'Your hand is cold,' she said.

'Yours too.' We smiled grimly at each other. I felt like we were two little girls in a fairytale as we entered the house together.

It was dim inside, with only the light from the door and a couple of narrow windows to see by. As my eyes adjusted I was able to make out more lumber and some broken chairs lying on the packed dirt floor. Just inside the door was a blackened hearth, jutting lengthwise into the room rather than laid parallel to the wall. At each corner of the hearth stood a square stone pillar about seven feet high, supporting arches of stone. Leading up from the arches was the same lumpy construction as outside, an ugly but serviceable pyramid to channel out the smoke.

I let go of Susanne's hand and stepped onto the hearth so I could look up the chimney. It was black above me; even when I stood on tiptoe, holding onto a pillar and craning my neck, I couldn't see an opening. 'Must be blocked,' I murmured. I felt dizzy suddenly, lost my balance and fell hard into the dirt.

Jacob was next to me in a second, giving me a hand up and brushing me off. 'Are you all right?' he asked, concern in his voice.

'Yes,' I replied shakily. 'I — I lost my balance, I think. Maybe the stone isn't even.'

I looked around for Susanne; she was gone. 'Where's —' I started to say before a sharp pain jabbed at my stomach, propelling me past Jacob and outside.

Susanne was doubled over in the yard, arms crossed over her abdomen. Jan stood next to her, speechless and staring. As I put my arm around her shoulder she gasped and a bright red flower appeared on the inner thighs of her pants, spreading rapidly down her leg.

For a second I panicked. Holy Mother, I thought, what do I do? Then I had a sensation I hadn't felt in months: my brain switched over to automatic, a familiar place where I knew exactly who I was and what I had to do.

I put both arms around her and said softly, 'Susanne, you must lie down.' She nodded, bent her knees and slumped forward in my arms. I lowered her carefully onto her side, then glanced up at Jan, still frozen in place. 'Jan, give me your jacket,' I commanded. He stared at me until I repeated myself loudly. He handed me his tan cotton jacket, the kind I associated with old men playing shuffleboard. I stuffed it under Susanne's head, then took off Jean-Paul's shirt and draped it over her like a blanket, covering her bloody groin. A red patch began to seep outward on the shirt's back. For a second I was mesmerized by the two colors, made the more beautiful by contrasting with each other.

I shook my head, squeezed Susanne's hand and leaned toward her. 'Don't worry, you're all right. Everything will be OK.'

'Ella, what is happening?' Jacob was towering over us, his long face screwed up with worry. I glanced at Jan, still paralyzed, and made a quick decision. 'Susanne has had a —'

What a time for my French to fail me; Madame Sentier had never prepared me for using words like miscarriage. 'Susanne, you must tell them. I don't know the word in French. Can you do that?'

She looked at me, eyes full of tears. 'All you have to do is say it. That's all. I'll do the rest.'

'*Une fausse couche,*' she murmured. The two men stared at her, bewildered.

'Now,' I said evenly. 'Jan, do you see that house down there?' I pointed to the nearest farm, a quarter of a mile down the hill. Jan didn't respond until I spoke his name again, sharply this time. Then he nodded.

'Good. Now, run there, quickly, and use their telephone to call the hospital. Can you do that?'

Finally he snapped out of it. 'Yes, Ella, I will hurry to that farm for to telephone the hospital,' he said.

'Good. And ask the people at the farm if they can help us with their car, in case an ambulance can't come. Now go!' The last word was like a whip cracking. Jan crouched down, touched the ground with one hand and took off like he was in a playground race. I grimaced. Susanne has to get rid of this guy, I thought.

Jacob had knelt next to Susanne and placed his hand on her hair. 'Will she be all right?' he asked, trying to muffle his desperation.

I addressed my answer to Susanne. 'Of course you'll be all right. It probably hurts a little now, yes?'

Susanne nodded.

'That will stop soon. Jan has gone to call an ambulance to come and get you.'

'Ella, this is my fault,' she whispered.

'No. It's not your fault. Of course it's not your fault.'

'But I didn't want it and maybe if I had this wouldn't have happened.'

'Susanne, it's not your fault. Women have miscarriages all the time. You didn't do anything wrong. You had no control over this.'

She looked unconvinced. Jacob was staring at the two of us like we were speaking in Swahili.

'I *promise* you. It's not your fault. Believe me. OK?'

Finally she nodded.

'Now, I need to examine you. Will you let me look at you?'

Susanne held my hand tighter and tears began to roll down the side of her face. 'Yes, it hurts, I know, and you don't want me to look, but I have to, to make sure you're all right. I won't hurt you. You know I won't hurt you.'

Her eyes darted to Jacob, then back to me; I understood. 'Jacob, take Susanne's hand,' I ordered, transferring her thin hand into his. 'Help her onto her back and sit here next to her.' I positioned him so he was facing her and couldn't see what I was doing.

'Now, talk to her.' Jacob looked at me helplessly. I thought for a moment. 'Do you remember you told me you have one good student of piano? Who plays Bach? What will he play for the next concert? And why? Tell Susanne about him.'

For a second Jacob looked lost; then his face relaxed. He turned to Susanne and began to speak. After a moment she relaxed as well. Trying to move her as little as possible, I managed to wriggle her pants and underwear down her legs far enough to get a look, mopping up the blood with Jean-Paul's shirt. Then I pulled her pants up again, leaving them unzipped. Jacob stopped talking. They both looked at me.

'You've lost some blood, but the bleeding has stopped now. You'll be fine.'

'I'm thirsty,' Susanne said softly.

'I'll look for some water.' I stood up, pleased to see they were both calm. I circled the farmhouse, looking for an outdoor spigot. There wasn't one; I would have to go back inside.

I slipped into the *devant-huis* and stood in the doorway of the house. Sunlight was falling in a thin beam across the hearth stone. In the shaft of light I could see thick dust, kicked up by our visit. I looked around for a source of water. It was very quiet; I couldn't hear anything, no comforting sounds like Jacob's voice or the wind in the pines above us or cowbells or a distant train. Just silence and the sheet of light on the slab before me. It was a huge piece of stone; it must have taken several men to set it in place. I looked at it more closely. Even discolored by soot it was clearly not local stone. It looked foreign.

In a corner opposite the door there was an old sink with a tap. I doubted it worked but for Susanne's sake I would have to try it. I walked around the hearth, heart racing, hands clammy. When I reached the sink I wrestled with the tap for a minute before I managed to turn it. For a moment nothing happened; then there was a sputter and the tap began to shake violently. I stepped back. A great spurt of dark liquid suddenly gushed out into the sink and I jumped, cracking the back of my head against the corner of one of the pillars holding up the chimney. I cried out sharply and whirled around, stars shooting before my eyes. I sank to my knees next to the hearth and pulled my head down. The back of my head was damp and sticky. I took several deep breaths. When the stars disappeared I lifted my head and lowered my arms. Drops of blood left the broken psoriasis patches in the creases of my elbows and rolled down my arms to meet the blood on my hands.

I stared at the tracks of blood. 'This is the place, isn't it?' I said aloud. '*Je suis arrivée chez moi, n'est-ce pas?*'

Behind me the water stopped.

9. The Chimney

Isabelle stood silent in the *devant-huis*. She could hear the horse shifting in the barn; from the house came the sounds of digging.

— Marie? she called softly, uncertain if she should say the name aloud, who might hear it. The horse whinnied at the sound of her voice, then stopped moving. The digging continued. Isabelle hesitated, then pushed the door open.

Etienne was working on a long hole near the slab of granite, extending from its base out into the room. It was not along the far wall where he had earlier decided the hearth would go, but near the door. The floor was packed hard and he was having to slice violently at it with his spade to loosen the dirt.

When the light from the door fell on him he glanced up, saying: — Is she — then stopping himself when he recognized Isabelle. He straightened up.

— What are you doing here?

— Where is Marie?

— You should be ashamed, La Rousse. You should be on your knees praying for God's mercy.

— Why are you digging on a Holy Day?

He ignored the question.

— Your daughter has run off, he said loudly. Petit Jean has gone to look for her in the woods. I thought you were he, coming back to say she is safe. Aren't you concerned about your own shameful daughter, La Rousse? You should be looking for her too.

— Marie is *all* I'm concerned about. Where did she go?

— Behind the house, up the mountain. Etienne turned back to the hole and began to dig again. Isabelle watched him.

— Why are you digging there rather than against the far wall, where you said the hearth was to go?

206

He straightened up again and raised the spade above his head. Isabelle jumped back quickly and Etienne laughed.

– Don't ask stupid questions. Go and find your daughter.

Isabelle backed out of the room and pulled the door closed. She remained in the *devant-huis* for a moment. Etienne had not begun digging again and it was very quiet, a silence full of secrets.

I am not alone with Etienne, she thought. Marie is here, somewhere nearby.

– Marie! she began to call. Marie! Marie! She went out into the yard, still calling. Marie did not appear – only Hannah, laboring up the path. Isabelle had not waited for her outside Chalières, but had left her with Jacob and run along the path toward the farm until she had been sure Hannah could not catch up. Now when she saw Isabelle the old woman stopped, leaning on her stick and breathing hard. Then she lowered her head and hurried past her daughter-in-law to the house, banging the door shut behind her.

It wasn't easy getting Lucien drunk. He gazed at me across the table and drank his beer so slowly that I had to let my gulps trickle back into my glass to wait for him to catch up. We were the only customers in a bar in the center of town. American country and western played over the sound system; the waitress read a newspaper behind the counter. Moutier on a rainy Thursday in early July was as dead as a stop sign.

I had a flashlight in my bag, but I was relying on Lucien to have tools in case we needed them. He didn't know it yet, though; he sat tracing patterns in the wet glass rings left on the table, looking uncomfortable. I had a long way to go to get him to do what I wanted. I'd have to resort to desperate measures.

I caught the waitress's eye. When she came over I ordered two whiskeys. Lucien stared at me with big hazel eyes. I shrugged. 'In America we always have whiskey with beer,' I lied airily. He nodded and I thought of Jean-Paul, who would never have let me get away with such a ridiculous statement. I missed his prickly, sarcastic edge; he was like a knife, cutting through the haze of uncertainty, saying what needed to be said.

When the waitress brought two shots, I insisted that Lucien drink his in one go rather than sip it delicately. When he finished it I ordered two more. He hesitated, but after the second he visibly relaxed and began to tell me about a house he'd built recently. I let him run on, though he used a lot of technical words I didn't understand. 'It's halfway up the mountain, on a slope – always harder to build,' he explained. 'And then there were problems with the concrete for *l'abri nucléaire*. We had to remix it twice.'

'*L'abri nucléaire?*' I repeated, not sure of the French.

'*Oui.*' He waited while I looked it up in the dictionary I kept in my bag.

'A *nuclear shelter*? You built a nuclear shelter in a house?'

'Of course. It's required. It's the law in Switzerland that every new house has a shelter.'

I shook my head as if to clear it. Lucien misunderstood my gesture. 'But it's true, every new house has a nuclear shelter,' he repeated more fervently. 'And every man does his national service, did you know that? When he is eighteen a man serves for seventeen weeks in the army. And after that, for three weeks every year in the reserves.'

'Why is Switzerland so military if it's a neutral country? You know, like during World War II?'

He smiled grimly. 'So that we *can* remain neutral. A country cannot be neutral unless it has a strong army.'

I came from a country with a huge military budget and no sense of neutrality at all; it seemed to me that the two had little to do with each other. But I wasn't here to talk politics; we were getting further and further away from my intended topic. I had to find a way to get onto the subject of chimneys.

'So what's this nuclear shelter made of?' I asked awkwardly.

'Concrete and lead. You know, the walls are a meter thick.'

'Really?'

Lucien began to explain in detail how a shelter was constructed. I closed my eyes. What a nerd, I thought. Why on earth am I getting him to help me?

There was no one else. Jacob was too shaken by Susanne's

miscarriage the day before to go back to the farm and Jan wasn't a rule-breaker. Another wimp, I thought grimly. What is it with these men? Again I wished Jean-Paul were here: he would argue with me about the usefulness of what I wanted to do, he would question my sanity, but he would back me if he knew it was important to me. I wondered how he was. That night seemed so long ago now. One week.

He wasn't here; I had to rely on the man at hand. I opened my eyes and interrupted Lucien's soliloquy. '*Ecoute*, I want you to help me,' I said firmly, deliberately switching to the familiar form in French. Up until now I'd persisted in remaining formal with him.

Lucien stopped, looking surprised and suspicious.

'Do you know the farm near Grand Val with the old chimney?'

He nodded.

'We went to see it yesterday. It used to be my ancestors' farm.'

'Really?'

'Yes. There's something I need to get from it.'

'What?'

'I'm not sure,' I replied, then added quickly, 'but I know where it is.'

'How can you know where it is when you don't know what it is?'

'I don't know.'

Lucien paused, peering into his empty shot glass. 'What do you want me to do?' he asked after a moment.

'Come with me to the farm, to look around. Do you have any tools?'

He nodded. 'In my truck.'

'Good. We might need them.' He looked alarmed and I added, 'Don't worry, we don't have to break in or anything – there's a key to the lock on the door. I just want to look around. Will you help me?'

'You mean now? Right now?'

'Yes. I don't want anyone to know I'm going there, so it has to be at night.'

'Why don't you want anyone to know?'

I shrugged. 'I don't want people to ask questions. To talk.'

There was a long silence. I braced myself for his no.

'OK.'

When I smiled, Lucien returned it hesitantly. 'You know, Ella,' he said, 'that's the first time you've smiled all evening.'

It was beginning to rain when Isabelle entered the woods. The first drops filtered through the new leaves on the beech trees, shaking them gently and filling the air with a soft, rustling sound. A musky smell rose from the dampening mix of dead leaves and pine needles.

She began to climb the slope behind the house, calling Marie's name occasionally, but more often standing still and listening to the sounds behind the rain: crows cawing, the wind in the pines further up the mountain, horse hooves on the path toward Moutier. She didn't think Marie would go far – she didn't like being alone or away from home. But she had never been shamed before either, in front of so many people.

It comes with your new hair, Isabelle thought, and with being my daughter. Even here. Yet I have no magic to protect you with, nothing to keep you safe from the cold and the dark.

She headed further up, reaching a ridge of rock halfway up the mountain and turning west along it. She knew she was being drawn to a particular place. She entered the little clearing where she and Jacob had kept the goat all summer. She had not been back since Jacob traded the goat for the cloth. Even now there were signs that an animal had been kept here: the remains of a shelter of branches, a ragged bed of straw and pine needles, droppings dried into hard pellets.

I thought I was so clever with my secrets, Isabelle brooded somberly, looking at the goat's bed. That no one would ever know. It seemed a long time ago to her, a winter away.

Once she had visited one secret place she knew she would go to the other. She did not try to fight the impulse, even knowing it was unlikely Marie would be there. When the ridge descended toward the gorge she threaded her way through the rocks to the spot where Pascale had knelt and prayed. Here there was no trace of the secret: the blood had been absorbed in the ground long ago.

– Where are you, *chérie*? she said softly.

When the wolf stepped from behind the rock, Isabelle jumped and screamed, but did not run. They faced each other, the flames of the wolf's eyes alert and penetrating. It took a step toward Isabelle and stopped. Isabelle stepped backwards. The wolf stepped forward again and Isabelle found herself moving backwards down through the rocks. Fearful of falling, she turned around but kept glancing over her shoulder as she walked to make sure the wolf came no closer. It kept the same distance from her, slowing down or stopping when she did, speeding up when she did.

It is driving me like a sheep, Isabelle thought, forcing me to go where it wants. She tested this by veering to one side. The wolf jumped to that side and ran close to her until she turned forward again.

They came out from the rocks to the path by the edge of the trees that led from Moutier to Grand Val, the way back to the farm. Trotting toward her from the Moutier direction was the Tourniers' horse, carrying Petit Jean and Gaspard. It was the horse she had heard moving in the barn and, she now understood, galloping along the path earlier.

Isabelle turned to look at the wolf. It was gone.

Lucien had an old Citroën truck stuffed with tools – exactly what I'd hoped. It rattled and coughed down the main street so loudly I was sure the entire population had come to their windows to watch our departure. So much for discretion.

It had just begun to rain, a fine mist that slicked the streets and made me pull my jacket tight around me. Lucien switched on the windshield wipers; they scraped against the windshield, setting my nerves on edge. He drove cautiously through town, not that he needed to: at nine-thirty not a soul was on the streets. By the train station, the only place showing any signs of life, he turned onto the road toward Grand Val.

We were silent during the drive. I was grateful that he didn't ask a lot of questions the way I would have if I were in his position: I didn't have any answers for him.

We turned into a small road which dipped under the railroad tracks and headed up a hill. At a cluster of houses Lucien swung onto a dirt road I recognized from our walk that morning. He drove about 300 yards, stopped and switched the engine off. The windshield wipers came to a blessed halt, the truck coughed several times, then with a long wheeze went dead.

'It's over there.' Lucien pointed to our left. After a moment I could make out the outline of the farm fifty yards away. I shivered; it was going to be hard to get out of the truck and walk up there.

'Ella, can I ask you something?'

'Yes,' I replied reluctantly. I didn't want to tell him everything, but I knew I couldn't expect him to help me blindly.

He surprised me. 'You are married.' It was more a statement than a question, but I confirmed it with a nod.

'It was your husband who called the other night, during the fondue.'

'Yes.'

'I was married too,' he said.

'*Vraiment?*' I sounded more surprised than I'd intended. It was like his telling me he suffered from psoriasis: it made me feel guilty that I'd assumed he wouldn't have the kind of life I did, with stress and romance.

'Do you have children?' I asked, trying to give him back his life.

'A daughter. Christine. She lives with her mother in Basle.'

'Not too far from here.'

'No. I see her every other weekend. And you, do you have children?'

'No.' My elbows and ankles started to itch, the psoriasis demanding attention.

'Not yet.'

'No, not yet.'

'The day I found out my wife was pregnant,' Lucien said slowly,

'I had been planning to tell her I thought we should separate. We'd been married two years, and I knew things weren't going well. For me, anyway. We sat down to tell each other our big news, our thoughts. She went first. After she told me I couldn't tell her what I'd been thinking.'

'So you stayed together.'

'Until Christine was a year old, yes. It was like hell, though.'

I don't know how long it had been growing in me, but I realized suddenly that I felt nauseous, my stomach swimming in concrete. I swallowed and took a deep breath.

'When I heard you on the phone with your husband it reminded me of phone calls I used to have with my wife.'

'But I hardly said anything to him!'

'It was your tone.'

'Oh.' I stared out at the dark, embarrassed.

'I'm not sure my husband is the right man to have children with,' I said then. 'I've never been sure.' Saying it aloud, to Lucien of all people, felt like breaking a window. The very sound of the words shocked me.

'It is better that you know now,' Lucien said, 'so that if you can help it you don't bring a child into a world without love.'

I swallowed and nodded. We sat listening to the rain; I concentrated on calming my stomach.

'Do you want to steal something from there?' he asked suddenly, nodding toward the farm.

I thought about it. 'No. I just want to find something. Something that is mine.'

'What? You left something there yesterday? Is that it?'

'Yes. The story of my family.' I sat up straight. 'You'll still help me?' I asked briskly.

'Of course. I said I would help you, so I'm going to help you.' Lucien met my eyes with a steady gaze.

He's not so bad, I thought.

It seemed that Petit Jean was not going to stop. Isabelle stepped into the middle of the path, forcing him to pull up the horse. She reached up and grasped the bridle. The horse pressed its muzzle into her shoulder and snorted.

Neither Petit Jean nor Gaspard would look her in the eye, though Gaspard removed his black hat and nodded at her. Petit Jean sat tensely, eyes fixed ahead, waiting impatiently to be released.

— Where are you going? she asked.

— Back to the farm. Petit Jean swallowed.

— Why? Have you found Marie? Is she safe?

He did not reply. Gaspard cleared his throat, keeping his blind eye toward her.

— I'm sorry, Isabelle, he mumbled. You know I would have nothing to do with this but because of Pascale. If she had not made the dress I wouldn't be obliged to help now. But — he shrugged and put his hat back on. I'm sorry.

Petit Jean hissed between his teeth and pulled savagely at the reins. Isabelle lost her grip on the bridle.

— Help with what? she shouted as Petit Jean kicked the horse into a flying start. Help with what?

As they galloped away Gaspard's hat fell off and rolled into a puddle. Isabelle watched them disappear down the path, then leaned over and picked up the hat, shaking it free of mud and water. She held it loosely in her fingers as she followed the path home.

It was raining harder. We ducked into the *devant-huis*, my flashlight picking out the padlock on the door. Lucien gave it a brief tug. 'This was put here to keep *les drogués* out,' he announced.

'There are, um, *druggies* in Moutier?'

'Of course. There are druggies everywhere in Switzerland. You don't know this country very well, do you?'

'That's for sure,' I muttered in English. 'Jesus. So much for appearances.'

'How did you get in yesterday?'

'Jacob knew where the key is hidden.' I looked around. 'I didn't notice where. It shouldn't be hard to find, though.'

We used the flashlight to check all the obvious places in the *devant-huis*.

'Maybe Jacob accidentally took it with him,' I suggested. 'We were all upset yesterday. It would have been an easy thing to do.' I felt vaguely relieved that I wouldn't have to go through with this after all.

Lucien looked at the tiny windows on either side of the door; their broken panes of glass could easily be pushed in, but neither of us would fit through them. The windows at the front of the house were also small and high up. He took the flashlight from me. 'I will look for a bigger window around the back,' he said. 'You can wait here alone?'

I forced myself to nod. He ducked out of the *devant-huis*, disappearing around the corner. I leaned against the doorway, hugging myself to keep from shivering, and listened. At first I could hear only the rain; after a while other sounds began to emerge – traffic on the main road below us, a train whistle – and I felt a little comforted by the normal world so close.

I heard what sounded like a shriek from inside the house and jumped. 'It's only Lucien,' I told myself, but stepped out into the yard anyway, rain and all. When the light flashed through the window next to the door and the face appeared I stifled a scream.

Lucien beckoned me to the window and handed me the flashlight through the jagged pane. 'I'll meet you at the window at the back.' He disappeared before I could ask him if he was all right.

I headed around the house as Lucien had a few minutes before. It was hard turning the corner: the side and back of the building were private territory, the part hidden from public view. Circling the house I was stepping into another, unknown world.

It was muddy at the back of the house; I had to pick my way between puddles to find drier, firmer footing. When I saw the open window and Lucien's dark outline just inside I stepped too quickly and slid to my knees.

He leaned out. 'Are you all right?' he asked.

I staggered to my feet, the flashlight beam swinging wildly. The knees of my pants had soaked up two circles of mud. 'Yes. Fine,'

I muttered, flapping the pants legs to shake off whatever mud I could. I handed him the flashlight, which he kept trained on the window sill while I scrambled in.

It was cold inside – colder, it seemed, than outside. I pushed the wet hair out of my eyes and looked around. We were in a tiny room at the back of the house, a bedroom or storage room, empty except for a pile of lumber and a couple of broken chairs. It smelled musty and damp, and when Lucien shone the flashlight up into the ceiling corners we could see tatters of cobwebs fluttering in the draft from the open window. He pushed it closed; the frame made the shrieking sound I had heard a few minutes before. I almost asked him to open it again, to leave an escape route free, but stopped myself. There's nothing to escape from, I told myself firmly, my stomach somersaulting.

He led the way to the main room, stopped by the hearth and shone the flashlight on the chimney. We looked at it for a long time in silence.

'It's impressive, isn't it?' I said.

'Yes. I have lived in Moutier all my life and heard about this chimney, but I have never seen it.'

'When I saw it yesterday I was surprised that it is so ugly.'

'Yes. Like those *ruches* I saw on television. From South America.'

'*Ruches*? What's a *ruche*?'

'A house of bees. You know, where they make honey.'

'Oh, a hive. Yes, I know what you mean.' Somewhere, probably in a *National Geographic*, I had seen the tall, lumpy beehives he was referring to, encased in a greyish cement that hid a ridged form, like a cocoon before it hatched, graceless but functional. An image of one of the ruined farms in the Cévennes flashed through my head: the perfectly placed granite, the elegant line of the chimney. No, this was nothing like that; this was made by people desperate for a chimney at all, where anything would do.

'It's strange, you know,' he said, staring at the hearth and chimney. 'Look at its position in relation to the rest of the room. It's not where you would expect a hearth to be. It does not set the room up the way it should. It makes it – awkward. Uncomfortable.'

He was right. 'It's too close to the door,' I said.

'Much too close. You almost walk into it when you come in. That is very inefficient – so much heat would escape whenever the door is opened. And the draft from the door would make the fire burn fast and it would be hard to control. Dangerous, maybe. You would expect it to be against the far wall, there.' He pointed. 'It's strange that people have lived here for hundreds of years and put up with it in that position all that time.'

Rick, I thought suddenly. Rick would be able to explain this. This is his territory, these interior spaces.

'What do you want to do now?' Lucien sounded baffled. What had seemed straightforward in my imagination was infinitely more absurd in reality, in the dark and the damp.

I took the flashlight from him and began going over the chimney methodically, the four square pillars at the corners of the hearth, the four arches between the pillars that held up the chimney.

Lucien tried again. 'What do you want to find?'

I shrugged. 'Something – old,' I replied, standing on the hearth stone and gazing up the tapering tunnel. I could see remains of birds' nests on ledges formed by jutting rocks. 'Maybe something – blue.'

'Something blue?'

'Yes.' I stepped off the stone. 'Now, Lucien, you build things. If you were going to hide something in a chimney, where would you hide it?'

'A blue thing?'

I didn't answer; I just stared at him. He looked at the chimney. 'Well,' he said after a moment, 'most parts of the chimney would get too hot and things would burn up. Maybe further up the chimney. Or –' He knelt down and placed his hand on the hearth stone. He rubbed his hand over it and nodded. 'Granite. I don't know where they got this stone; it isn't local.'

'Granite,' I repeated. 'Like in the Cévennes.'

'Where?'

'It's a part of France, in the south. But why granite?'

'Well, it's harder than limestone. It spreads heat more evenly.

But this slab is very thick, so the bottom of it would not get so hot. You could hide something under it, I suppose.'

'Yes.' I nodded, rubbing the bump on my forehead. It made sense. 'Let's lift the granite.'

'It's much too heavy. We would need four men to lift it!'

'Four men,' I repeated. Rick, Jean-Paul, Jacob and Lucien. And one woman. I looked around. 'Do you have a, a – in English it's block and tackle.' He looked blank, so I got paper and pen from my bag and sketched a crude pulley system.

'Ah, *un palan!*' he cried. 'Yes, I have one. Here, in my truck. But even so, we would still need more men to pull it.'

I thought for a moment. 'What about your truck?' I asked. 'We could attach *le palan* here, then attach it to the truck and use that force to pull up the stone.'

He looked surprised, as if he had never considered his truck for more noble purposes than transportation. He was silent for a long time, looking at the position of everything, measuring with his eyes. I listened to the dripping outside.

'Yes,' he said finally. 'Maybe we can do that.'

'We *will* do it.'

When she got to the farm Isabelle quietly tried the door of the house. It was bolted from the inside. She could hear Etienne and Gaspard grunting and straining, then stopping and arguing. She did not call out to them. Instead she went into the barn, where Petit Jean was rubbing down the horse. He barely reached the horse's shoulder but he handled the animal confidently. He glanced at Isabelle, then continued rubbing. She saw him swallow again.

Like the man on the road when we were leaving the Cévennes, she thought, remembering the man with the pronounced Adam's apple, the torches, Marie's brave words.

– Papa told us to stay here so we wouldn't get in the way, Petit Jean announced.

– We? Is Marie here?

Her son jerked his head toward a pile of straw in the darkest corner of the barn. Isabelle hurried over.

– Marie, she said quietly, kneeling at the edge of the pile.

It was Jacob, curled in a ball and wedged into the corner. His eyes were open wide but he didn't seem to see her.

– Jacob! What is it? Have you found Marie?

Draped over his knees was the black dress Marie had worn earlier over the blue one. Isabelle crawled over and snatched it from him. It was sodden, heavy with water.

– Where did this come from? she demanded, examining it. It had been torn at the neck. The pockets were full of stones from the Birse.

– Where did you find it?

He looked dully at the stones and said nothing. She gripped his shoulders and began to shake him.

– Where did you find it? she cried. Where?

– He found it here, she heard from behind her. She looked over at Petit Jean.

– Here? she repeated. Where?

Petit Jean gestured around him. In the barn. She must have taken it off before she ran off into the woods. She wanted to show off her new dress to the devil in the woods, eh, Jacob?

Jacob flinched beneath Isabelle's hands. She let go of him.

Lucien backed the truck up as close to the house as possible. He ran the rope from a small metal loop under the truck's rear fender through the *devant-huis* and the little window next to the door – all the broken glass knocked out so it wouldn't cut the rope – and into the house. He attached the block to a structural beam running across the room and ran the rope from the little window up through the block's pulley and down to the hearth stone, tying the end to one point of a triangular metal frame. Clamps were attached at the other two points.

Then we dug around one end of the stone until we'd exposed the base. It took a long time because the floor was packed hard. I hacked at it with a shovel, stopping now and then to wipe the sweat out of my eyes.

Lucien positioned the metal frame over the end of the stone and fixed the clamps around it, wedging their teeth into the dirt under the bottom. Finally we went around the stone with the shovel and a crowbar, loosening the dirt around it.

When everything was ready we argued about who would stay inside and keep the block and tackle in place and who would go in the truck.

'You see, this is not set up well,' Lucien said, looking anxiously at the rope. 'The angle is not good. The rope will rub against the window, there, and against the chimney arch, there.' He flashed light on these points of friction. 'The rope could fray and break. And the force is not even on both clamps because we could not hang the block directly over the stone, but at the side, on the beam. I have tried to compensate for it but the pull on each side is still different and the clamps could easily slip. And the beam. It may not be strong enough to carry the weight of the stone. It is best that I watch it.'

'No.'

'Ella –'

'I will stay here. I will watch the rope and the clamp, and *le palan*.'

The tone of my voice made him back down. He moved to the little window and looked out. 'OK,' he said quietly. 'You stand here with the flashlight. If the rope begins to fray, or the clamps slip, or there is any reason that I should stop the truck, point the light on the mirror there.' He aimed the flashlight at the side mirror on the left of the truck. It flashed back at us. 'When the stone is lifted far enough,' he continued, 'flash the light in the mirror also, so I will know to stop.'

I nodded and took the flashlight from him, then lit the way to the back window for him, bracing myself for the screech when he forced the window up. He glanced at me before disappearing. I smiled weakly; he didn't smile back. He looked worried.

I took up my position by the little window, tense with nerves. At least my queasiness had disappeared with all the activity and I felt I was in the right place, as absurd as the situation was. I was glad I was there with Lucien: I didn't know him well enough to have to explain myself the way I would with Rick or Jean-Paul, and he was interested enough in the mechanics of the task not to ask too many questions about *why* we were doing it.

It had stopped raining, though there were still dripping sounds everywhere. The truck sputtered to a start and sat shaking while Lucien switched the headlights on and revved the engine. He stuck his head out of the window and I waved. Slowly, slowly the truck inched forward. The rope came to life, the slack taken up, the line quivering. The block hanging from the beam swung out toward me. There was a cracking sound as the beam took the strain of the pull from the truck; I jumped back, terrified that the house would fall down around me.

The beam held. I trained the flashlight back and forth along the rope, to the block, down to the clamps around the stone, back along the rope, down through the window and out to the truck. There was a lot to keep an eye on. I concentrated, my body tight as a spring.

I'd let the flashlight fall for several seconds on one of the clamps when it began to slide from the stone. I quickly flashed the light through the window to the mirror. Lucien stopped the truck just as the clamp came free from the stone and the metal frame hurtled up toward the block, knocking into the chimney before smashing into the beam. I shrieked and pressed my back against the door. The frame clattered to the floor. I was rubbing my face with my hands when Lucien poked his head through the little window.

'Are you all right?' he asked.

'Yes. It was just one of the clamps, it slipped from the stone. I'll put it back on.'

'Are you sure?'

'Of course,' I replied. Taking a deep breath, I walked over to the frame.

'Let me see it,' Lucien said. I brought it to him to examine. Luckily the metal wasn't damaged. He watched from the window while I placed it around the stone and tightened the clamps as I'd seen him do. When I finished I shone the light on it and Lucien nodded.

'Good. You know, maybe we *can* do this.' He went back to the truck; I returned to the window as before.

We began again.

Isabelle crouched in the straw and looked out through the *devant-huis*. The rain was falling hard now and the sky was dark. It would be night soon. She watched her sons. Petit Jean continued to brush the horse, glancing around nervously. Jacob sat studying the stones from Marie's dress. He licked them, then looked up at his mother.

— They chose the ugliest stones, he said softly. The grey ones, with no color. Why would they do that?

— Be quiet, Jacob! Petit Jean hissed.

— What do you mean, you two? Isabelle cried. What are you keeping from me?

— Nothing, Maman, Petit Jean replied. Marie has run away, you know. She's going back to the Tarn to meet the devil. She said so.

— No. Isabelle stood up. I don't believe you. I don't believe you!

The clamps slipped twice more, but the third time they kept their grip on the stone. Lucien inched the truck forward slowly and steadily, making a tremendous racket but maintaining an even pull. I had the flashlight on the block when I heard the sound, a sucking noise, like a foot being pulled from mud. I moved the light and saw the hearth separating reluctantly from the dirt, rising an inch, two inches, three inches, steadily. I watched, frozen. The beam began to groan. I left the window, crouched next to the stone and shone the light into the crack. There was a terrible din now, with both the beam and the block groaning, and the truck outside straining, and my heart pounding. I looked into the dark space under the hearth.

They heard the boom of rock hitting the ground and froze. Even the horse went still.

Isabelle and Petit Jean moved toward the door, Jacob uncurling himself to follow them. Isabelle reached the door and tried it. As she pushed, the bolt was slid across and the door opened by Étienne, red-faced and sweating. He smiled at her.

– Come in, Isabelle.

She started at the sound of her name, then stepped past him. Hannah was on her knees next to the newly set hearth, eyes closed, candles placed on the stone. Gaspard stood back, head bowed. He did not look up when Isabelle and the boys came in. I have seen Hannah like that before, she thought. Praying at the hearth.

I saw a flash of blue, a tiny piece of blue in that dark hole. Then the stone had been lifted five inches, and I stared and stared without understanding, and then it was six inches, and then I saw the teeth and I knew. I knew and I began to scream and at the same time I reached into the grave and touched a tiny bone. 'That's a child's arm!' I shouted. 'That's –' I reached in further and took the blue between my fingers and pulled out a long thread wound around a strand of hair. It was the Virgin blue and the hair was red like mine and I began to cry.

She stared at the hearth, placed so strangely in the room.

He couldn't wait, she thought. He couldn't wait for others to help and he let the stone drop where it would.

It was a huge slab, set too close to the entrance. They were crowded between it and the door, she and Etienne and Petit Jean and Jacob. She stepped away from them and began to circle the hearth.

Then she saw a flash of blue on the floor. She fell to her knees, reached out to it and pulled. It was a piece of blue thread and it came from beneath the stone. She pulled and pulled until it broke off. She held it up to the candle for them to see.

I heard the snap and a sizzling of rope in the air. Then with a vast boom the stone fell back in place, the clamps smashing into the beam. I knew I'd heard that boom before.

★

– No! Isabelle cried, and threw herself onto the hearth, sobbing and banging her head against the stone. She pressed her forehead against the cold granite. Clutching the thread against her cheek she began to recite: – *J'ai mis en toi mon espérance: Garde-moi donc, Seigneur, D'éternel déshonneur: Octroye-moi ma délivrance, Par ta grande bonté haute, Qui jamais ne fit faute.*

Then there was no more blue; all was red and black.

'No!' I cried, and threw myself onto the hearth, sobbing and banging my head against the stone. I pressed my forehead against the cold granite. Clutching the thread against my cheek I began to recite: '*J'ai mis en toi mon espérance: Garde-moi donc, Seigneur, D'éternel déshonneur: Octroye-moi ma délivrance, Par ta grande bonté haute, Qui jamais ne fit faute.*'

Then there was no more blue; all was red and black.

10. The Return

I stood on the stoop for a long time before I could bring myself to ring the doorbell. I set down my travel bag, the gym bag next to it, and looked at the door. It was nondescript, cheap plywood with a peephole at eye height. I glanced around: I was in a complex of houses, small and new, with grass but no trees except for a few spindles trying to grow. It wasn't so different from new American suburbs.

I rehearsed what I was going to say one more time, then rang the bell. As I waited my stomach began fluttering and my hands grew sweaty. I swallowed and rubbed my hands on my pants. I could hear thumps coming from inside; then the door swung open and a small blond girl stood on the threshold. A black and white cat pushed past her legs and onto the steps, where it stopped in the act of sloping off and pushed its nose against the gym bag. It sniffed and sniffed until I nudged it away with my toe.

The girl wore bright yellow shorts and a T-shirt with juice spilled down the front. She hung onto the doorknob, balancing on one foot, and stared at me.

'*Bonjour*, Sylvie. Do you remember me?'

She continued to stare. 'Why is your head purple?'

I touched my forehead. 'I hit my head.'

'You must put a bandage on it.'

'Will you put one on for me?'

She nodded. From inside a voice called, 'Sylvie, who's there?'

'It's the Bible lady. She's hurt her head.'

'Tell her to go away. She knows I won't buy one!'

'No, no!' Sylvie shouted. 'The *other* Bible lady!'

There was a click-click-click down the hall, then Mathilde appeared behind Sylvie, wearing short pink shorts and a white halter top and holding a half-peeled grapefruit in one hand.

'*Mon Dieu!*' she cried. '*Ella, quelle surprise!*' She handed the grape-fruit to Sylvie, seized me and kissed me on both cheeks. 'You should have told me you were coming! Come in, come in.'

I didn't move. My shoulders were shaking, and I lowered my head and began to cry.

Without a word Mathilde put an arm around me and picked up the travel bag. When Sylvie picked up the gym bag I almost cried out, 'Don't touch it!' Instead I let her take it and my hand. Together they led me inside.

I couldn't face getting on a plane. I didn't want to be cooped up, but more than that, I didn't want to get home too fast. I needed more time to make the transition than a plane would give me.

Jacob came with me on the train to Geneva and put me on the bus to the airport, but three blocks out from the train station I got up and asked the bus driver to let me off. I went to a café and sat with a coffee for half an hour till I knew Jacob would be on a train back to Moutier, then went back to the station and bought a train ticket to Toulouse.

It had been hard leaving Jacob: not because I wanted to stay, but because it was so obvious to him that I wanted to get away as soon as possible.

'I'm sorry, Ella,' he murmured as we said goodbye, 'that your visit to Moutier has been so traumatic. It was meant to help you but instead it has hurt you.' He glanced at my bruised forehead, at the gym bag. He hadn't wanted me to take it with me, but I'd insisted, though I wondered vaguely if there would be problems with the sniffer dogs at the airport – another reason to take the train.

Lucien had brought the gym bag the previous morning when I finally woke up after the drugs the doctor pumped into me had worn off. He appeared at the end of my bed, unshaven, dirty and exhausted, and set the bag next to the wall.

'This is for you, Ella. Don't look in it now. You know what it is.'

I glanced dully at the bag. 'You didn't do it alone, did you?'

'A friend owed me a favor. Don't worry, he won't tell anyone.

He knows how to keep secrets.' He paused. 'We used stronger rope. The beam almost came down, though. The whole house almost collapsed.'

'I wish it had.'

As he was leaving I cleared my throat. 'Lucien. Thank you. For helping me. For everything.'

He nodded. 'Be happy, Ella.'

'I'll try.'

They left my bags in the hall and led me to the backyard, a patch of lawn fenced off from the neighbors on both sides and scattered with toys and a plastic wading pool. They made me lie in a plastic lawn chair, and while Mathilde went back inside to get me something to drink Sylvie stood at my shoulder, gazing at me steadily. She reached out and began patting my forehead lightly. I closed my eyes. Her touch, and the sun on me, felt good.

'What's that?' Sylvie asked. I opened my eyes. She was pointing at the psoriasis on my arm; it was red and swollen.

'I have a problem with my skin. It's called psoriasis.'

'Soar-ee-ah-sees,' she repeated, making it sound like the name of a dinosaur. 'You need a bandage there too, *n'est-ce pas*?'

I smiled.

'So,' Mathilde began when she'd handed me a glass of orange juice, sat down on the lawn beside me and sent Sylvie in to change into her bathing suit. 'Where have you been to get such bruises?'

I sighed. The prospect of explaining everything was daunting. 'I've been in Switzerland,' I began, 'visiting my family. To show them the Bible.'

Mathilde wrinkled her face. 'Bah, the Swiss,' she said.

'I was looking for something,' I continued, 'and –'

A shrill scream came from the house. Mathilde jumped up. 'Ah, that will be the bones,' I said.

It was hardest leaving Susanne. She came into my room not long after Lucien left the gym bag. She sat on the side of the bed and nodded toward the bag without looking at it.

'Lucien told me about it,' she said. 'He showed me.'

'Lucien is a good man.'

'Yes.' She looked out the window. 'Why was it there, do you think?'

I shook my head. 'I don't know. Maybe —' I stopped; thinking about it made me shake, and I was trying hard to make them think I was well enough to leave the next day.

Susanne put a hand on my arm. 'I should not have mentioned it.'

'It's nothing.' I changed the subject. 'Can I say something frank to you?' In my weakness I was feeling honest.

'Of course.'

'You must get rid of Jan.'

The shock in her face was of recognition rather than surprise; when she began to laugh I joined in.

Mathilde came back out, holding a weeping Sylvie by the hand.

'Tell Ella you're sorry for looking at her things,' she ordered.

Sylvie regarded me suspiciously through her tears. 'I'm sorry,' she mumbled. 'Maman, please let me play in the pool.'

'OK.'

Sylvie ran to the pool as if eager to get away from me.

'I'm sorry about that,' Mathilde said. 'She is a curious little thing.'

'It's OK. I'm sorry it scared her.'

'So that — those — that is what you found? What you were looking for?'

'I think her name was Marie Tournier.'

'*Mon Dieu*. She was — from the family?'

'Yes.' I began to explain, about the farm and the old chimney and the hearth, and the names Marie and Isabelle. About the color blue and the dream and the sound of the stone dropping into place. And the color of my hair.

Mathilde listened without interrupting. She examined her bright pink nails, picking at her cuticles.

'What a story!' she said when I'd finished. 'You should write it down.' She paused, started to say something else, then stopped herself.

'What?'

'Why have you come here?' she asked. '*Ecoute*, I'm glad you came, but why didn't you go home? Wouldn't you want to go home when you are upset, to your husband?'

I sighed. All that to tell her too: we would be here for hours. Her question reminded me of something. I glanced around. 'Is there a – have you got a – where is Sylvie's father?' I asked awkwardly.

Mathilde laughed and waved her hand vaguely. 'Who knows? I haven't seen him in a couple of years. He was never interested in having children. He didn't want me to have Sylvie, so –' She shrugged. '*Tant pis*. But you haven't answered my question.'

I told her everything else then, about Rick and Jean-Paul. Though I didn't cut any corners, it took less time to tell her than I'd expected.

'So Rick doesn't know where you are?'

'No. My cousin wanted to call and tell him I was coming home, but I wouldn't let him. I told him I would call Rick from the airport. Maybe I knew I wouldn't make it back.'

In fact I'd sat on the train from Geneva in a stupor, not thinking about my destination at all. I'd had to change trains in Montpellier, and while I'd been waiting I'd heard a train announced, with Mende listed as a stop. I'd watched it come in, people get off and on. Then it had just sat there, and the longer it had sat not going the more it had taunted me. Finally I'd picked up my bags and stepped onto it.

'Ella,' Mathilde said. I looked up; I'd been watching Sylvie splashing in the pool. 'You really need to talk to Rick, *n'est-ce pas*? About all of this.'

'I know. But I can't bear calling him.'

'Leave that to me!' She jumped up and snapped her fingers. 'Give me the phone number.' I did, reluctantly. 'Good. Now you watch Sylvie. And don't come inside!'

I leaned back in the chair. It was a relief to let her take charge.

★

Luckily children forget quickly. By the end of the day Sylvie and I were playing in the pool together. When we went inside Mathilde had hidden the gym bag in a closet. Sylvie said nothing more about it; she showed me all her toys and let me braid her hair into two tight plaits.

Mathilde would say little about the phone call. 'Tomorrow night, eight o'clock,' she explained cryptically, handing me an address in Mende, just as Jean-Paul had with La Taverne.

We ate dinner early because of Sylvie's bedtime. I smiled when I looked at my plate: it was like food I'd eaten when I was young, definite without being fancy. There was no pasta in special sauces or oils or herbs, no fancy bread, no blending together of tastes and textures. Here was a pork chop, string beans, creamed corn and a baguette; it was comfortingly straightforward.

I was starving, but when I took a bite of pork I almost spat it out: it tasted of metal. I tried the corn and the beans; they tasted of it too. Though I was hungry, I couldn't bear the taste and feel of anything once I had it in my mouth.

It was impossible to hide my discomfort, particularly since Sylvie had decided to link her eating with mine. Whenever I took a bite of my pork chop she took one of hers; when I drank, she drank. Mathilde wolfed everything down without noticing our pace, then chided Sylvie for taking so long.

'But Ella is eating so slowly!' Sylvie cried.

Mathilde glanced at my plate.

'I'm sorry,' I said. 'I'm feeling a little funny. Everything tastes – metallic.'

'Ah, I had that when I was pregnant with Sylvie! Horrible. But it only lasts a few weeks. After that you eat anything.' She stopped. 'Oh, but you –'

'I think it may be the medication the doctor put me on,' I interrupted. 'Sometimes there are traces of it still in the system. I'm sorry, I just can't eat.'

Mathilde nodded. Later I caught her giving me a long appraising look.

I fit into their lives surprisingly easily. I'd told Mathilde I would leave the next day – not that I knew where to go. She waved it off. 'No, you stay with us. I like having you here. It's normally just Sylvie and me, so it's good to have company. As long as you don't mind sleeping on the couch!'

Sylvie made me read book after book to her at bedtime, excited by the novelty, brusquely correcting my pronunciation and explaining what some of the phrases meant. In the morning she pleaded with Mathilde to let her stay home from the summer camp she was attending. 'I want to play with Ella!' she shouted. 'Please, Maman. Please?'

Mathilde glanced at me. I nodded slightly. 'You'll have to ask Ella,' she said. 'How do you know she wants to play with you all day?'

Once Mathilde had left for work, yelling instructions over her shoulder, the house was suddenly quiet. I looked at Sylvie; she looked at me. I knew we were both thinking of the bag of bones hidden in the house.

'Let's go for a walk,' I said brightly. 'There's a playground nearby, yes?'

'OK,' she said, and went off to pack all the things she would need into a bear-shaped knapsack.

On the way to the playground we passed a row of stores; when we reached a pharmacy I paused. 'Let's go in, Sylvie, I need to get something.' She obediently entered with me. I led her over to a display of soaps. 'You choose one,' I said, 'and I'll get it for you as a present.' She became engrossed in opening the boxes and sniffing at the soaps, and I was able to talk to the pharmacist in a low voice.

Sylvie chose lavender, holding it as we walked so she could smell it, until I convinced her to put it in her bear bag for safekeeping. At the playground she ran off to her friends. I sat on the benches with the other mothers, who looked at me suspiciously. I didn't try to talk to them: I needed to think.

In the afternoon we stayed at home. While Sylvie filled her pool I went to the bathroom with my purchase. When I came down she jumped into the water and splashed around while I lay on the grass and looked up at the sky.

After a while she came and sat beside me. She played with an old Barbie doll, whose hair had been cut raggedly, talking to her and making her dance.

'Ella?' she began. I knew what was coming. 'Where is that bag of bones?'

'I don't know. Your mother put it away.'

'So it's still in the house?'

'Maybe. Maybe not.'

'Where else could it be?'

'Maybe your mother took it to work with her, or gave it to a neighbor.'

Sylvie looked around. 'Our neighbors? Why would they want it?'

Bad idea. I changed tack. 'Why are you asking me about it?'

Sylvie looked down at the doll, pulled its hair, shrugged. 'Don't know,' she mumbled.

I waited for a minute. 'Do you want to see it again?' I asked.

'Yes.'

'Are you sure?'

'Yes.'

'You won't scream or get upset?'

'No, not if you are here.'

I got the bag from the closet and brought it outside. Sylvie was sitting with her knees pulled up under her chin, watching me nervously. I set the bag down. 'Do you want me to – lay it out so you can see it, and you wait inside and I'll call you when it's ready?'

She nodded and jumped up. 'I want a Coke. Can I have a Coke?'

'Yes.'

She ran inside.

I took a deep breath and unzipped the bag. I hadn't actually looked in it yet.

When it was all ready I went and found Sylvie; she was sitting in the living room with a glass of Coke, watching television.

'Come,' I said, holding my hand out to her. Together we went to the back door. From there she could see something in the grass. She pressed into my side.

'You don't have to look at it, you know. But it won't hurt you. It's not alive.'

'What is it?'

'A girl.'

'A girl? A girl like me?'

'Yes. Those are her bones and her hair. And a little bit of dress.'

We walked over to it. To my surprise Sylvie let go of my hand and squatted down next to the bones. She looked at them for a long time.

'That's a pretty blue,' she said at last. 'What happened to the rest of her dress?'

'It —' Rotted — another word I didn't know. 'It got old and was destroyed,' I explained clumsily.

'Her hair is the same color as yours.'

'Yes.'

'Where does she come from?'

'Switzerland. She was buried in the ground, under a chimney hearth.'

'Why?'

'Why did she die?'

'No, why was she buried under the hearth? Was it to keep her warm?'

'Maybe.'

'What was her name?'

'Marie.'

'She should be buried again.'

'Why?' I was curious what she would say.

'Because she needs a home. She can't stay here forever.'

'That's true.'

Sylvie sat down in the grass, then stretched out alongside the bones. 'I'm going to sleep,' she announced.

I thought about stopping her, saying that it was inappropriate, that she might have nightmares, that Mathilde would find us and think I would make a terrible mother, letting her daughter sleep next to a skeleton. But I didn't say any of these things. Instead I lay down on the other side of the bones.

'Tell me a story,' Sylvie commanded.

'I'm not very good at telling stories.'

Sylvie rolled onto her elbow. 'All grown-ups can tell stories! Tell me one.'

'OK. Once there was a little girl with blond hair and a blue dress.'

'Like me? Did she look like me?'

'Yes.'

Sylvie lay down again with a satisfied smile and closed her eyes.

'She was a brave little girl. She had two older brothers, and a mother and a father and a grandmother.'

'Did they love her?'

'Most of them, except for her grandmother.'

'Why not?'

'I don't know.' I stopped. Sylvie opened her eyes. 'She was an ugly old woman,' I continued in a hurry. 'She was small and wore black all the time. And she never spoke.'

'How could the girl know the grandmother didn't like her if she never spoke to her?'

'She – she had fierce eyes, and she'd glare at the little girl in a way she didn't at anyone else. So the girl knew she didn't like her. And it was worse when she wore her favorite blue dress.'

'Because the grandmother wanted it for herself!'

'Yes, the cloth was very beautiful but there was only enough to make a dress for a little girl. When she wore it she looked like the sky.'

'Was it a magic dress?'

'Of course. It protected her from the grandmother, and from other things too – fire and wolves and nasty boys. And drowning. In fact, one day the girl was playing by the river and fell in. She went under water, and she could see fish swimming below her and she thought she was going to drown. Then the dress puffed up with air and she floated to the surface and was safe. So whenever she wore the dress her mother knew she would be safe.'

I glanced over at Sylvie; she was asleep. My eyes lit on the fragments of blue between us.

'Except for one time,' I added. 'And it only takes once.'

I dreamed I was standing in a house that was burning to the ground. There were pieces of wood falling and ashes blowing everywhere. Then a girl appeared. I could only see her out of the corner of my eye; if I looked at her directly she disappeared. A blue light hovered around her.

'Remember me,' she said. She turned into Jean-Paul; he hadn't shaved in days and looked rough, his hair grown out so it curled at the ends, his face and arms and shirt covered with soot. I reached out and touched his face, and when I took my hand away there was a scar from his nose to his chin.

'How did you get this?' I asked.

'From life,' he replied.

A shadow crossed my face and I woke up. Mathilde was standing over me, blocking the evening sun. She looked like she'd been there for a while, her arms crossed, studying us. I sat up. 'I'm sorry,' I said, blinking. 'I know this must look bizarre.'

Mathilde snorted. 'Yes, but you know, I'm not surprised. I knew Sylvie would want to see those bones again. It looks like she's not scared of them anymore.'

'No. She surprised me, she was so calm.'

Our voices woke her; Sylvie rolled over and sat up, cheeks flushed. She looked around, her eyes coming to rest on the bones.

'Maman,' she said, 'we're going to bury her.'

'What? Here in the yard?'

'No. Her home.'

Mathilde looked at me.

'I know just the place,' I said.

Mathilde let me take her car into Mende. It was strange to think I'd been there only three weeks before; a lot had happened since then. But I had the same feeling now walking around the grim cathedral and the dark narrow streets of the old town. It wasn't a welcoming place. I was glad Mathilde lived further out, even in a treeless suburb.

The address turned out to be the same pizzeria I'd eaten in before. It was almost as empty as last time. I felt calm walking in, but when I saw Rick sitting alone with a glass of wine, frowning at the menu, my stomach turned over. I hadn't seen him in thirteen days; it had been a long thirteen days. When he looked up and saw me, he stood up, smiling nervously. He was wearing work clothes, a white button-down shirt, a navy cotton blazer and docksiders. He looked big and healthy and American in that dark cave of a place, like a Cadillac crawling through a narrow street.

We kissed awkwardly.

'Jesus, Ella, what happened to your face?'

I touched the bruise on my forehead. 'I fell,' I said. 'It's no big deal.'

We sat down. Rick poured me a glass of wine before I could say no. I politely touched it to my lips without swallowing. The smell of acid and vinegar almost made me gag; I set it down quickly.

We sat in silence. I realized I would have to start the conversation.

'So Mathilde called you,' I began feebly.

'Yeah. God, she talks fast. I didn't really understand why you couldn't call me yourself.'

I shrugged. I could feel tension gathering in my stomach.

'Listen, Ella, I want to say a couple things, all right?'

I nodded.

'Now, I know this move to France has been hard for you. Harder for you than for me. Me, all I had to do was work in a different office. The people are different but the work is similar. But for you, you don't have a job or friends, you must feel isolated and bored. I can understand that you're unhappy. Maybe I haven't paid enough attention to you because I've been so busy with work. So you're bored and, well, I can see there'd be temptations, even in a little hick town like Lisle.'

He glanced at the psoriasis on my arms; it seemed to throw him momentarily.

'So I've been thinking,' he continued, getting back on track, 'that we should try and start over.'

The waiter interrupted him to take our order. I was so nervous that I couldn't imagine eating anything, but for form's sake I ordered the plainest pizza possible. It was hot and close in the restaurant; sweat formed on my forehead and hands. I took a shaky sip of water.

'So,' Rick continued, 'it turns out there's an easy way to do that. You know I was in Frankfurt at meetings over this housing project?'

I nodded.

'They've asked me to oversee it, as a joint project between our company and theirs.' He paused and looked at me expectantly.

'Well, that's great, Rick. That's great for you.'

'So you see? We'd move to Germany. Our chance to start over.'

'*Leave France?*'

My tone surprised him. 'Ella, you've done nothing but complain about this country since you arrived. That the people aren't friendly, that you can't make friends, that they treat you like a stranger, that they're too formal. Why would you want to stay?'

'It's home,' I said faintly.

'Look, I'm trying to be reasonable. And I think actually I'm being pretty good about it. I'm willing to forgive and forget this whole thing with – you know. All I'm asking is that you move away from him. Is that unreasonable?'

'No, I guess it's not.'

'Good.' He looked at me and his goodwill momentarily slipped. 'So you're admitting something happened with him.'

The hard knot in my stomach moved and beads of sweat broke on my upper lip. I stood up. 'I have to find a bathroom. I'll be back in a minute.'

I managed to walk away from the table calmly, but once I reached the bathroom and shut the door I let go and vomited, long gasping retches that shook my whole body. It felt like I'd been waiting to do it for a long time, that I was throwing up everything I'd eaten in France and Switzerland.

Finally I was completely empty. I sat back on my heels and leaned against the wall of the cubicle, the light set into the ceiling shining on me like a spotlight. The tension had been flushed away; though exhausted, I was able to think clearly for the first time in days. I began to chuckle.

'Germany. Jesus Christ,' I muttered.

When I got back to the table our pizzas had arrived. I picked mine up, set it on the empty table next to us and sat down.

'You all right?' Rick asked, frowning slightly. 'Structure sound?'

'Yup.' I cleared my throat. 'Rick, I have something to tell you.'

He looked at me apprehensively; he really didn't know what I might say.

'I'm pregnant.'

He jumped. His face was like a television where the channels changed every few seconds as various thoughts passed through him.

'But that's *wonderful*! Isn't it? That's what you wanted, wasn't it? Except –' The doubt in his face was so painful that I almost reached across and took his hand. It occurred to me then that I could lie and that would solve everything. That was the open door I was looking for. But I was never good at lying.

'It's yours,' I said at last. 'It must have happened just before we started using contraceptives again.'

Rick jumped up from his seat and came around the table to hug me. 'Champagne!' he cried. 'We should order champagne!'

He looked around for the waiter.

'No, no,' I said. 'Please. I'm not feeling well.'

'Oh, right. Listen, let's get you home. We'll go now. Do you have your stuff with you?' He glanced around.

'No. Rick. Sit down. Please.'

He did, the uncertain look back in his face. I took a deep breath.

'I'm not coming back with you.'

'But – isn't that what this is all about?'

'What's all about?'

'This dinner. I thought you were coming back with me. I've got the car and everything.'

'Is that what Mathilde told you?'

'No, but I assumed —'

'Well, you shouldn't have.'

'But you're having my baby.'

'Let's leave the baby out of this for a moment.'

'We can't leave the baby out of it. It's there, isn't it?'

I sighed. 'I guess so.'

Rick gulped the last of his wine and set his glass down. It made a cracking noise against the table. 'Look, Ella, you've got to explain something to me. You haven't said why you went to Switzerland. Did I do something wrong? Why are you being like this with me? You seem to be implying something's wrong with *us*. That's news to me. If anyone should be upset it's *me*. You're the one running around.'

I didn't know how to say it nicely. Rick seemed to sense this. 'Just tell me,' he said. 'Be straight with me.'

'It happened when we moved here. I feel different.'

'How?'

'It's hard to explain.' I thought for a moment. 'You know how you can buy an album and be obsessed with it for a while, play it all the time, know all the songs. And you think that you know it so well and it's special to you. Like for instance the first album you ever bought when you were a kid.'

'The Beach Boys. *Surf's Up.*'

'Right. Then one day you just stop playing it — not for any reason, it's not a conscious decision. You just suddenly don't need to listen to it anymore. It doesn't have the same power. You can hear it and know that they're still good songs, but they've lost their magic over you. Just like that.'

'That's never happened with the Beach Boys. I still feel the same way when I listen to them.'

I brought my hand down hard on the table. 'God dammit! *Why* do you do that?'

The few people in the restaurant looked up.

'What?' Rick hissed. 'What did I do?'

'You aren't *listening* to me. You take the metaphor and mangle it. You just won't listen to what I'm trying to say.'

'What *are* you trying to say?'

'I don't think I love you anymore! That's what I'm trying to say, but you won't listen!'

'Oh.' He sat back. 'Why didn't you just say it, then? Why did you have to drag the Beach Boys into it?'

'I was trying to explain with a metaphor, to make it easier. But you insist on looking at it from your perspective.'

'How else am I supposed to look at it?'

'From *my* point of view! Mine!' I rapped on my chest with my knuckles. 'Can't you ever look at things from *my* point of view? You act so nice and easygoing with everyone, but you always get your way, you always make people see it from your point of view.'

'Ella, do you want to know what I see from your point of view? I see a woman who's lost, directionless, doesn't know what she wants, so grabs at the idea of a baby as something to keep her busy. And she's bored with her husband so she fucks the first offer she gets.'

He stopped and looked away, embarrassed now, realizing he'd gone too far. I'd never heard him be so frank.

'Rick,' I said gently. 'That's not my point of view, you see. That is most definitely *your* point of view.' I began to cry, as much from relief as anything else.

The waiter came over and silently cleared away our untouched pizzas, then placed the bill on the table without being asked. Neither of us looked at it.

'Is this – change in your feelings temporary or permanent?' Rick asked when I'd stopped crying.

'I don't know.'

He tried again. 'This album thing you talked about. Does it ever change back? You know – do you ever get reobsessed with it?'

I thought about it. 'Sometimes.' But never for very long, I added to myself. The feeling never really returns.

'So maybe the situation will change.'

'Rick, all I know is that right now I can't come back with you.' I could feel tears gathering behind my eyes again.

'You know,' I added, 'I haven't even told you what happened in Switzerland. And in France too. What I found out about the Tourniers. A whole story. I could tell a whole story – filling in some gaps here and there. You see, it's like this whole different life is going on with me that you don't know anything about.'

Rick pinched his nose at the top of his brow between his thumb and forefinger. 'Write it down,' he said. He glanced at my psoriasis again. 'Right now I gotta get out of here. It's too hot in here.'

When I got back Mathilde was still up, reading a magazine in the living room, her long legs propped up on the glass coffee table. She looked up at me inquiringly. I flopped down on the sofa and stared at the ceiling.

'Rick wants to move to Germany,' I announced.

'*Vraiment?* That's sudden.'

'Yes. I'm not going with him.'

'To Germany?' She made a face. 'Of course not!'

I snorted. 'Tell me, do you like any other country besides France?'

'America.'

'But you haven't even been there!'

'Yes, but I'm sure I'd love it.'

'It's hard to imagine going back. California would seem so alien.'

'Is that what you're going to do?'

'I don't know. But I'm not going to Germany.'

'Did you tell Rick you're pregnant?'

I sat up. 'How did you know?'

'It's obvious! You're tired, food bothers you, though you eat a lot when you do eat. And when you're not talking you look like you're listening to something inside you. I remember it well from Sylvie. So who is the father?'

'Rick.'

'You are sure?'

'Yes. We had been trying to conceive for a while, then we stopped, but obviously not before I got pregnant. Now that I think about it, I've had the symptoms for a few weeks.'

'And Jean-Paul?'

I turned onto my stomach and pressed my face into one of the sofa cushions. 'What about him?'

'Are you going to see him? Talk to him?'

'What can I say to him that he'd want to hear?'

'*Mais* – of course he would want to hear from you, even bad news. You haven't been very kind to him.'

'Oh, I don't know about that. I thought I was being kind *not* contacting him.'

To my relief Mathilde changed the subject. 'I'm taking Wednesday off,' she said, 'to go to Le Pont de Montvert, as you suggested. We'll take Sylvie too. She loves it up there. And of course you can see Monsieur Jourdain again.'

'Oh, I can't wait.'

She shrieked and we began to laugh.

Wednesday morning Sylvie insisted on helping me dress. She came into the bathroom where I'd been changing into white shorts and an oatmeal-colored shirt and leaned against the sink, watching me.

'Why do you wear white all the time?' she asked.

Oh, God, here we go again, I thought. 'This shirt is not white,' I stated. 'It's – like the color of cereal.' I didn't know how to say oatmeal.

'No, it isn't. My cornflakes are orange!'

I'd eaten three bowls of cornflakes earlier and was still hungry. '*Alors*, what would *you* like me to wear?'

Sylvie clapped her hands and ran into the living room, where she began looking through my bag. 'All your clothes are white or brown!' she cried, disappointed. She pulled out Jean-Paul's blue shirt. 'Except this. Wear this,' she commanded. 'How come you haven't worn this before?'

Jacob had washed the shirt for me in Moutier. The blood had mostly come out, but left a rusty outline on the back. I thought it wasn't noticeable unless you looked for it, but Mathilde spotted it immediately when I put it on. I caught her raised eyebrows and craned my neck to look down at my back.

'You don't want to know,' I said.

She laughed. 'A life full of drama, eh?'

'It wasn't like this before, I promise!'

Mathilde glanced at her watch. 'Let's go, Monsieur Jourdain will be waiting for us,' she said. She opened the hall closet, took out the gym bag and handed it to me.

'You really called him?'

'Listen, Ella, he is a good man. He has good intentions. Now that he knows your family really was from the area, he'll treat you like a long-lost niece.'

'Is Monsieur Jourdain the man who called me Mademoiselle? With the black hair?' Sylvie asked.

'No, that was Jean-Paul. Monsieur Jourdain was the old man who fell off his stool. You remember?'

'I liked Jean-Paul. Will we see him?'

Mathilde grinned at me. 'Look, this is his shirt,' she said, pulling at one of the shirt tails.

Sylvie gazed up at me. 'Then why are *you* wearing it?' I blushed and Mathilde laughed.

It was a beautiful day, hot in Mende but crisp and cool the further into the mountains we drove. We sang all the way there, Sylvie teaching me the songs she'd learned at her camp. It felt strange singing on our way to a burial, but not inappropriate. We were bringing Marie home.

When we pulled up to the *mairie* in Le Pont de Montvert, Monsieur Jourdain appeared immediately in the doorway. He shook hands with all of us, even Sylvie, and held on to my hand for a moment. 'Madame,' he said, and smiled at me. He still made me nervous; maybe he knew that, for his smile had a desperate air, like a child who wants to be accepted as an adult.

'Let's have coffee,' he said hurriedly, and ushered us down to the café. We ordered coffees and an Orangina for Sylvie, who didn't stay long at the table once she discovered the café's cat. We adults sat in awkward silence for a minute before Mathilde slapped the table and cried, 'The map! I'll just get it from the car. We want to show you where we're going.' She jumped up and left us alone.

Monsieur Jourdain cleared his throat; for a second I thought he was going to spit. 'Listen, La Rousse,' he began. 'You know I said I would try to find out about some of the family listed in your Bible?'

'Yes.'

'*Alors*, I found someone.'

'What, a Tournier?'

'Not a Tournier, no. Her name is Elisabeth Moulinier. She is the granddaughter of a man who lived in l'Hôpital, a village not far from here. It was his Bible. She brought it here when he died.'

'Did you know her grandfather?'

Monsieur Jourdain pursed his lips. 'No,' he said shortly.

'But – I thought that you knew everyone around here. Mathilde said so.'

He frowned. 'He was a Catholic,' he muttered.

'Oh, for God's sake!' I burst out.

He looked embarrassed but stubborn too.

'Never mind,' I muttered, shaking my head.

'Anyway, I told this Elisabeth you would be here today. She is coming to see you.'

'That's –' What is it, Ella? I thought. Great? Do you want to be connected with this family?

'That was kind of you to arrange it,' I said. 'Thank you.'

Mathilde returned then with the map and we spread it out on the table.

'La Baume du Monsieur is a hill,' Monsieur Jourdain explained. 'There are some ruins of a farm, here, you see?' He pointed to a tiny symbol. 'You go now and I will bring Madame Moulinier to you there, in an hour or two.'

★

When I saw the car parked at the side of the road, dusty and battered, my stomach lurched. Mathilde, I thought. She does love making phone calls. I glanced at her. She pulled up behind it, trying to look innocent, but I could see the trace of a self-satisfied smile. When she caught my eye she shrugged.

'Why don't you go on ahead?' she said. 'Sylvie and I will have a look at the river, won't we, Sylvie? We'll come find you later. Go on.'

I hesitated, then picked up the gym bag, a shovel and the map, and started up the path. Then I stopped and turned around. 'Thanks,' I said.

Mathilde smiled and waved a hand at me. '*Vas-y, chérie.*'

He was sitting on the crumbled remains of a chimney, his back to me, smoking a cigarette. He was wearing the salmon-colored shirt; the sun gleamed in his hair. He looked so real, so at home with himself and his surroundings that I almost couldn't look at him, it hurt so much. I felt a rush of longing for him, to smell him and touch his warm skin.

When he saw me he flicked his cigarette away but remained sitting. I set down the bag and the shovel. I wanted to put my arms around him, press my nose into his neck and burst into tears, but couldn't. Not until I had told him. The effort to keep from touching him was almost unbearable, and so distracting that I missed his first words and had to ask him to repeat them.

He didn't repeat them. He just looked at me for a long time, studying my face. He tried to remain expressionless, but I could see it was a struggle for him.

'Jean-Paul, I am so sorry,' I murmured in French.

'Why? Why are you sorry?'

'Oh.' I linked my hands behind my neck. 'There's so much to tell you, I don't even know where to begin.' My jaw began to tremble and I pressed my elbows into my chest to keep myself from shaking.

He reached over and touched my bruised forehead.

'How did you get this?'

I smiled grimly. 'From life.'

'Tell me about it, then,' he said. 'And about why you are here with that.' He nodded at the bag. 'Tell me in English. You speak in English when you need to, and I speak in French when I need to.'

I'd never thought of doing it that way. He was right: it would be too much to say what I had to say in French.

'The bag is full of bones,' I explained, crossing my arms and resting my weight on one hip. 'Of a girl. I can tell from the size and shape of the bones, plus there are remains of what looks like a dress, and hair. I found them under the hearth of a farm they say was the Tournier farm for a long time. In Switzerland. I think they're the bones of Marie Tournier.'

I stopped my halting explanation and waited for him to challenge me. When he didn't I found myself trying to answer his unspoken questions. 'In our family names have been passed down even up to the present. There are still Jacobs and Jeans, and Hannahs and Susannes. It's like a commemoration. All the original names still survive, except for Marie and Isabelle. Now I know you'll think I'm making something out of nothing, and with no proof, but I think that meant they did something wrong, they died or were shunned, or something. And the family dropped their names.'

Jean-Paul lit a cigarette and drew on it deeply.

'There are other things, the kind of evidence you'll be suspicious of. Like her hair, the hair there in the bag, is the same color as mine. As mine turned when I came here. And when we were lifting the hearth stone and it fell back it made this noise I've heard in my nightmare. This big groaning boom. Exactly the same. But mostly it's the blue. The bits of dress are exactly the blue I dreamed of. The Virgin blue.'

'The Tournier blue,' he said.

'Yes. It's all coincidence, you'll say. I know how you feel about coincidence. But there's too much of it, you see. Too much for me.'

Jean-Paul stood up and shook his legs, then began pacing around the ruin. He walked all the way around it.

'This is the Mas de la Baume du Monsieur, yes?' he asked when he returned to me. 'The farm listed in the Bible?'

I nodded. 'We're going to bury the bones here.'

'May I look?' Jean-Paul gestured at the bag.

'Yes.' He had an idea: I knew him well enough to read the signs. It was oddly comforting. My stomach, jittery since seeing the Deux Chevaux, settled down and demanded food. I sat on the rocks and watched him. He knelt and opened the bag, spreading it wide. He looked for a long time, touched the hair briefly, fingered the blue cloth. He glanced up, looking me up and down; I remembered I was wearing his shirt. The blue and the red.

'I didn't wear it deliberately, really,' I said. 'I didn't know you would be here. Sylvie made me wear it. She said I wasn't wearing enough color.'

He smiled.

'Hey, speaking of which, it turns out Goethe stayed in Moutier for a night.'

Jean-Paul snorted. 'That is no great boast. He stayed everywhere for a night.'

'I suppose you've read everything by Goethe.'

'What was it you said once? You would bring up someone like Goethe right now.'

I smiled. '*Touché.* Anyway, I'm sorry I took your shirt. And it got – I had kind of an accident with it.'

He scrutinized it. 'It looks all right to me.'

'You haven't seen the back. No, I'm not going to show it to you. That's another story.'

Jean-Paul zipped the bag shut.

'I have an idea,' he said. 'But it may upset you.'

'Nothing can upset me more than everything already has.'

'I want to dig here. By the chimney.'

'Why?'

'Just a theory.' He crouched by the remains of the hearth. There wasn't much left of it. It had been a large slab of granite, like the one in Moutier, but it had cracked down the middle and was crumbling away.

'Look, I don't want to bury her right there, if that's what you're thinking,' I said. 'That's the last place I want to put her.'

'No, of course not. I just want to look for something.'

I watched him shift bits of stone for a while, then got down on my knees and helped him, avoiding the larger rocks, careful of my abdomen. At one point he glanced at my back, then reached over and traced the outline of blood on the shirt with his finger. I remained hunched over, my arms and legs pricked with goosebumps. Jean-Paul moved his finger up my neck and onto my scalp, where he spread his fingers and pulled them through my hair like a comb.

His hand stopped. 'You do not want me to touch you,' he said; it was a statement rather than a question.

'You won't want to touch me when you've heard everything. I haven't told you everything yet.'

Jean-Paul dropped his hand and picked up the shovel. 'Tell me later,' he said, and began to dig.

I wasn't really surprised when he found the teeth. He held them out to me in silence. I took them, opened the gym bag and got out the other set. They were the same size: children's teeth. They felt sharp in my hands.

'Why?' I said.

'In some cultures people bury things in the foundations of houses when they're built. Bodies of animals, sometimes shoes. Sometimes, not often, humans. The idea was that their souls would remain with the house and scare away evil spirits.'

There was a long silence.

'They were sacrificed, you mean. These children were sacrificed.'

'Maybe. Probably. It is too much of a coincidence to find bones under the hearths of both houses for it to be accidental.'

'But — they were Christian. They were supposed to be God-fearing, not superstitious!'

'Religion has never completely destroyed superstition. Christianity was like a layer over the older beliefs — it covered them but they didn't disappear.'

I looked at the two sets of teeth and shivered. 'Jesus. What a family. And I'm one of them. I'm a Tournier too.' I was beginning to shake.

'Ella. You are far away from them,' Jean-Paul said gently. 'You belong to the twentieth century. You are not responsible for their actions. And remember that you are as much a product of your mother's family as your father's.'

'But I'm still a Tournier.'

'Yes, but you do not have to pay for their sins.'

I stared at him. 'I've never heard you use that word before.'

He shrugged. 'I was brought up Catholic, after all. Some things are impossible to leave behind entirely.'

Sylvie appeared in the distance, running in a zigzag, distracted by flowers or rabbits, so that she looked like a yellow butterfly flitting here and there. When she saw us she made a beeline for us.

'Jean-Paul!' she cried. She ran over to stand next to him.

He crouched beside her. '*Bonjour, Mademoiselle*,' he said. Sylvie giggled and patted his shoulder.

'Have you two been digging already?' Mathilde picked her way through the rocks in pink slingbacks, swinging a yellow *panier*. '*Salut, Jean-Paul*,' she said, grinning at him. He smiled at her. It occurred to me that if I had any sense I'd bow out and let them be together, give Mathilde some fun and Sylvie a father. It would be my own sacrifice, an atonement for my family's sins.

I stepped back. 'I'm going to look for a place to bury the bones,' I announced. I held out my hand. 'Sylvie, do you want to come with me?'

'No,' Sylvie said. 'I'm going to stay here with Jean-Paul.'

'But – maybe your mother wants to be alone with Jean-Paul.'

I immediately realized I'd made a mistake. Mathilde began to laugh her high shriek.

'Really, Ella, you are so stupid sometimes!'

Jean-Paul said nothing, but pulled a cigarette from his shirt pocket and lit it with a smirk on his face.

'Yeah, I am stupid,' I muttered in English. 'Very, very stupid.'

★

We all agreed on the spot, a grassy patch next to a boulder shaped like a mushroom, not far from the ruins. It would always be easy to find because of the shape of the rock.

Jean-Paul began to dig while we sat nearby and ate lunch. Then I took a turn with the shovel, then Mathilde, until we'd made a hole about two feet deep. I began to lay the bones out. We'd dug room enough for two, and though Jean-Paul had found only the teeth among the ruins, I set them in their place as if the bones of the whole body were there too. The others watched, Sylvie whispering to Mathilde. When I finished I pulled a blue thread from the remains of the dress and put it in my pocket.

As I stood up Sylvie came over. 'Maman said I should ask you,' she began. 'Could I bury something with Marie?'

'What?'

Sylvie pulled the bar of lavender soap from her pocket.

'Yes,' I said. 'Take it out of its wrapping first. Do you want me to put it in for you?'

'No, I want to do it.' She lay down next to the grave and, stretching out her arm, dropped the soap into place. Then she stood up and brushed the dirt off her front.

I didn't know what to do next: I felt I should say something but didn't know what. I glanced at Jean-Paul; to my amazement he'd bowed his head, closed his eyes and was whispering something. Mathilde was doing the same, and Sylvie imitated them both.

I looked up and saw a bird high above us, fluttering its wings so that it hovered in place.

Jean-Paul and Mathilde crossed themselves and opened their eyes at the same time. 'Look,' I said, and pointed upwards. The bird was gone.

'I saw it,' Sylvie declared. 'Don't worry, Ella, I saw the red bird.'

After we filled in the dirt we began piling small rocks on the grave to keep animals from taking away the bones, building it into a rough pyramid about eighteen inches high.

We'd just finished when we heard a whistle and looked around.

Monsieur Jourdain was standing at the ruins, a young woman at his side. Even from that distance it was obvious she was about eight months pregnant. Mathilde glanced at me and we grinned. Jean-Paul saw the exchange and gave us a puzzled look.

Oh, God, I thought. I still have to tell him. My stomach tightened.

When they got close the woman stumbled. I stood frozen.

'*Mon Dieu!*' Mathilde breathed.

Sylvie clapped her hands. 'Ella, you didn't tell us your sister was coming!'

She reached me and stopped. We studied each other: the hair, the shape of the face, the brown eyes. Then we stepped together and kissed the other's cheeks: one, two, three times.

She laughed. 'You Tourniers always kiss three times, as if two were not enough!'

Late in the day we decided to come down from the mountain. We would have a drink at the bar, then go our separate ways: Mathilde and Sylvie to Mende, Elisabeth to her home near Alès, Monsieur Jourdain to his house around the corner from the *mairie*, Jean-Paul to Lisle-sur-Tarn. Only I didn't know where I was going.

Elisabeth and I walked together to the cars.

'You will come stay with me?' she asked. 'Come now if you want.'

'Soon. I have some – things to sort out. But I'll come in a few days.'

At the cars she and Mathilde looked at me expectantly. Jean-Paul looked off at the horizon.

'Um, you go ahead,' I said to them. 'I'll get a lift with Jean-Paul. We'll see you there.'

'Ella, you are coming home with us, aren't you?' Sylvie asked anxiously. She began to pat my arm.

'Don't worry about me, *chérie*.'

When the cars disappeared down the road Jean-Paul and I found ourselves on either side of his car. 'Can we take the roof down?' I asked.

'*Bien sûr.*'

We unhooked the clasps on each side, rolled the roof back and fastened it. When we were done, I leaned against the side of the car and rested my arms along the top ridge of the window. Jean-Paul leaned against the other side.

'I have something to tell you,' I said. I swallowed the lump in my throat.

'In English, Ella.'

'Right. OK. In English.' I stopped again.

'You know,' he said, 'I had no idea I could be so miserable about a woman. It has been almost two weeks you go away. Since then, I can't sleep, I can't play piano, I can't work. The old women tease me at the library. My friends think I am crazy. Claude and I fight over stupid things.'

'Jean-Paul, I'm pregnant,' I said.

He looked at me, his whole face a question. 'But we —' He stopped.

I thought again about lying, about how much easier it would be to lie. I knew he would see through it.

'It's Rick's,' I said softly. 'I'm sorry.'

Jean-Paul took a deep breath. 'There is nothing to be sorry about,' he said in French. 'You wanted to have a baby, yes?'

'*Oui, mais —*'

'Then there is nothing to be sorry about,' he repeated in English.

'If it's with the wrong person, there's plenty to be sorry about.'

'Does Rick know?'

'Yes. I told him the other night. He wants us to move to Germany.'

Jean-Paul raised his eyebrows.

'What do *you* want to do?'

'I don't know. I have to think about what's best for the baby.'

Jean-Paul pushed himself off the car and walked to the other side of the road, where he stood looking out over the fields of broom and granite. He reached over, picked a stalk of broom and squeezed the bitter yellow flowers between his fingers.

'I know,' I whispered so he wouldn't hear me. 'I'm sorry. It's too much, isn't it?'

When he came back to the car he looked resolute, even stoic. This is his finest hour, I thought. Unexpectedly I smiled.

Jean-Paul smiled back at me.

'What's best for the mother is usually what's best for the baby,' he said. 'If you are unhappy the baby will be also.'

'I know. But I've lost sight of what's best for me. I wish I at least knew where home was. It's not in California anymore. And Lisle — I don't think I can go back there. Not right now. Or Switzerland. Certainly not Germany.'

'Where do you feel most comfortable?'

I looked around.

'Here,' I said. 'Right here.'

Jean-Paul opened his arms very wide.

'*Alors, tu es chez toi. Bienvenue.*'

Epilogue

I stared up at the sky, a pale blue washed out by late September sun. The Tarn was still warm; I lay on my back, arms stroking out from my sides, breasts flattened, hair floating in the river like leaves around my face. I looked down: my belly was just beginning to push above the water. I cupped the mound with my hands.

There was a rustling of paper from the bank.

'What happened to Isabelle?'

'I don't know. Sometimes I think she left Moutier and returned here to the Cévennes. She found her shepherd and had her baby, and lived happily ever after. She even went back to being Catholic so she could worship the Virgin.'

'Happy ending.'

'Yes. But you know, I don't think that's what really happened. More often I think she died starving in a ditch somewhere, fleeing from the Tourniers, a baby dead in her womb, forgotten, her grave unmarked.'

There was silence.

'But you know the worst fate, even worse than that, and yet the most likely?'

'What can be worse than that?'

'She lived with it. She stayed in Moutier and lived with her daughter's body under the hearth for the rest of her life.'

Isabelle kneels at the crossroads. She has three choices: she can go forward, she can go back, or she can remain where she is.

— Help me, Holy Mother, she prays. Help me to choose.

A blue light surrounds her, giving her solace for the briefest moment.

I sat up abruptly, crouching on the long smooth rock of the river bed, my breasts regaining their roundness. The baby had woken and begun to wail like a kitten. Elisabeth lifted him from his blanket on the river bank and guided his mouth to her breast.

'Has Jean-Paul read this?' She patted the manuscript next to her.

'Not yet. He will this weekend. It's his opinion I'm the most nervous about.'

'Why?'

'It's the most important to me. He has definite opinions about history. He'll be very critical of my approach.'

Elisabeth shrugged. 'So? It's *your* history, after all. *Our* history.'

'Yes.'

'Now, what about the painter you were telling me about? Nicolas Tournier.'

'The red fish, you mean.'

'What?'

'Nothing. He has a place, no matter what Jean-Paul thinks.'

Jacob reaches the crossroads and finds his mother on her knees, bathed in blue. She does not see him and he watches her for a moment, the blue reflected in his eyes. Then he looks around and takes the road leading west.

Acknowledgments

I would like to thank the following people (in alphabetical order, that great leveller) for their help: Juliette Dickstein; Jonathan Drori; Susan Elderkin; Jonny Geller; James Greene; Kate Jones; my cousin Jean Kleiber, who first told me about chimneyless farms and other things Swiss; Lesley Levene; Madame Christine Martinez of Florac, who without knowing it gave me a crash course in French village life; and Vicky Singer.

Most useful were *Montaillou* and *The Peasants of Languedoc* by Emmanuel Le Roy Ladurie, *The Return of Martin Guerre* and *Society and Culture in Early Modern France* by Natalie Zemon Davis, *Protestants du Midi*, *1559–1598*, by Janine Garrisson, and *Moutier à travers les âges* by Ph. Pierrehumbert.

Most of the places in the book may exist, but none of the people does.